The Despicables

Silent Oath©

Robert Lester Simmons

Published by Donahue Publishing

First Edition

ISBN: 979-8-89864-031-6

For information about special discounts for bulk purchases, please contact Donahue Publishing at info@donahuepublishing.co.

www.donahuepublishing.co

Acknowledgments

A personal note to my family and friends who embarked with me on my long and arduous journey in writing this book. Without your support and input, the inspiration for this book would surely be impossible.

All things are possible with God in faith. Glory be to the Father, the Son and the Holy Ghost.

Table of Contents

The Despicables

Prologue

"So God created man in his own image, in the image of God created he him; male and female created he them."

— Genesis 1:27

"A corporation is an artificial being, invisible, intangible, and existing only in contemplation of law."

— Chief Justice John Marshall, Dartmouth College v. Woodward (1819)

In the beginning, GOD created man in His image.

And in 1886, man returned the favor.

On May 10th of that year, the Supreme Court of the United States declared that corporations were persons under the Fourteenth Amendment. Not metaphorically. Not symbolically. Legally, actually, constitutionally: persons.

But these were not persons GOD made.

These were persons man conjured—artificial beings with the rights of the living but none of the constraints of flesh. They could not bleed. They could not die. They could not be imprisoned. They felt no guilt, harbored no conscience, and bore no soul.

They were immortal by design. Invincible by law. And they would outlive nations.

The corporate person was Satan's greatest innovation: a perfect vessel for evil that could never be judged by GOD, for it had no spirit to save or condemn. It was legal fiction that became the most powerful reality on earth.

Where GOD breathed life into dust and called it sacred, man breathed ink into paper and called it a person. Where GOD gave His creation free will and moral responsibility, man gave his creation limited liability and eternal existence. Where GOD's persons could repent, man's persons could simply rebrand.

The corporation became the Antichrist's answer to the Incarnation: not GOD made flesh, but evil made law.

And like all great deceptions, it hid in plain sight. Wrapped in the language of progress, commerce, and innovation. Baptized in the holy water of capitalism. Blessed by the priests of Wall Street. Defended by the prophets of the law.

But the Despicables knew the truth[9].

They had always known.

Long before 1886, long before America, long before even Rome or Babylon, they understood that power belonged not to those who commanded armies, but to those who commanded the machinery of legitimacy. Kings could be overthrown. Emperors could be assassinated. But institutions? Institutions were eternal.

And so, they built their empire not on thrones, but on corporate charters. Not with swords, but with signatures. They learned to hide behind the veil of the corporate person: to commit atrocities without culpability, to steal without stealing, to murder without killing, to enslave without chains.

The corporate person could do what no human could: exist in multiple places simultaneously, accumulate wealth without limit, influence elections without voting, and escape justice by simply dissolving and reforming under a new name.

It was the perfect camouflage for ancient evil.

The Despicables

The Despicables did not invent the corporation. But they perfected it. They transformed it from a tool of commerce into a weapon of spiritual warfare. They understood what the righteous refused to see: that in creating the corporate person, mankind had given Satan a body that could walk the earth indefinitely, legally, invincibly.

A body that paid no wages to morality.

A body that recognized no authority but profit.

A body that served no master but Mammon.

The corporate person was not merely amoral. It was structurally, systematically, legally designed to maximize self-interest without regard for human consequence. Its fiduciary duty was not to GOD, not to justice, not to the common good—but to shareholder value. Period. By law.

To be a good corporation was to be a good servant of greed.

And greed, as the Despicables well knew, was the engine of Hell.

They had names, these corporate persons. Pan American Insurance Company. Genesis Financial. Moldavu Capital. And ten thousand others, spanning continents and centuries, an unholy communion of legal fictions that controlled more wealth than nations, wielded more power than kings, and answered no law but their own.

They were the principalities and powers that the Apostle Paul warned about: "For we wrestle not against flesh and blood, but against principalities, against powers, against the rulers of the darkness of this world, against spiritual wickedness in high places."

The corporate person was the high place made law.

The ruler of darkness gives a charter.

Spiritual wickedness grants legal personhood.

And the Despicables? They were the bloodline that shepherded this abomination for generations. They were the human persons who served the corporate persons, who fed them, sustained them, and used them as vessels for an evil older than memory.

They trafficked in souls by calling it Human Capital Acquisition.

They stole futures by calling it Risk Management.

They destroy lives by calling it Strategic Restructuring.

They turn children into commodities, neighborhoods into profit centers, and nations into subsidiaries.

They turn races, a human invention against each other.

And the law protects them. Because the law they wrote said: corporations are persons.

But they were not GOD's persons.

They were something else.

Something that walks like power, talks like progress, and dresses like legitimacy. They are evil persona.

Something that wears a suit and tie, sits in boardrooms, shakes hands with presidents, and donates to charity.

Something that smiles with perfect teeth and has no mouth.

Something that looks you in the eye and has no soul.

The corporate person is Satan's spawn.

And the Despicables are its priests.

But there are others. Others who remember that GOD's persons—the flesh and blood kind, the kind that loves, suffers, bleeds and prays—are made in His image for a reason. Others who understand that no amount of legal fiction changes the truth[9]: that evil, no matter how it disguises itself, is always evil.

Others who know that corporate persons are charters by man.

But they could also be judged by GOD.

This is the story of that judgment.

This is the story of how one man, born of GOD's image, hunted by Satan's spawn, discovered he was never meant to serve the Despicables.

He is meant to dismantle them.

One corporation at a time.

One bloodline at a time.

One truth[9] at a time.

Because in the end, the corporate person—for all its power, all its immortality, all its legal invincibility—has one fatal flaw:

It cannot pray.

And the man who could?

His name was Malik Andrew Madison.

And he is about to remind the Despicables that no weapon formed against GOD's persons shall prosper.

Not even the ones wearing Armani or through legal documents.

Not even the ones listed on the New York Stock Exchange.

Not even the ones that claimed, by law, to be persons.

The war is ancient.

But the reckoning just began.

"Thou art of purer eyes than to behold evil, and canst not look on iniquity: wherefore lookest thou upon them that deal treacherously, and holdest thy tongue when the wicked devoureth the man that is more righteous than he?"

— Habakkuk 1:13

Significance of Truth

Spiritually, the number 9 symbolizes completion, enlightenment, and universal love. It represents the end of a cycle and the attainment of wisdom, calling for service to humanity and alignment with higher purpose. In many traditions, it embodies divine order, transformation, and the fulfillment of spiritual law—the harvest of one's deeds before renewal.

All digits return to 9, symbolizing that truth is the sum of all things—every path, when reduced, leads back to truth.

Proof of Constancy (the Law of Nine):

Any multiple of 9, when its digits are added and reduced, always returns to 9: $9 \times 3 = 27 \rightarrow 2 + 7 = 9$

Meaning:

Nine is incorruptible—it always returns to itself. Symbolically, truth—like 9—cannot be altered or destroyed; it remains constant no matter how it's multiplied or divided.

Neil deGrasse Tyson's Three Kinds of Truth

In his discussion on truth, physicist Neil deGrasse Tyson posits that truth can be categorized into three distinct types, which helps to clarify the source and validity of different claims in society:

1. **Objective Truth:** This is truth based on evidence and verifiable fact, independent of belief. It is discovered through scientific analysis and experimentation, and its validity applies universally, whether one believes in it or not (e.g., the laws of physics, the shape of the Earth).

2. **Personal Truth (Spiritual/Religious):** This is a profound, deeply felt conviction that is true *for the individual*. Tyson classifies religious and spiritual beliefs here, noting that while these convictions are valid and deeply meaningful to the person holding them. They are truths "in your bones", they cannot be verified, repeated, or objectively proven to compel belief from an external party.

3. **Political Truth:** This is a truth that becomes accepted or asserted as fact simply because it has been repeated incessantly. Its power comes from volume and persistence, not from evidence or personal conviction. Tyson highlights that this type of truth is manufactured and is often used to manipulate public opinion (e.g., propaganda or campaign slogans).[1]

---

[1] *(Source: Neil deGrasse Tyson, The Joe Rogan Experience, Episode #1159, August 22, 2018, https://www.youtube.com/watch?v=vGc4mg5pul4.)*

Chapter One
The Ritual

For the Despicables, ritual was never mere ceremony. Each act, whether cloaked in incense, blood, or silence, served as a binding contract with unforeseen forces. They did not pray for forgiveness, for that was a sign of weakness and allegiance to a god other than themselves. Nor did they worship with humility. Their rituals were transactions, designed to harness power, manipulate destiny, and enslave the will of others.

Every symbol etched, every chant whispered, every torch extinguished was part of a vast machinery of control. To the outside world, these rituals looked archaic, remnants of forgotten faith. But within the secret halls where they gathered, the rituals became the very architecture of their empire. They were the engines that drove their shadow dominion. They believed that through repetition and sacrifice, they could bend economies, topple nations, and command loyalty beyond reason.

The rituals also served another purpose: remembrance. Each rite was a reenactment of their ancient covenant, tracing their lineage back to Babylon, Athens, Mesopotamia, Jerusalem, Rome, and the hidden councils of the Middle Ages. They invoked not merely gods, but the memories of kings, merchants, priests, cardinals, popes and warlords whose bloodlines ran through them. In this way, their gatherings were not only about power in the present, but also about binding themselves to a continuity of dominion, a reminder that their authority was inherited and eternal.

Yet perhaps the most insidious purpose of their rituals was psychological. They created belonging and fear all at once. The participants, trapped by spectacle and secrecy, found themselves unable to imagine life outside this world order. Rituals hardened their hearts, sustained their resolve, suppressed their doubts, and fused their identity to the collective will of the Despicables.

The common people, though excluded from the inner sanctum, played their own role in this grand theater. They were both audience and unwitting participants, their daily struggles and hopes channeled into support for the very system that kept them subjugated. Information collected about their inner thoughts from online information to know their most intimate personal details. All ways to keep the public under constant surveillance.

Thus, those invited or coerced into their inner sanctum made their rituals not superstition. They were architectures of empire, the choreography of control, and the living testament that man could play God, if only he was willing to pay the cost to their souls. Though the uneducated and poor had no chance of sharing in the Despicables' vast wealth, they supported the Despicables even in instances where it was clear they would not be beneficiaries of their largesse. This did not matter to these disciples as they saw the Despicables as protectors in a changed world that had changed not to their liking.

The ritual chamber itself bore witness to centuries of such ceremonies, its stone walls scarred by ancient symbols, its air thick with the residue of countless offerings. Tonight, like so many nights before, the Despicables would gather once more, their modern suits and digital devices, a stark contrast to the primordial forces they sought to command.

Chapter Two
Two Wives, Two Silos

"However, each one of you must love his wife as he loves himself and the wife must respect her husband."

— Ephesians 5:33

They say you never forget your first love, except in my case, it was not the love I remembered. It is also said that a wife and husband must be equally yoked. And so it is also true about the relationship between an employee--employer which should be equally yoked. Sometimes a publicly traded corporation operates two silos: one good, one bad. This was the case with Pan American Insurance Company ("PAINCO") where the Despicables infiltrated and jockeyed for control and power.

Malik Andrew Madison

Malik Andrew Madison was a man whose presence entered a room before he did. With the smooth, sculpted features and luminous brown skin that recalled a younger actor, Terrence Howard. Malik carried himself with the self-assured calm of a man who had weathered storms: and learned from each one. His eyes, a cool hazel-gray, seemed to study and measure the world with the precision and eyes of an artisan, a scholar, and a survivor. When he spoke, his tone was low, deliberate, and magnetic: each word carefully chosen, as if he already thought five sentences ahead.

He stood just under six feet tall, lean but strong, with a quiet elegance in his posture: equal parts boardroom and backstreet. The faintest trace of a South Side Chicago accent colored his otherwise polished diction. A reminder that no Ivy League degree could erase where he originated.

Malik was an undergraduate from Harvard: a man who bore the mark of the Ivy League not in arrogance but in articulation. His time there honed his intellect, sharpened his vision, and deepened his conviction that brilliance often blooms in unlikely soil. He met his first wife, Monica Mitchell, when he was a senior at a Kappa Alpha Psi dance on the campus of Northeastern University. She was a freshman pledge at the time with Alpha Kappa Alpha sorority. Petite with a countenance and the looks of actress Kerri Washington. They formed an instant connection and attraction though for different reasons.

She saw dollar signs as in her "Mrs." degree and Malik saw a sense of difference in their demeanor and approach to life that interestingly appealed to him. For 3 years they commuted back and forth from Boston and Chicago until Monica's matriculation from Northeastern. During those 3 years, Malik pursued his law degree at DePaul University College of Law evening program. They married that July of Monica's graduation from college. His upbringing was so markedly different to Monica's family.

Yet his real education didn't begin in lecture halls, courtrooms or boardrooms It began in the modest home of his parents, Andrew and Hannah Madison. His father, a broad-shouldered construction worker with calloused hands and a gentle soul, believed in the dignity of labor. His mother, Hannah Mitchell Madison: a beautician by trade and a housekeeper by necessity: believed in the power of transformation, not just of hair and home, but of spirit. Together, they worked two jobs each, sacrificing sleep and comfort so that their only son of their five children-might ascend where they could not.

Malik's maternal lineage was steeped in quiet resilience and ancestral memory. His grandmother Ellen was the daughter of Adisa, a name that in old African tongues meant one who makes her meaning clear. From Adisa's daughter Ellen came Hannah, and through Hannah, five children, one named Malik. Malik inherited not only ambition but a sense of sacred duty: to redeem the sacrifices of those who came before. In his veins flowed generations of survival, resistance, and a whisper of destiny that he could neither ignore nor fully understand.

To those who knew him in the courtroom or the corporate corridors of power, Malik was a strategist, a closer, the man who could turn a negotiation with a single glance or pause. But those closest to him at work knew another truth[9]: beneath the composed exterior lived a man haunted by legacy, driven not merely by success but by purpose. He carried the invisible weight of his ancestors like a well-tailored suit, moving through life with equal parts, grace and gravity of his arguments.

No, his real-life education took hold when he met Monica Mitchell. During their college, Malik lied on his back watching Monica as she applied her make up to her face, ever so delicately and sensually before the mirror of vanity in their bedroom. They were going to Faneuil Hall in downtown Boston for a night out. As if it was a ritual to mesmerize a young not yet worldly Malik Andrew Madison to hide her evil self from him. It was all part of the education of Malik's rites of passage. Malik liked his girls a bit racy with a bit of an edge.

It was the show. Marrying Monica Mitchell was like hitching a horse on a freight wagon.

Beautiful, delicate, always center stage, but she was not built for the pull or to last. She was a show horse manufactured as a viper to seduce men. Her constant request to look directly into her open eyes while speaking to her or during lovemaking cast a spell on the looker, as if to reveal the eyes are the window to the soul. Though Malik found out Monica did not have a soul. She never was going to move in cadence, like two horses pulling up a steep hill. No, Monica added to the weight, not just literally, not just spiritually, but financially and in every way humanly possible. She drained you emotionally and mentally.

To say Monica Mitchell was evil; did not do her wicked ways justice. Monica was always atop the wagon, never pulling it. Always demanding and wanting more, ever so pristine and above the fray. That was her theater, always commanding more. By the time Monica and Malik divorced, he had earned a Ph.D. in the signs of deception, dishonesty, cruelty, and topped it all off with a good dose of psychology. Malik learned from Monica how to spot a sociopath in his midst.

Her conduct and thinking bordered on the sociopathic spectrum with narcissism and the inability to understand empathy and sympathy as a perceived strength. To Monica, these attributes of empathy and sympathy were the antithesis to weakness and represented weak character traits for the stronger to exploit and dominate another person. In Monica's world, these people are often referred to as "low IQ" simply because they don't ascribe to the values of grift, graft, corruption and undue influence as strengths and the path of least resistance to prosperity.

At 4'9", 98 pounds, Monica was like a miniature Iman, the Ethiopian-born model. Shining, sharp-eyed and demure. Demure on the outside which held or detracted from her selfish nature inside. She was like fine Italian leather on the outside, but inside the belt held the hardness of raw suede. All of it belied by her street smarts, her cunning nature and her lack of conscience. Monica was raised, if not born, without conscience. She had the lit of Harlem and the cadence of Bedford Stuyvesant. She was like a surgeon with a dull scalpel. Street smarts, if you will, like Malik never encountered.

Monica once told Malik this during one of their many heated arguments. As he chastised her shortcomings, usually concerning some type of deception, she said, "I do not understand you.

You know I was raised not to have a conscience." And she really did not.

You cannot claim to have much of a conscience if you abandon your dying mother, stricken with emphysema, left to lie in her own filth. It was her mother's elder daughter who flew from Florida to New York to place their mother in hospice care. Their mother died within a month after. That moment became Monica's rite of passage into the Despicables: the initiation into a world defined by a lack of conscience. And in that dark curriculum, Monica graduated with honors. Throughout their brief marriage, Malik literally would pay for his own contribution for ignoring the obvious. Because that's just how it was with the Despicables: cruelty was their badge of honor.

Except, he did not fully know the full extent and implications to her statements.

While Malik worked full time as an account executive at a pharmaceutical company and attending evening law school, Malik thought of Monica as his partner as they built a future together. It was shortly after their marriage, that Malik discovered he had not married a partner, but a show horse. A "wannabe" stay-at-home mom who wanted a child right away. To say, Monica and Malik had marital difficulties was an understatement. Every day was a constant struggle and battle to get Monica to keep her word. It was rather tiring. The constant bickering and conflict seemed totally unnecessary. But not Monica. It was just her nature.

And indeed, it happened. Monica became pregnant within a year of their marriage. It was a marriage destined to fail. Malik begged Monica to delay pregnancy until after he completed law school. He also saw the signs trouble awaited their marriage. It was apparent even on the day of their wedding. As he dressed in his tuxedo along with his groomsmen, Malik's father came into the dressing room, walked up to him and adjusted his bow tie. He gave Malik only a handful of lessons throughout life.

As he straightened Malik's tie, his father said to him, "Son, I will tell you one more time. All that glitters is not gold." He looked Malik directly in his eyes. It was no secret that very few of Malik's family members or friends particularly cared for Monica. She was not quite the girl one took easily, as she held things close to the vest.

Malik replied, "I know Dad, but we have all the guests outside and I am just going to put my best foot forward and hope for the best."

He said," Alright then," and then he left him. Malik's dad came from the streets as well.

Malik saw many of the failings of Monica, but she was the finest girl he ever dated and in his own way he loved her. He could not say the same about Monica as Malik was not sure she understood or appreciated love. She had a way of making a person feel foolish and safe at the same time.

Monica as Delilah

Monica's insistence that a man look directly into her eyes during lovemaking was more than intimacy; it was both an interrogation and coronation. The eyes, for her, are both the mirror and the reflection in the window of the soldier. They are where a man's hidden truths[9] flicker when his body is too distracted to guard his soul. In this way, Monica's gaze resembled Deliliah's questions of Samson while he slept to find out the secrets of his powers. She shared Samson's secrets of power with the Philistines. In Malik's case, with the Despicables.

Just as [0]Deliliah waited until Samson's body lay at rest, vulnerable, to press him for the secret of his great strength, Monica uses the moment of passion: the release of defenses: to compel a man's truth[9]. Where Deliliah asked with words, Monica asked with the eyes. Where Delilah cut Samson's hair, Monica cut deeper, severing the illusion a man may weave about himself.

Monica seized his gaze as if binding him in chains yet unseen, and with each fatal meeting of eyes she served her curse: striking not the body, but the vanity of Malik's soul. Each view into her eyes was meant to syphon his strength as she planned her wound of his pride. She would deliver a narcissistic injury at her time, manner and means. An injury she intended him to carry like Delilah's shears upon Samson's strength for the rest of his life. Deliah asked Samson while he slept about his secrets to share with the Philistines. Monica had Malik gaze into her eyes to recruit and cultivate him as a Despicable.

Bedford Stuyvesant

Malik still remembered the coldness of her sisters the first time he met them. That day in Bedford Stuyvesant, he had just met her "family." Her pseudo-grandfather received him in his kitchen in his multi-million-dollar brownstone. Surrounded by what appeared to be bodyguards as he sat on the landing in the kitchen before a burning wood-burning fireplace. They exchanged pleasantries. One cannot say they had a meaningful conversation, but certainly a respectful one as his bodyguards hovered near him. It was one of three times Malik met her grandfather in the entire eight years he was with Monica.

On their way back from Bedford Stuyvesant, after their visit to Monica's grandfather's home in Brooklyn, they veered off Atlantic Avenue, just as the molten sun began to shimmer off the brick facade of the numerous brownstones. Malik, half lost in his private thoughts, barely noticed the shift in rhythm outside the moving car until the music hit. Shoulder to shoulder, skin to skin was a large Caribbean parade blocking the streets. The synchronized pulse of a calypso band vibrated through the car windows like thunder wrapped in tin foil. Then they slowed, then stopped. As their SUV eased from Atlantic Avenue onto Nostrand Avenue in Bedford Stuyvesant, they were swept into the Caribbean parade as the calypso music beat outside the car and inside their heads. Without warning they were swept into the Caribbean Day parade: a panorama of sound, sweat, feathers, and fire.

The streets pulsated as if the ancestors themselves descended from the heavens in the masquerade, draped in gold lame' and crimson plumes. Dancers from Trinidad, Jamaica, Barbados, and Haiti danced their way through with a sway enough to cause a baby in a cradle to lull to sleep. Hips rolling in sync with ancient rhythms that defied centuries of bondage and migration. The air was thick with incense and smoke from barbecued jerk chicken, oil drum fire pits blazing beside makeshift grills. Mangoes, roti, rum punch: everything was for sale and offered with a shout and a wink.

Malik cracked the window, letting the pungent scent of sweat, spice, and spiritual warfare seep into his senses. Flags of every island snapped in the humid late August wind, wrapping around bodies like living scriptures. The trucks bore the loudspeakers stacked to the heavens, preaching not sermons but soca and dancehall, as if salvation was found in the rhythm, not church.

Then they saw her: a woman crowned in white feathers, her chest bare, except for pearls and body paint, holding aloft a banner that read: "WE ARE CARRIBBEAN, THE SPIRIT LIVES ON!" Malik's thoughts wandered to the many stories told by Monica's family about Bedford-Stuyvesant.

They came on ships, on flights, on borrowed hopes. From Kingston, Port of Spain, Castries, Nassau, Bridgetown, the Caribbean diaspora spilled into New York like the waves from the Atlantic Ocean, not crashing, but rising. It began in earnest in the 1910s and 1920s, trickled quietly at first: Jamaican merchants, Barbadian dock workers, Trinidadian clerks, all drawn by the story that "New York paid Black men to work." They brought with them their varied traditions, voodoo, numbers racket and Caribbean shine, all culminated into one lively Caribbean culture, yet maintained their native individuality. Bedford Stuyvesant was their Ellis Island.

By the 1940s, ships like the Empire Windrush brought not just laborers but scholars, nurses, soldiers: Black men in British uniforms who fought Hitler hard only to face Jim Crow in Harlem. They sought dignity in a foreign language. And Bed-Stuy, with its aging brownstones, and open stoops, Jewish-owned groceries, offered them both a challenge and a painted canvas of many black hues.

They brought more than hues and labor. They presented their culture as a resistance, a revolution of sorts. Steel drums echoed off Malcolm X Boulevard. Carnival costumes, made in Crown Heights basements, dazzled on Eastern Parkway each September. The smell of oxtail, curry goat, and callaloo wafted from vinyl-covered kitchens. Churches became embassies: Mt. Zion Apostolic, St Paul's Pentecostal, and countless storefront sanctuaries where Patois and Creole replaced King's English and French.

They were carpenters and seamstresses by day trade, revolutionaries, and prophets by heritage. The West Indian Day Parade became their annual celebration and combined legacy that joined the Caribbean nations. Though each nation had its own designated flag on West Indian Day Parade, all separate Caribbean nations came together as one. Flags wrapped around torsos; faces painted in the colors of the ancestral soil. Soca, reggae, and calypso were not music: they were declarations of survival.

Caribbean Rhythm

But it was not all joyful. The Caribbeans in Bed-Stuy had to wrestle with the dual gaze: too "Black" to be American, too foreign to be trusted by Black Americans who fought their own wars in Brownsville and the Bronx. Yet over time, those divisions blurred. Schoolyards turned Trini boys into Knick fans. Dominican girls fell in love with Barbadian boys. The dialects mixed like spices in a Jambalaya stew.

By the 1980s, Bedford-Stuyvesant was not just Black. It was Caribbean Black.

The surnames on mailboxes read Thomas, Baptiste, Sinclair, and DeSouza. The neighborhood pulsed with a quiet confidence: not flashy, not desperate: but deeply rooted. A place where grandmothers still swept their stoops before sunrise, where the bodegas' radios played Bob Marley beside "Big Daddy Kane."

Beneath the reggae posters and storefront flags, under the visible rhythm of Carnival and street fairs, there thrived another current: a subterranean Caribbean culture in Brooklyn. It was unofficial, unlicensed, and often unspoken, but only by those that knew: it was more real than anything else.

In the basements of corner row houses and behind metal grates of shuttered shops, unregulated sound systems rattled brick walls with dub, soca, and dancehall. These were not commercial parties. They were coded rituals. Men with dreadlocks tucked under Rasta caps controlled the turntables like shamans, spinning vinyl that spoke in tongues: riddims laced with resistance and sexual freedom.

To get in, you had to know someone. Not just someone: the right someone. Passwords changed weekly. Entry was through alleys, back doors, or side gates where incense masked the smell of sexuality mixed with smoke. Inside, bodies swayed, shoulders rolled, and eyes locked. There were no bouncers, only watchers. This was more than music. It was a spiritual reclamation of space.

In whispered corners of the underground, Obeah women and Bush doctors still practiced the old ways. Not publicly: these weren't New Age boutiques offering sage then, smoke shops today. These were elders whose reputations moved by word of mouth. Their remedies passed on in brown paper bags. Their prayers were muttered in broken tongues. And their warnings rarely ignored.

Some said there was a "healer in Crown Heights" who could bless a man before court or curse a landlord who displaced tenants. Whether truth[9] or urban myth, her name was never spoken in vain.

Others still lit blue candles at midnight, called on Papa Legba at the crossroads, or washed their thresholds in rum and Florida water.

The underground Caribbean culture didn't just preserve religion: it preserved rebellion.

Vendors sold jerk chicken, callaloo, and ital stew out of illegal kitchens, reachable only by word of mouth. These pop-up kitchens weren't listed in the phonebooks. And are not even today on WhatsApp or Yelp. They were loyalty-based economies, where cash was king, and silence was a contract.

Policy

There were underground money economies as well: "susu" or "pardna" clubs where Caribbean immigrants pooled savings, far from the eye of banks or the IRS. Women carried cash in the pockets of their bras and kept ledgers in their heads or handwritten notebooks passed at nail salons and barbershops.

The law barely knew it existed, and if it did, it didn't understand the economy. To people in the hood, it wasn't a crime. It was cultural protection. Self-reliance in exile. Patois, Creole, broken English: all spoken with a purpose. In court, Caribbeans straightened their accents. In the street, they used their Caribbean words like a hidden weapon. To speak raw Patois in the open was a declaration: "I am not from here. FAFO."

Language in the underground was like bearing armor and not just about communication. It was identity warfare: a way to gate keep who was inside and who did not belong, before you entered the lion's den.

In the shadows of brownstone-lined streets and behind bodegas stocked with Red Stripe and codfish, an underground economy pulsed in Bed-Stuy: one that quietly funded funerals, storefront churches, college tuitions, and barbershops for decades. It was also an informal banking system that allowed money to flow into investments only to return intricately back to the investors.

In the mid-1920s and well into the 1980s, Bedford-Stuyvesant, Brooklyn: home to one of the largest African American and Caribbean populations in New York: was a vibrant epicenter of both cultural life and informal economies. Among the most notable was the "numbers racket", an underground lottery system with deep roots in the Black and Caribbean communities.

The numbers racket began in Harlem around 1910 with Stephanie St Clair ('Queenie' in Manhattan aka 'Madam St Clair' in Harlem). Queenie was from Martinique and ran her numbers racket in Harlem from about 1910 to about 1969 until her death. Ellsworth 'Bumpy' Johnson took over the business from her. Casper Holstein from the Virgin Islands and Ellsworth 'Bumpy' Johnson, initially 'Queenie's' enforcer, cornered the numbers racket in Harlem after Queenie died.

Around the 1940s, the numbers racket made its way from Harlem to Bed Stuy with the emergence of 'Bumpy' Johnson who expanded his business from Harlem into Bed Stuy. It was a flourishing business from the 1930s through the 1970s. For a time, Blacks and Caribbeans prevented the Puerto Ricans from the numbers racket. Puerto Ricans slowly arrived in Bed Stuy around the 1970s. Blacks and Caribbeans had to cut them in as runners, collectors, security, or muscle or to police the streets, but rarely as bankers. Eventually the Puerto Ricans started their own numbers racket.

The genius of the 'numbers' lay in its simplicity. Winning digitism to something every player could check for themselves: no tricks, no mystery. Open a newspaper and there it was. Casper Holstein refined the game by linking his policy racket to the daily stock market figures, giving the play an air of legitimacy. Other bankers followed suit, drawing their winning numbers from widely available reports and publications. The system gave the players confidence, knowing the results were fixed not by the banker's whim but by sources they could verify in print.

To the Caribbean immigrants who came from islands like Jamaica, Trinidad, Barbados, and the Dominican Republic, the numbers game was more than just a gamble. It was a cultural carryover and a survival mechanism, closely resembling "play whe" in Trinidad or the "drop pan" lottery in Jamaica. These island-born systems, adapted to urban America, gave the newly arrived a way to participate in an economy that had largely shut them out.

And at the center was the Caribbean connection to the "numbers game", an underground lottery-like system or as it was referred to as a "policy racket." A racket that began with hope and ended, for some, in power or prison. Monica's family was cursed with power.

Long before Powerball, Mega Millions and Pick 3, the numbers racket or policy as it was known in the neighborhood was the people's lottery. You would find Caribbean women, often from Jamaica or Trinidad, taking bets at laundromats, beauty parlors, or corner groceries. They weren't gangsters, but bankers in a parallel economy.

The game was simple: A player picked a three-digit number. If the number hit, the payout was 600 to 1. Unlike the state-run lotto, the winnings were delivered in cash, same day, by a runner, usually a teenage boy or nephew on a bike.

The operation was run by "bankers", "tellers", "runners", "pick-up men", and "security": a decentralized network of local community figures who often doubled as barbers, beauty salon owners or bodega workers. Women, especially Caribbean matriarchs, played crucial roles as tellers and runners, trusted with collecting bets and payouts. The bankers, pick-up men and security were generally men who provided the necessary pressure and "muscle" when needed. The revenue stream and profit margins were extreme in the numbers racket.

In Bed-Stuy, other Black and Caribbean cultures, the numbers were not viewed from a criminals' standpoint because these operators were seen as benefactors in their neighborhoods. They provided emergency loans, paid rent, and funded community programs and funeral costs. In an era where banks redlined Black and Caribbean neighborhoods, the numbers were their de facto financial institutions. This truly was a testimony about the strength and faith in self-reliance and resilience that Black and Caribbean culture lost over the years.

The Despicables were everywhere. Just as a thriving economy emerged and as gentrification arrived in the urban centers of Black and Caribbean communities, the Despicables arrived for their "cut." This arrangement only flourished as an underground economy with the Despicable's tacit approval, though still illegal. The Despicables, unlike the Black and Caribbean "numbers" entrepreneurs, operated with a layer of legitimacy: because of approvals enabled by bribes to local precincts and political fixers. In Bed-Stuy, the line between criminality and community service was often blurred. The money flowed from backroom parlors to storefront churches, from dice games to nightclubs like the legendary Slave Theater. These enterprises opened the doors to large investments by traditional bankers, all under the control of the Despicables.

There were occasional crackdowns and arrests, usually right before a citywide election, because of the uncertainty whether the Despicables had sufficiently corralled the incoming administration in its street illegal commerce activity. Or until they put the right controls, surveillance, bribes, harassment, intimidation, and other forms of undue influence in place to guarantee alliance and allegiance.

Occasionally, rival factions fought for turf or when a political boss needed a public win that required the unique services of the Despicables. But for the most part, the numbers racket was tolerated, even protected. Some say it kept the streets calmer, giving folks something to hope for, a chance for a little joy and security, even if fleeting.

By the 1990s, the New York State lottery coupled with the proliferation of the drug trade siphoned away customers from the street game. Government regulation sanitized what was once intimate and dangerous. But the legacy of the numbers racket remains etched in Bed-Stuy's cultural DNA. It represented the resilience of Caribbean immigrants and Black Americans who turned exclusion into enterprise. The numbers migrated and flourished in the Bronx, Queens and Manhattan for a while until it was replaced by more enterprising rackets like drugs and other unlawful activities. In a broader sense, it represented a choice between a "Road Less Traveled" or the "Path of Least Resistance."

Even today, elders in the neighborhoods still speak in hushed tones about who "hit" big back in the day, or which runner never got caught, or which local church was built with quiet donations from the underground economy.

And even when the gentrification crept in like a slow fire: Starbucks replacing rum bars, brownstones flipped for white-collar invaders: the rhythm of the Caribbean never fully left. It lingers in the way people still speak, the way they stress their season of truth[9], the way they carry both a homeland and a borough on their backs. But, like urban folklore, the evil influx of drugs brought back the memory of Bed-Stuy under the rule of the Despicables, still operated in the shadows and received their cut of the underground economy.

Malik's thoughts drifted away as they arrived back at Monica's parents' home.

Sisterhood

When they arrived back at her parents' home, Malik immediately went to the family's den off the living room. Within twenty minutes her two sisters came into the den and for literally 15 minutes or more, they simply stared at Malik with no offer of conversation. Malik, not one to back down, sat there on the couch staring back at Monica's two sisters, returning their vacuous stare with as much conviction as they showed him. Both were exquisitely beautiful like Monica, each one a represented porcelain doll of quality, petite and unassuming but for the blank stares.

It was as if they tried to intimidate him or to turn him into a stone from their unusual antics. Like Lot's wife in the biblical story of Sodom and Gomorrah, to say anything or to break his returning gaze with even a blink, meant Malik surely would turn to stone.

Their faces only showed the darkness and wickedness in their eyes. Malik's first indication was foul with Monica's family. Things were never as they seemed or normal by any objective standards. You might ask: "Why did not Malik pay attention to the warnings? Or if he did, why did he stay with Monica?" It is said that "youth is wasted on the young." Perhaps, it was as simple as stubbornness or maybe even immaturity.

The fact of the matter was despite the warnings, Malik stayed because to leave would defy his destiny and to fulfill his purpose in life. Though at the tender age of twenty-six he had no appreciation of his purpose or manifest destiny in life. So, in Malik's own way, he was selfish like Monica.

However, over time and as things revealed themselves to him, Malik realized he had not married into a family. He soon learned he had married into a syndicate. Perhaps, it was the large sums of cash her parents retrieved from a closet upstairs. They often would provide him with money to take Monica on a nice date when they visited them. More on that in a moment. There was a certain intrigue and fascination surrounding Monica's family. Until one day she completely lost her luster.

The Flight

And that day, when Monica stood at the door of their home in Chicago with their eight-month-old daughter, Jordan, in her arms with a sneer and wicked smile on her face, she boldly pronounced:

"Now that I have your baby, I will never be broke," Monica said as she laughed in Malik's face.

That was the day the dagger was thrust into his heart. Except his efforts to stave the wounds were futile. She thrust the blade of words into his mind and heart. Malik's efforts to remove that narcissistic injury were futile. As he pulled the blade from his heart, only his hand grasped its handle. The first of many callouses formed as protection over his heart. He lost another part of innocence. His experiences with Monica and her family marked a seminal point in his life as part of his personal truth[9]. That even his wife betrayed him. There would be other layers to peel away while at the same time the miseducation of Malik Andrew Madison started. This became part of Malik's personal truths[9], among others throughout his life, that helped form him.

April Fools' Day

It was "April Fool's Day" when Malik returned home to find it being ransacked. They were like professional movers. It was a disservice to brand them "U-Haul" as he entered their condo from a day-long study session for the Illinois Bar examination. It looked as if these folks had done this before. As Malik walked into their home, he saw Monica and her father rifling through their home, boxing up Jordan's and Monica's things. Barely enough time to utter a word or mount a defense, the shock of it all demobilized him. He was "bum rushed" without any clarity about what he should or could do. It was a mid-Sunday afternoon, so Malik was faced with limited legal options. She was taking his daughter across state lines.

And then suddenly it occurred to Malik. This was the plan all along as he recalled Monica once said: "When people do not do what we want, we take their children from them." For years, Malik resisted her family's efforts to enroll him in their dastardly deeds. They needed a street wise attorney to represent them in their dastardly deeds.

Maybe it was the constant harangue that Jordan was Monica's daughter, as if Malik's role was relegated to sire. It all came to a head that dreadful day. Malik felt hoodwinked, bamboozled and used.

All her evening trips out of the house when he returned home from a full day of work and law school made sense. Forced to tend to their daughter Jordan, it only made him grow closer to their daughter. He grew close to his daughter only for Monica's family to snatch Jordan from him. That was the plan and then everything he thought they had together become suspect. But, Malik refused to be controlled and relocate with her to New York. To do that, meant he would enter the kitchen and cast him into the fire of evil.

Monica knew fully a bond of attachment would form between him and his daughter. When it formed, then only to snatch Jordan from his hands just when Malik learned to love her more. It was certainly a bitter pill that he swallowed. The day Malik lost his innocence.

And, then just like that, they were gone. Left alone in their home. Left alone with his shock. Left alone foolish. For the rest of the day, all Malik did was walk around the home, like a zombie. Though at work, he hid his separation and despair from his colleagues and the office. He was paralyzed and understandably confused.

For the next nine months after they left, Malik was on autopilot. Thankfully he was in his last semester of law school. In July, he was scheduled to sit for the Illinois Bar examination. However, the sense of embarrassment and loneliness took its toll on him physically, mentally, emotionally but not spiritually. It made that dreadful day more impactful that she left Malik on April 1. April Fools' Day. She created a "fool's paradise" for them.

But, after nine months of conversations and separation, Malik finally convinced Monica to return to their home in Chicago. He accepted all the blame for the difficulties in their marriage.

They returned to Chicago and at least for a short time Malik was happy to have Jordan back. He still had his reservations about Monica. Perhaps, it was the forewarning that Malik's mom said to him when he told her Monica returned to Chicago.

She said, "Son, a woman does not stay away from her man for nine months, unless something else is going on." How did she know?

He took her comment seriously while at the same time realized his mother never cared for Monica. Nevertheless, Malik became vigilant over his emotions and expectations over Monica. He even asked GOD to give him a sign whether his marriage to Monica was truly sanctioned before GOD's eyes. And, then GOD gave Malik his answer.

It was not even a full month before Monica announced she was returning to New York. For that week, Malik kept asking her, "What is wrong?"

Monica simply said: "It's not you."

"WTF, does 'it's not you' mean?" Malik racked his brain as everything seemed fine when they returned.

This girl was good at twenty-two; she was a viper. Two days after he said farewell to Monica and Jordan at O'Hare Airport, a telephone bill arrived. Call it gut or intuition, Malik immediately opened the telephone bill. Over 30 calls to some number in New York appeared on the bill and during times Malik was at work or out of the house or at church.

Malik immediately dialed the number. On the third ring, a man answered the telephone. Although he tried to deny the affair, his protestations and explanations were lame. Even a wife can betray a husband.

Within 6 months of their second marital separation, Malik divorced Monica. She ended up as the concubine of the wealthy man Malik confronted on the telephone. The three of them had a tumultuous relationship. It got to the point for his own sanity and to safeguard his new marriage, he was estranged from Jordan a long time. Ten years later, out of blue Monica reached out to Malik. Jordan wanted a relationship with her father. His second wife, Denai, expressed her reservations, but they agreed to the reconciliation. They put their best foot forward.

Denai

Denai Madison, the second wife of Malik Madison, moved through life with the precision of a finely tuned Cartier timepiece: measured, deliberate, and unflinchingly composed. Every action, every word, carried intention. Her confidence was quiet but unmistakable, the kind that made even the most arrogant executive pause and listen.

She possessed the intellect of a sage: earned not in lecture halls but in the hard classrooms of Houston streets. From a secretary's desk, she climbed the corporate ladder to become Senior Vice

President, Treasury at PAINCO: without a single framed diploma on her wall, yet every bit the diplomat in how she carried herself.

Though she hadn't traveled widely, her mind had journeyed everywhere. She devoured books: thousands of them: on subjects as varied as Gitner's economic theories to Hitler, Shelly Winters to Einstein's musings on relativity. She could hold a conversation with anyone, about anything, and leave them wondering how she knew so much.

It was that blend of intellect, poise, and quiet strength that first caught Malik's attention in the PAINCO cafeteria. She reminded him of a young Diahann Carroll: elegant, luminous: with the unbending resolve of Angela Bassett. There was a weight in her gaze, the kind that told him she survived storms he could only imagine.

As an adopted child of parents whose marriage fractured soon after her arrival, Denai learned early that survival was a solo act. Life hardened her edges but polished her will and presentation. She had both presentation and facility. Malik knew instinctively that if his back was ever against the wall, Denai would be the one standing beside him: back-to-back, facing the storm together.

They married two years after their first meeting. Three years later came Kendall: their miracle, their anchor, the living proof that, amid chaos and ambition, love could still be built brick by deliberate brick.

Kendall was, as Denai often said, "the joy that made the struggle worth it."

Malik Madison built his life on dualities. Two careers, two callings, two loves: and two silos, each walled off from the other like nations with uneasy treaties.

In one, there was Denai: the steady compass that kept his world aligned. Her strength wasn't loud, but it was the kind that endured when storms came. She was disciplined, wrapped in elegance, a woman who could turn chaos into order simply by showing up. When Malik came home to her, he could exhale. She was beautiful as well, except for the calm center of their spinning world.

Then there was Monica: beautiful too, volatile, intoxicating. With Monica, the air was charged, heavy with passion and danger. She stirred something primal in him, something that whispered of risk and reward, of a world beyond rules and restraint. She didn't love gently, if at all. She consumed. Malik knew that being with her was like handling electricity: you couldn't hold it for long without being shocked and burned, but oh, how intoxicatingly alive the pain was. With Monica it felt like you were without Novocain as the dentist removed your molars.

He recalled his college days in Boston whenever they would go out; he would lie dressed on her bed watching Monica apply her make-up to her face. It was a bit of theatre and painting at the same time. Theater because it was like an act in a play where Monica played the muse. Painting as she applied the mask to hide the evil within her. In either case, Malik was mesmerized by Monica's ritual adoring her beauty while slowly he surrendered his heart to her.

If Denai Madison was the embodiment of calm precision, Monica Mitchell was the storm that preceded it. Where Denai's power flowed like measured water through stone, Monica's surged like fire through oil: beautiful, dangerous, and unpredictable.

Their stories didn't begin with her but generations before, in the red clay fields of rural Mississippi. In the late 1940s, Monica's grandmother: Hattie Mitchell, barely fourteen and already a mother of two: left those dusty roads behind, following the Great Migration north to New York. She carried nothing but a tattered satchel, a photograph of her children, and a will forged in hardship.

To survive, she did whatever required to make it. Housekeeping, barmaid work, street hustles, odd jobs that blurred the line between survival and sin: she did them all. Without a high school education, she learned that the world rarely rewarded virtue, but it respected hustle. And so, she hustled. She always kept a man nearby, not for love but for leverage: "just in case I ever need spare change," she would say with a sly, tired grin.

Somewhere along the way, she crossed paths with Bumpy Johnson and fell into his Harlem network, running numbers and collecting debts. It was there she met Monica's "play grandfather," a Jamaican hustler with street smarts but no schooling. Together, they built their own rival operation in Bedford-Stuyvesant: a shadow enterprise that flirted with danger at every turn, competing with Queenie, Bumpy, and Casper Holstein's legendary racket.

Theirs was a world of whispered threats and midnight escapes. The family lived on the run, constantly shifting from one safe house to another: sleeping behind locked gates, hearing the rattle of machine-gun fire in the distance like a twisted lullaby. The fear of being kidnapped, or worse, was a constant companion. Sometimes they'd disappear not because someone was after them: but because they were after someone else's child to settle a debt.

That fear: sharp, generational, and never quite silenced: etched itself into Monica's bloodline. She learned early that love was conditional, loyalty was currency, and survival meant striking first. It was that inheritance of dysfunction she carried into every relationship she touched, including her marriage to Malik Madison.

Monica had beauty that could silence a room, but it was the kind that warned you not to look too long. Her conscience had been buried long ago, somewhere between the gunfire and the running. She didn't love so much as she possessed. She didn't trust: she calculated.

Where Denai built silos to protect, Monica built them to control. Denai's walls held loyalty and resolve. Monica's life was made of secrets, jealousy, and scars too deep to heal.

Two women. Two silos.

And Malik Madison caught somewhere in between: was learning that love, like empire, can be divided by its own foundations.

He had once tried to rationalize it all: to explain his divided heart as some complex manifestation of need. One woman grounded him; the other ignited him. Denai spoke to his reason, Monica to his rebellion. Each reflected a part of himself he could never reconcile: the man who wanted to build and the man who wanted to burn.

But life, he learned, doesn't permit such symmetry for long.

The two silos he'd constructed to separate his worlds: his home with passion with Denai, his passion never really a home with Monica: were beginning to crumble. Secrets leaked through cracks like water through concrete. The more he tried to contain them, the more they eroded the foundation beneath him. It never makes sense to have a house that is not a home.

At night, Malik would sometimes wake in a cold sweat, unsure which woman he had dreamed. In those moments, his mind played cruel tricks: Denai's voice calling him from the shadows, Monica's perfume lingering in the sheets.

He was a man divided: by love, by guilt from the estrangement from his daughter, Jordan, by the weight of choices that could no longer be neatly partitioned.

And yet, he told himself, every empire whether a marriage between two people or a corporation with competing interests begins with two silos: one of grain, the other of secrets. One sustains life; the other destroys it.

Malik Madison built both with his wives but also found himself within two silos at PAINCO.

And in time, he would come to learn which of these various silos would collapse first. There were the two silos at PAINCO that Malik and Denai now fought. Malik felt another but different type of storm brewing.

Moldavu Ltd.

Denai Madison had always been precise. Deliberate. The kind of woman who noticed patterns others overlooked. She asked many questions and left nothing to wonder or chance. As Vice President of Treasury Operations, Pan American Insurance Company ("PAINCO"), her mind was a finely tuned instrument designed to track liquidity, detect financial anomalies, and anticipate corporate risk. But lately, the numbers did not sit right. On paper, it appeared that PAINCO was a legitimate operation. However, while digging deeper into the corporate finances and legal documents, it became readily apparent that a "deep state" operation ran a second silo within PAINCO simultaneously.

She ran her hand slowly across the printout before her. Line by line, wire transfer by transfer: something was wrong. On paper, it appeared to be a boutique investment firm based in a nondescript office building in Valleta, Malta. Its balance sheets scrubbed clean, its filings precise, and its directors: a carousel of lawyers and accountants: seemed almost interchangeable. Its

CEO was a woman named Marilyn Raynor. Yet behind the neat façade, Moldavu was a vault for the Despicable's darkest ambitions. Moldavu Ltd. was not just another affiliate. Its movements were erratic. And substantial. Too substantial. Millions moved in and out of the company without adequate capitalization and documentation. Offshore accounts. Round-trip transactions.

And something that looked like layering: classic signs of money laundering.

The company formed in the wake of the Cold War, forged out of the Soviet Black Market and the Balkan smuggling networks that thrived on chaos. Arms, oil, and stolen art all passed through Moldavu's shell accounts. What was once a loose consortium of smugglers became, through careful cultivation, a global holding company with tentacles buried deep in London, Zurich, Hong Kong, and Dubai.

Denai discussed this information with Malik. For Malik, the revelation came not from the headlines, but from rumors: a coded wire transfer that bore Moldavu's imprint, a chance slip of a customs agent's tongue, the sudden disappearance of a friend who asked too many questions. He learned that Moldavu was not simply laundering money: it was laundering history. Dictators, oligarchs, even certain "respectable" Western financiers trusted Moldavu to hide their spoils.

The Despicables used Moldavu Ltd. as both shield and sword. Shield, because its layers of shell corporations and offshore trusts made any investigation drown in paperwork. Sword, because through Moldavu, they could destabilize currencies, finance coups, or bankrupt rivals under the guise of legitimate market operations.

The Despicables

Many once-stable blue-chip Fortune 100 companies collapsed not merely because they failed to adapt to market changes or advancing technology: but because they were betrayed from within.

Corporate raiders, often disguised as trusted allies, infiltrated their ranks only to reveal themselves later as hostile suitors' intent on plundering what they could. They stripped assets, gutted pensions, laid off employees in droves, and left proud institutions in ruin.

Sears, Enron, Bear Stearns, and Lehman Brothers all fell victim to this brand of corporate warfare: systematically dismantled by government seizures, opportunistic competitors, or the invisible hand of greed. They were kindred spirits of a sort: rivals bound by mutual guilt and survival instinct.

Financial historians noted that Sears relied heavily on its 'financial services group' (which included Allstate, Dean Witter Reynolds, and Coldwell Banker) to offset retail losses in the 1980s and early 1990s. In 1992, Sears reported that its financial services subsidiaries generated the bulk of its total operating income, effectively subsidizing its failing department stores. Today, Allstate appears strong; Sears is defunct while Allstate remains a Fortune 100 personal lines insurance giant, headquartered in Illinois. Sears, after its disastrous merger with Kmart under Eddie Lampert, filed for bankruptcy in 2018, with only a handful of stores left operating under the Sears trade name.

Until its demise, Sears used its crown jewel, Allstate, as a lifeline: draining the insurer's cash reserves to keep its retail empire afloat. But tides and alliances in the investment community of Wall Street shift quickly. Today, Allstate appears as a symbol of resilience, while Sears exists only as a faded memory of what once was.

When one company saw the regulatory and or enforcement bullet such as an investigation come its way, a simple step aside and let a competitor take the hit. In industries where nearly everyone's hands were dirty. It was often a rival who 'whistle-blew' first, offered up another's sins to shield its own. Politics and business, after all, have always made for strange and treacherous bedfellows.

Some said the very name "Moldavu" was a corruption of an old Slavic word meaning "to swallow whole." And indeed, that was its nature. Moldavu swallowed institutions and digested people into capital.

Malik realized then that Moldavu was not merely a company. It was a citadel of principalities, the kind the Apostle warned of in Ephesians: powers and rulers of darkness hiding behind corporate seals and glossy annual reports. It was a Despicable's edifice, its foundation laid in greed and blood, its shareholders not men but demons clothed in Armani suits. The scriptures warn there are principalities both good and bad waging war above us. These are not necessarily human battles as we know them, but spiritual warfare of sorts. Those below these spiritual battles are merely pawns and assets to be traded as wars wage.

Moldavu treated people as human capital although it can be accused it traded them as chattel as well. Moldavu cloaked its crimes in the sterile language of commerce. In its ledger, human lives and broken bodies were disguised as assets and addictions. Other matters involving weapons, military and wars became balance sheet line items such as machinery. Like what the street called pimps and pushers, Moldavu rebranded as strategic partners.

Human trafficking was entered under the pseudonym "Human Capital Acquisition." To the outside world, it looked like a benign consultancy in global recruitment. In truth[9], it was a pipeline of stolen girls from Eastern Europe, young men from the Caribbean, and migrant workers from Africa: catalogued, priced, and moved across borders like commodities.

Sex trafficking appeared as "Hospitality and Entertainment Services." High-rise brothels in Dubai and hidden villas in the Balkans were listed as "resort properties." The company's financial reports even projected "repeat customer engagement" as if debauchery were just another service industry.

Gun smuggling was reclassified as "Defense Logistics." Moldavu handled shipments of AK47s, rocket launchers, and drones, all re-labeled as "industrial equipment" or "agricultural machinery." Weapons that would topple governments hidden in shipping manifests next to crates of tractors and irrigation pumps.

Narcotics were sanitized as "Pharmaceutical Ventures." Moldavu's subsidiaries posed as research labs and drug wholesalers, their ledgers hiding the true cargo: cocaine from Columbia, heroin from Afghanistan, methamphetamine from Mexico and China. The streets overflowed with poison, while Moldavu's, parent company, PAINCO, and its shareholders toasted their "growth markets."

But that was precisely the type of information that tipped Malik and Denai off that something was afoul with Moldavu. In a rate of return and profit margin environment of approximately 6% in the financial services industry, Moldavu's return on equity was close to 25% and was marketed as a high-risk capitalization fund to investors. Its profit margins were extreme.

Even the street-level commerce: counterfeit luxury goods, blood diamonds, stolen cars: was swept into categories like "Retail Expansion," "Precious Metals," and "Logistics Optimization." Every crime had a corporate pseudonym, every sin a quarterly dividend.

Malik understood then that Moldavu was not just a money laundering machine. It was laundering mortality itself. By giving evil an executive gloss, they blurred the line between the boardroom and the back alley. The balance sheets of Moldavu were not accounts. They were confessions written in codes, where suffering was reduced to metrics and damnation wore the smile of a CEO. PAINCO trafficked in information too.

Moldavu's digital dominion was even more frightening. If Moldavu's shell corporations hid crimes in the shadows of finance, its offshore artificial intelligence laboratories brought these shadows into the blinding light of the digital age. From a discreet server farm nestled on an island near India, Moldavu ran what appeared to be a cutting-edge data analytics subsidiary. It was the surveillance arm of the Despicables: a machine designed to expose, exploit, and enslave the very soul of humanity.

The system tapped into the pulse of the internet. Every search query, every late-night purchase, every half-deleted message communicated and fed into Moldavu's algorithms. Social media chatter became a harvest field, where addictions and weaknesses were tagged, sorted, and filed away. Pornography habits, drug cravings, gambling slips, even the secret rendezvous of married men: all cascading, captured, and available virtually by AI. Man created God on earth just as Satan promised as his version of a 'person' in the form of the corporation. The Despicables were Satan's disciples on earth.

For the Despicables, the equation and motivation were simple: desire equals leverage. Moldavu weaponized the old adage: "You are only as sick as your secrets." Because it used the information to blackmail, corrupt and apply undue influence on its victims and targets to cause them to do things they otherwise avoided. A comment in the wrong ear could destroy a marriage. A leak of the wrong screenshot could topple a politician. A carefully planted rumor could unravel a life.

Their algorithms did not just monitor: they manipulated. Packages ordered online were mysteriously delayed or redirected. Mail delivered by the US Post Office already opened, and suggested someone in the facility monitored mail. Email messages sent, delivered, opened, monitored, delayed, and redirected if Moldavu needed leverage. Encrypted conversations "accidentally" unsent or undeliverable when the Despicables wanted paranoia to spread. Access to social media accounts suspended if chat messages or posts hinted at the source of unfavorable information about the Despicables. Even shipments of life-saving medicine could vanish from supply chains, only to reappear when a target agreed to bend the knee.

This was no longer simple surveillance. It was orchestration, but not a symphony of melodies. Moldavu's artificial intelligence function became the conductor of depravity, where each person's private compulsions were notes to be played, and every hidden urge was an instrument of control and subtle messaging. Access to home security cameras and sending software patches to open the camera and voice recorder on cell phones, laptops, computers, and handheld devices provided the Despicables with unfettered access to the private lives of people. This included the conduct and thoughts of their victims and targets. This was unabashedly an invasion of the public's privacy and a subversion of the US Constitution on all fronts.

Malik and Denai realized the horror: the Despicables did not need to create sins: they only needed to expose the ones that already lurked inside the human heart. And once revealed, those secrets bound men and women more tightly than shackles or chains ever could. Moldavu Ltd. had perfected a new form of slavery: one where the chains were invisible, the guards were algorithms, and the prison was the mind itself. In this sense, human beings simply served as electronic chattel to be used and then disposed of in whatever manner the Despicables wanted.

Denai and Malik were not paranoid. They were exacting. Between the two of them, they knew the internal controls better than anyone. This was not just financial engineering: it was intentional concealment.

And that terrified them.

Denai leaned back in her chair and closed her eyes, trying to find grounding in the sound of Miles Davis. The notes soothed her but could not wash away the chill in her bones.

Her cell phone vibrated with another message from Malik. One word: "Ready?"

She typed back, "Almost."

Denai had always stayed in the lines. A Black woman in corporate finance did not get far by rocking the boat. It was especially true for Malik, as senior corporate attorney, Mergers and Acquisitions, PAINCO. Now the storm raged and the tides rose, as they realized the only way to survive was to become the very uncovered peril they once insured against. The 'risk of ruin' the insurers feared would not come from a modeled Category 5 hurricane tearing through a metropolis like Tampa: but from an uncovered insurance man-made insurance peril called 'Madison-Mitchell.'

Denai turned to the safe in the corner, entered the code, and retrieved a thick manila envelope. Inside: bank statements, encrypted USBs, and a sealed letter addressed to Monica.

Then, she stood, straightened her blazer, and walked downstairs to join Malik for the night. There was no going back.

They both despised PAINCO for the way it treated their customers and used its employees. As to the latter, the Madisons held disdain for PAINCO's treatment of Black executives who occupied their positions largely to serve diversity goals. They both despised PAINCO for the way it treated their customers and used its employees. As to the latter, the Madisons held disdain for PAINCO's treatment of Black executives who were like a frantic crowd in and out of a revolving door of a Filene's Basement Christmas clearance sale. Often, PAINCO would hire a Black senior executive to simply carry out one of its "right-sizing" strategies of its workforce. Invariably, it was mostly Blacks and other minorities who took the brunt of layoffs.

Within a couple of years of its implementation, soon the Black executive would be shown the door with, of course, a lucrative stock option bundle. Or alternatively, Blacks deserved and earned promotions but were passed over numerous times given some trumped-up excuse for the omission. So, it was not that difficult or unreasonable for the Madison family to concoct a scheme to destroy PAINCO when it became necessary and righteous to do so. Their family purposefully placed in harm's way became the righteous justice PAINCO deserved.

By that time, Malik accepted a transfer to PAINCO's New York City office while his family remained in Chicago and would join him in their home in Asbury Park, New Jersey a year later. In the interim, strange and concerning things were happening to and around Malik after he worked in NYC.

Chapter Three
The Blood Oath

"…maintaining love to thousands, and forgiving wickedness, rebellion and sin. Yet he does not leave the guilty unpunished; he punishes the children and their children for the sin of the parents to the third and fourth generation."

— Exodus 34:7

The ritual chamber was thick with incense and dread. A man knelt at the center of the circle, a hood on his head wearing a black robe, bowed beneath the torchlight. Around him, the Despicables stood in their black robes, silent as stone. The High Voice, dressed in an attire like that of the man kneeling, intoned the three paths: voluntary membership, a blood offering, or the blood oath.

While the Despicables appeared to give the recruit, victim or target, a real choice, there was never one. Voluntary membership generally was for people who shared the same values and needed control as the Despicables. It was the other two choices that left the recruit in twisted nightmarish knots. For a blood offering was reserved for those who did not shy away from killing and death. The blood oath was slightly better because the recruit could offer up a family, friend or colleague for membership. In truth[9], nothing was ever voluntary and short-term with the Despicables. It was a lifetime family membership.

But the man did not answer. His silence answered itself. He would not yield, yet he would not refuse outright. The Despicables already knew the cost.

Within the Order, it was understood: if one would not serve, another must. Family blood was the guarantee. Someone always had to bear the mark or burden.

That night, the man returned home. His son, who was close to graduating from Columbia University, sat at the kitchen table, home for summer break. Textbooks stacked beside him as he filled out applications for graduate business school. He looked up, expecting the familiar comfort of a father's presence. But what entered the room was something else… a man weighed down by the weight of his commitment to the Order.

The father poured two glasses of bourbon and slid one across the table. The boy blinked, confused. "Dad, I don't drink."

"You will tonight because you face your rite of passage. You know about our family heritage and our commitment to it." The father took a long, deep gulp of bourbon, the sensation burning his throat.

The son frowned, the unease growing.

"There is a price to pay for the luxury we enjoy. A debt of sorts that our blood owes. I could not pay for it. So, it falls to you. We discussed this once on our hunting trip when you were sixteen," he continued.

The son shook his head, further confused. "What do you mean?"

His father's eyes were wet, but unflinching. "You've been chosen. The Despicables named the oath. They require a death or assassination."

The words dropped like stones between them. The son's heart raced. "Dad, you cannot ask me to..." he replied with a plaintive wail. His all-American collegiate looks showed a frown of consternation as he looked back at his father.

"I'm not asking," the father cut in, his voice cracking. "It's already decided. You are my offer to secure our family's continued future. One family member must always be willing to take the fall. If I don't offer your services, they'll take someone else. Your sister, perhaps your mother."

The boy's breath caught in his throat. He felt trapped, the walls of his own home closing around him. His father reached across the table, gripped his hand with desperate strength.

"They've given you an assignment. You will travel to Hartford from Penn Station. The target is a CEO of one of the largest life and health insurers in the nation. He'll be at a conference at the Thompson Hotel. You must carry out the blood oath to continue our family legacy and security." He looked away from his son. He never thought this day would come.

The young man recoiled, shaking his head. "Dad, I am about to graduate college next Spring, and I'm supposed to be going to grad school next fall!" He shouted at his father.

"And you still may if you carry out the assignment exactly as planned. This is not about what you want. It's about our survival as a family." The father took the last swig of bourbon from his glass.

Tears welled in the young man's eyes. His father's voice softened, almost pleading now. "Son, this is how it's always been. Every generation. Someone in the family must commit to the Order to prove our allegiance to the Order. It was mine once and my father before that and his. It's your turn now."

The young man sat frozen, his dreams dissolving into dust. Somewhere deep inside, something hardened. It needed to for him to complete the assignment. He nodded slowly, silently.

"This will guarantee your future and status in life. You will be fine. Everything is planned to minimize the risk of your identity and from getting caught…"

After the conversation with his father, the young man burst out of the house in a storm of confusion, fear, and anger. He couldn't tell which emotion ruled him, everything blurred together, a mental tornado ripped through the quiet order of his thoughts and left only wreckage behind.

Randolph "Randy" James Iannucci slammed open the car door of his 2025 BMW Z4 convertible. The night air hit him like a slap, but it wasn't enough. He needed movement—speed—to outrun the words that still echoed in his head. He threw the car into reverse and shot down the driveway like a bat out of hell.

He knew exactly where to go. Harlem—and the boroughs beyond— always was his refuge. When the world pressed too hard, his friends Jamal, Tito, and Antonio knew how to loosen its grip. Maybe, if luck was on his side, he'd run into that girl Gina again. That would ease the tension coiled in his chest.

He sped down the Southern State Parkway toward the Long Island Expressway, merging onto I-495 West with the familiar hum of late-night traffic. Fifteen minutes later, the Grand Central Parkway swallowed him whole, carried him across the RFK (Triborough) Bridge and into Manhattan. By the time he reached 125th Street via the Harlem River Drive, nearly an hour and a half passed—but the city's rhythm already began to work on him.

The drive itself was a mosaic of New York's many faces— each distinct yet woven into one pulse. Long Island's manicured lawns and tree-lined streets faded behind him, gave way to the sprawled arteries of the city. On a Saturday night, traffic was a coin toss; tonight, it flowed. The steady thrum of engines and the blur of green exit signs—Hicksville, Westbury, Mineola—became his soundtrack. Gas stations flashed by diners and strip malls fell away, and the horizon drew tight as the skyline of Queens and then Manhattan teased his eyes from afar.

Crossing from Nassau County into Queens, the world compressed. Apartment blocks replaced houses, the roads widened, and neon replaced stars. The ghostly towers of the 1964 World's Fair still stood defiant, waiting for their reckoning with time. Above, planes dipped and rose like restless spirits, lights winked as they descended toward LaGuardia or Kennedy. To the left, the Bronx skyline glowed faintly; to the right, the Chrysler Building gleamed—a silver relic, beautiful and unbowed.

Then came the Harlem River Drive—a winding vein of motion, light, and concrete. The bridges rose like sentinels in the night: Willis Avenue, Third Avenue, Madison Avenue. And beyond them, Harlem.

Randy pulled up to the Lambda Lounge, one of his usual haunts. If his friends weren't there, he'd drift to the Shrine, Harlem Nights, or Angel of Harlem—each a familiar port in the storm.

Harlem was his secret playground. His family and his White Long Island circle had no idea how deep his roots ran here. In the clubs, the regulars knew him well. They called him "White Chocolate." At first, he bristled at the nickname—but eventually, he wore it like a badge. After all, in truth[9], he was White… and he did have a taste for chocolate.

"Hell… that was less than a secret than what he was about to carry." He chuckled at the thought, killed the engine, and stepped out into the Harlem night.

Randolph "Randy" James Iannucci was the kind of young man who turned heads without even trying. He carried the effortless confidence of someone who was always told he had it all—and for the most part, he did. With the clean-cut, all-American good looks of a young actor Patrick Schwarzenegger, he embodied the charm and privilege of Long Island's finest sons. His smile—broad, easy, and lined with perfectly white teeth—had the power to disarm or seduce in equal measure. There was a glint, almost a mischievous twinkle, in his hazel eyes that hinted at a boyish audacity that lurked beneath the polish.

Randy's body still bore the sculpted memory of his glory days as a high school quarterback—shoulders wide, waist trim, his frame molded like a modern Adonis. Even his casual movements carried an athlete's poise, that unspoken awareness of strength under control. He dressed sharp but never overdressed—jeans that fit just right, a clean shirt open at the collar, and a watch that cost more than most people's rent.

When he walked, it was with a confident swagger—a rhythm in his step that said he was both cheered and envied. Yet beneath the swagger was a subtle tension, the kind that came from expectations too heavy to escape. Randy was aware of his good looks. And though he wore that confidence like cologne, there was something else beneath it—an unspoken fragility, uncanny sensitivity and sensibility like the quiet ache of a man who still tried to define himself beyond what the world already saw.

He was the "cat's meow" but it rarely showed. Randy made everyone feel comfortable around him. Though life as he knew it was about to change. For now, he couldn't worry about it.

Chapter Four
The Gypsy

"Do not turn to medium or necromancers, do not seek them out, and so make yourself unclean by them; I am the Lord thy GOD."

— Leviticus 19:31

It was a Friday evening in Manhattan, and Malik was the last to leave the office. But this wasn't just any Friday night; it was the start of another double life. Behind the door of his executive suite office, he slipped out of his tailored suit and into a pair of shorts and a fitted golf shirt. In less than an hour, he would blend in like any other night runner, tourist, or delivery man. Bobbing, weaving, twisting and turning to avoid the onslaught of people on the heated pavements of Manhattan streets, Malik was deep in thought as he navigated the crowds like a drone on automatic pilot.

But this wasn't about exercise or errands. Malik had a job to do and it wasn't corporate.

This night's destination was the Village. The city glimmered with obvious luxury while Malik prepared to take something back from those who had taken too much of his family's future. His timing had to be flawless. By 5:00 AM, the meeting would be done.

He had a few hours. Just enough time to disappear into the shadows of the city's canyon of skyscrapers, complete the job, and then catch the early train out of Penn Station. He needed to be in Asbury Park, New Jersey, by 7:00 AM, as if nothing changed.

The Gypsy Warning

The steam rose from the city's manholes mingled with the scent of roasted nuts and stale beer as Malik walked aimlessly around the Village. His stride was calm but calculated… he had time, but not much. Then something… *someone*… stopped him cold. He noticed the woman the old man described when they met earlier.

She stood under a chipped red awning that read: "Madam Erzsebet: Fortune Told, Truths⁹ Revealed." She beckoned to him with a crooked finger. She waited for him and knew Malik would come. The man he met with earlier gave him the address for the next piece of his request.

He responded kindly as he stepped into the storefront, a bit hesitant at first.

The storefront cluttered and dim, the kind of place that made people cross the street and quicken their pace. A flickered neon sign blinked above the door. She stepped forward from the shadows, stooped, her frame wrapped in layers of scarves and velvet. Her face was a tapestry of time, deeply lined and weather-worn, like cracked porcelain. Her eyes, though clouded with age, gleamed with unsettling clarity.

"You..." she said in a thick, guttural accent.

"You walk with ghosts." She firmly said.

Malik paused. He had not spoken a word.

"Come," she beckoned with a gnarled finger, her gold bangles clinking as she turned. The door creaked open with a moan. Against his better judgment, he followed.

Inside, the air was thick and musty, almost humid. The front of the shop was crammed with relics; carved wooden saints, blown-glass evil eyes, faded books of Slavic tongue, and cracked icons of the Virgin Mary that looked centuries old. Dust floated like ash through a single beam of light that pierced the stained-glass window.

She moved with surprised speed, parted beaded curtains and led him to the back. A narrow hallway opened into a smaller room, cozier but no less cluttered. Candles flickered beside amulets and jars filled with herbs and bones. The table in the center covered in an old tapestry. She sat.

She spoke, eyes closed, her voice low but sharp.

"You carry the blood of Mitchell... on both sides."

His brow furrowed. He had not told her his name.

She opened her eyes slowly.

"Your ex-wife's family... her maiden line is Mitchell, yes?"

Malik said nothing.

"She is not your only tether. Your great grandmother, too. The name is old. Older than ships, older than slavery. Two lines split long ago. One bore watchers, called the Shilohs. The other... took darker paths. The Despicables."

Malik felt a sudden chill run down his chest.

"These two branches once were one. A tribe blessed and cursed. But now they are at war with spirits and signs, through people like you. Blood calls blood. One to protect, one to possess. Your divorce was not a separation, but a rejoining. An unholy alliance hidden in plain sight.

"Your ex-wife's grandmother formed an unholy alliance. This curse passed through your ex-wife's family to her and now it resides in your daughter." She took a long drag from her cigarette as the smoke rose above her.

Malik was immersed in shock. He had not told the gypsy anything about Monica's background. Yet here he sat before Madam Erzebet as she spun her yarn of truth[9].

She reached beneath the table and pulled out a small black mirror, no larger than a hand.

"You are a thread in their knot. You dream of drowning, yes?"

His mouth opened slightly. He *did* dream that.

She hissed, "Because your soul knows the war began."

Malik stared into the mirror. His reflection flickered once, twice, then steadied.

"Beware of the Mitchell name," she said. "Beware of those who smile with family teeth."

Then she was quiet. The candle behind her flickered and then went out.

Blood in the Roots

Madam Erzebet tapped her foot, steady and precise, like a seamstress who coaxed her machine to threaded yarn of forgotten centuries into the present fabric of life. Malik sat mesmerized by her tales. They called themselves the Al-Abd al-Dasa, a name meaning "The Servants of the Hidden One." A tribe of one hundred souls, born of Moorish and Romani breath, nestled deep in the green folds of the Balkan hills. They were musicians, prophets, midwives, and scribers. Warriors of spirit more than swords.

A sacred line. Shiloh-blooded.

But their kin, Dushev, betrayed them.

For coin. For favor. For power offered by the pale White men with ink-stained hands, silver, and silver tongues.

It was the winter of 1812 when the Dushev opened their mountain pass and allowed the Europeans in—Dutch traders, Portuguese scouts, emissaries from an empire of greed masked in the language of commerce. In a single night, they surrounded the Al-Abd al-Dasa, bound, and marched them in chains through the snow-covered valleys they had once called their new home.

No graves.

No goodbyes.

Only shadows.

From the Balkans they shipped them down the Danube, through Venice, into holding camps in Ghana, West Africa where their skin tone and color, olive and brown, quickly grouped and graded them under one word: slave.

The slave castles of Ghana sat high above the seas with cobbled roads which led to and from the seaport. They stood still as stone against the crashing waves of the Atlantic, their whitewashed walls pockmarked by time, sea salt, and sorrow.

The slave castles of Ghana.

Cape Coast Castle. Elmina Castle. Fort Christiansborg. Fort Amsterdam. Structures of European ambition and African torment. Bastions built not just to defend land, but to traffic souls, a trade to continue into even modern times. It was in the White Europeans' nature and culture to always own men. But inside these Ghanaian seaport castles they were simply cathedrals of suffering.

The castles were perched like gods along the Gulf of Guinea, sun-bleached during the day and ghost-haunted by night. From afar, they looked like fortresses of order but inside they were cathedrals of torture. Beneath their courtyards lay dungeons, stone-walled, windowless chambers where African men, women and children were herded like cattle. The air was thick with human waste, sweat, and despair. Hundreds crammed into rooms no larger than a modern living room. The only light came from a single grated hole in the ceiling, where the sun bore witness, and the rain could not cleanse what was done below.

The walls still echo.

"We were here," they seem to say."

"And we were taken."

Elmina, the oldest of them all, was built by the Portuguese in 1482, long before Columbus sailed west. It passed from hand to hand… Dutch, British, Danish, all eager to profit from the Transatlantic Slave Trade. Here, the currency was flesh. And business boomed.

The Papal Decree

The year was 1493, the dawn of conquest. In Rome, beneath frescoed ceilings and incense clouds, Pope Alexander VI sat upon the throne of St. Peter. His lips, anointed with sacred oil, carried words that stained centuries: a decree granted to kings the divine right to enslave the earth.

The slave trade grew exponentially like the announcement of a gold rush on newly discovered land that miners flocked to mine. In 1493, shortly after Columbus's voyage, Pope Alexander VI issued a series of papal bulls (decrees) that laid the foundation for European colonization and enslavement. The most famous and heinous of the decrees were the Inter Caetera (1493) which granted Spain and Portugal the right to colonize newly discovered lands in the Americas, provided they spread Christianity. It essentially gave the Iberian crowns divine sanction to conquer non-Christian lands worldwide. Religion, like other facets of human society, was always an economic system beyond just religious rivalry. While it appeared as the language of salvation, but it was inked with damnation.

With it, he carved the New World like meat on a table, gifted Spain and Portugal domination over lands they never saw and peoples they did not know. "To bring them to the faith," he proclaimed, but the Despicables smiled in the shadows, for they knew it was not faith but fortune that would bind the innocent in chains.

Yet this was not the beginning, only the coronation of cruelty. Four decades earlier, Pope Nicholas VI issued the Dum Diversas (1452) and Romanus Pontifex (1455) by Pope Nicholas V, which explicitly authorized the King of Portugal to enslave Saracens (Muslims), pagans, and other "enemies of Christ." The plan was to reduce them to perpetual slavery. What began as permission to plunder Muslim and African lives now swelled to a doctrine that would engulf the world: the "Doctrine of Discovery."

And so, the Church, keeper of souls, became the broker of bondage. The Pope's decree was more than law. It was covenant, signed not only with ink but with blood. It opened the door for kingdoms to build empires of flesh, sugar, tobacco, cotton, spices, gold, and death. It baptized slavery not as sin but as enterprise. It formed the very existence of the Despicables.

By 1492-1493, Pope Alexander VI did not proclaim slavery for the first time but legitimized and expanded it under Church authority. His decrees reinforced what historians call the "Doctrine of Discovery," which gave Christian nations the religious and legal justification to conquer, dispossess, and enslave non-Christians worldwide.

The Despicables

Captured from across the African interior, Ashanti, Ewe, Fante, Fulani, Igbo and, Yoruba, they marched in chains for days, weeks and months. Once inside the castles, they were sorted, branded, and held until ships arrived. Those deemed unfit as too sick, too broken, too rebellious discarded. The rest were led to a place that still exists.

It was a narrow arch, carved into the ocean-facing wall. Once you passed through it, there was no coming back. You were no longer African. No longer human in the eyes of your captors. You were now cargo, assigned to the hull of a ship bound for Barbados, Brazil, the Carolinas, or Virginia.

From that door, thousands, perhaps as many as 12.5 million souls, disappeared into history.

The castles had chapels, too.

Above the dungeons, European officers prayed while twirling beads in their hands.

They had communion. They baptized the sinners and sang hymns to the glory of their God.

They read Psalms, while the cries of the dying rose through the floors like incense. The African came to know that the devil wore collars and crosses.

Visitors come now with cameras and sandals, unaware that every stone beneath them absorbed blood. Some weep when they enter the dungeon. Others stand in silence and bewilderment, feeling a presence and sense of guilt, they cannot explain. Still others absorbed disquieted rage.

But the descendants felt the anger in their marrow. The castles were not ruins. They were wombs of trauma, the birth places of centuries of diaspora.

Beneath their courtyards sat several slave ships bound for the "Middle Passage." Sixteen died before the first week. Their bodies eventually, after days, finally tossed into the sea. Mothers, daughters, fathers and sons rested at the deep bottom of the Atlantic Ocean. In the bowels of the ship, one heard the weeping and screaming of the human cargo. A mother would shout out: "Kumbaya... Kumbaya..." and on the other side of the bow another shout from a man, "Kumbaya!" Translation: "Come by here Lord."

The sense of despair and fright was palpable because the Al-Abd-al-Dasa were not the only African tribe in the bowels of the slave ship. There were others which thus initiated the separation of Africans from each other which continued to the slave plantation, and some would say even until today.

It was seldom remembered that more than 16,000 slave ships carved their way across the Atlantic during the horrors of the Middle Passage. On their decks and in their holds, some 12.5 million Africans were torn from their motherland and delivered into bondage in the Americas.

What the records often obscure are the 1.8 million souls who never arrived, who perished in the stench and darkness of those floating tombs, their bodies claimed by the sea.

Unlike the celebrated voyages of Columbus's Santa Maria, Niña and Pinta, these thousands of slave ships carry no names taught in school, no monuments raised to memory. Their journeys remain largely unwritten, buried in the vaults of history, as though the erasure of their record could soften the magnitude of their crimes. Yet each vessel carried the promise of despair mixed with hope that survival in the new lands was possible and that GOD's providence looked over the slaves wherever. And each vessel was its own chapter in humanity's darkest ledger, and each wave that struck their hulls carried the silenced cries of a people whose suffering-built empires.

The Shilohs remembered this moment as one of the Despicables' earliest victories, when a shepherd of Christ was seduced into speaking Satan's tongue. The bulls of Rome were not the voice of GOD, but the echo of Lucifer's ambition disguised as holy writ. Satan's kingdom and dominion on earth.

From that day, the lash and the chain carried papal blessing. Ships christened with saints' names bore human cargo across the seas. And the Despicables laughed, for they had turned the keys of Heaven into the locks of Hell.

The greatest crime of the Despicables was not the lash nor the chain, but the lie and omission of facts. Unlike Columbus's ships, Santa Maria, Pinta and Nina, the names of these slaves' ships seemingly remain unrecorded thus furthering the slaves' story into the deep depths of annals of history. Sanctioned by the Catholic popes, the European slave traders, their allies in church and state did more than break the body of its slaves.

They broke the spirit of the captured souls. They doctored the Bible, taught the enslaved Africans only passages of obedience and withheld the fuller Word of GOD that proclaimed liberation, dignity, and justice. They twisted scripture into a tool of empire and silenced the truth[9] that condemned them.

They taught that bondage was natural, that servitude was ordained, that White masters stood as GOD's representatives on earth. This was no gospel; it was heresy. The greatest cruelty was not only in the flesh torn by lash, but in the lie planted in the mind: that the slave's highest calling was to obey, to suffer, and to forget the truth[9] of their divine purpose.

When folks speak of "missing books," the theory was about writings known in antiquity but excluded from the canon when church councils in Rome, Hippo, and Carthage finalized the Bible (4th and 5th centuries). These are often called the Apocrypha (hidden books) or Deuterocanonical books. Many of these contain teachings on justice, oppression, forgiveness, and divine wrath against the wicked words slave masters did not want in the minds of the enslaved.

Books like Enoch, Jubilees, Jasher, Wisdom of Solomon, Ecclesiasticus, Tobit and Maccabees included scripture and words that expand Exodus and warnings against corruption and judgment on oppressors. Other missing books condemned slavery as a sin against creation while others warned against violence, injustice, and unjust rulers because wisdom reigns over tyranny. Further, there are missing scriptures that talk specifically about the oppression of the poor and GOD's wrath against corrupt rulers. Because GOD favors righteousness through charity and mercy, not domination.

And most importantly, some of these books describe resistance against foreign oppressors, honoring martyrs who refuse to bow to tyrants. Other writings, preserved in Ethiopian and Gnostic traditions, also carried liberating themes such as the Gospels of Thomas, Magdalene and Shepherd of Hermes (kingdom is within, not bestowed by masters, challenges to male-dominated societies and the repentance of oppressors, respectively).

Wallace Plantation

The point is that the slave trader and then masters carved out a Bible of obedience, stripped away the books that thundered against slavery, trafficking, and exploitation. They taught submission as gospel and silence as salvation. But the true Word: the wisdom of Solomon, the cries of Maccabees, the visions of Enoch and Jubilees, all these were locked away, hidden from the slave, because they spoke of resistance, judgment, and the wrath of GOD upon the oppressor. The Despicables did not merely enslave the body. They attempted to enslave the soul.

When they arrived in America, they were offloaded into Virginia, branded with initials that erased their lineage, renamed with Biblical names, sold at auction to men who believed themselves to be GOD. From Virginia, they were placed in wooden wagons, hauled or walked shoeless, southward along what would become US Route 1. Down through the Carolinas. Into Georgia.

Waiting to bid on the soon-to-be slaves were family names like Holloway, Prentiss, Perdue, Hitchcock, Wallace, Langdon, Stallings, Graham, McConnell, and Weller, to name a few of the old Confederate plantation owners.

One African girl caught the interest of slave-owner Malcolm Wallace. She had no name they could pronounce. In what is now southeastern Mali, they called her Adisa, meaning the "clear one," because even as a child, her eyes held a fierce, untamed brightness. But by the time she stood shackled on the auction block in Savannah, Georgia, she was simply called Lot 27.

She was no more than 13. Five feet seven inches tall, 135 pounds, with almond-brown skin kissed by the sun and copper undertones, a rare Slavic-African blend, marked by high cheekbones, a slender nose, and full lips that trembled beneath fear and silence. Her hair fell in thick, wild curls down to her shoulders, uncombed since capture. Her wrists bore fresh welts. Her eyes were full of fear and bewilderment.

She stood trembling, barefoot on the wooden platform, flanked by two other girls, both younger, both weeping. Adisa did not cry. She simply moved forward.

Below her, gathered in linen and top hats, were the planters, slavers, and traders of Georgia's coastal elite. The sun was high.

The flies were thick. And among the bidders stood Malcom Wallace, a man of considerable means and unspeakable appetites.

A thick-bodied man with a permanent smirk and blue-gray eyes that flicked over human beings as if he were choosing horses or hunting dogs. He nudged the man beside him, Simon Pritchard, a slave owner from Augusta.

"That one's different," Malcolm said, his eyes narrowed. "Not like the rest. Something in her... exotic. Slavic, maybe? You see that skin? Like cinnamon cream."

Simon spat. "Pretty, sure. But she's too proud. Look at her jaw. That's trouble. You'll waste two months breaking her in."

"Then I'll enjoy the breaking," Malcolm said under his breath, licking his lips.

"I'm bidding on her," Simon said, a raised eyebrow. As if they engaged in a dirty saloon game of cards.

"Not today you are not."

The bidding began at $300.

Simon Pritchard raised his hand without hesitation.

Malcolm Mitchell followed at $400.

Simon went to $475, chewing a toothpick.

Malcolm barely blinked, "Six hundred."

The crowd quieted. Murmurs spread.

That was twice the amount what most field girls fetched.

The auctioneer paused, then looked at Simon.

"Let him have her," Simon muttered, as he stepped back with a scoff.

"You are overpaying for a whip's worth of trouble."

"Trouble," Malcolm said, eyes fixed on Adisa, "is precisely what I am buying."

As the gavel slammed down, Adisa flinched. The chain tugged. She was led down the steps, her head held unnaturally high.

Malcolm Wallace watched her walk.

"I'll keep her in the house," he said. "For a while."

He paid a bit more for the girl than he otherwise would, but he had special plans for her.

The Wallace Plantation sprawled across the red clay of central Georgia. Cotton fields as far as the eye could see. Rows of enslaved bodies bent beneath the scorching sun. And among them, two names endured: Malachi Mitchell and Elias Mitchell… given names twisted into surnames, carried by generations that followed.

The blood of the Al-Abd-al-Dasa never vanished. It merely hid, like a fire beneath ash. A habit, defense, and custom they learned as they hid among the Balkans when the Moors settled in that part of Eastern Europe.

In later generations, it whispered through the Mitchells.

It fought through Andrews. And in time, it reached the womb of a woman born a Mitchell, who would marry a man named Madison who in fact both were from the Mitchell lineage.

They would carry in his DNA the sorrow songs of the Dasa, the betrayal of the Dushev, and the silent rage of 100 stolen souls.

He was not just a man.

He was the return.

The reckoning is written in Balkan blood and southern soil. The curse and the cure. And now, centuries later, on American soil built from the stolen bodies and buried names, the war stirred again.

But with contracts. Algorithms. PowerPoint decks. Laws no one could read but everyone had to obey.

And Malik woke up.

Chapter Five
Adisa

"Then the Lord Said to Him, Know for Certain That Your Descendants Will Be Strangers In a Country Not Their Own, And They Will Be Enslaved And Mistreated Four Hundred Years."

— *Genesis 15:16*

What kind of human beats another within an inch of his life?

What manner of man beats another to within an inch of his life?

What kind of father strikes his own son until the breath of GOD trembles within him?

It is the same kind of man who defiles the innocent: who ravishes young boys and girls, leaving behind the wreckage of souls that will forever bear his sin.

The same kind of man who casts the scraps of his feast and the unwanted parts of fowl, pigs, and cattle to his slaves, offering the refuse of beasts as though it were mercy, when it is simply mockery.

The same kind of man that omitted scripture which taught against oppression, slavery, and obedience.

And what purpose does such cruelty and neglect serve?

It serves none but the appetite of darkness itself and to show man that cruelty has no bounds and the dark side must be fed as well. To show how far man will descend when he no longer sees GOD in the face of another.

For cruelty, when unrepented, becomes its own worship. The point is that the slave trader and then masters carved out a Bible of obedience, stripping away the books that thundered against slavery, trafficking, and exploitation. They taught submission as gospel and silence as salvation. But the true[9] Word: the wisdom of Solomon, the cries of Maccabees, the visions of Enoch and Jubilees: all these were locked away, hidden from the slave.

"That was the beginning," the old woman told Malik. "That was the wound. The seed of your line."

"Adisa was your great-great grandmother."

"Malcolm Wallace, he took her body, and from her womb he bred blood that still runs in you."

Malik could not speak.

After the Auction Block

The sun barely rose when Malcolm summoned Adisa from her quarters in the "Big House."

The plantation was quiet in the morning haze. The sugarcane fields still dripped with the morning dew. From the "Big House," the field hands looked like dark brush strokes against the green horizon, bent and steady, already breaking their backs for the day's quota. There were about 500 slaves that Malcolm Wallace owned: men, women, and children, which in plantation business represented a modest operation. But, enough to keep the Wallaces in a comfortable living.

Adisa was not yet assigned to field work; Malcolm claimed her as his "house girl," though no one misunderstood what that really meant. In the three years since he first brought her to the Wallace Plantation, she learned English quite well. She proved his instincts about her intellect and beauty.

He sensed this the day he bought her in Virginia. He knew that day she would be no ordinary slave.

But, this morning, he did not lead her back to his room. Malcolm and his wife, Polly, did not sleep in the same room. They stopped sharing the same bed shortly after the birth of their last child, Paul. Polly was a fair-skinned pale White woman who after each childbirth, found sustaining daily life too difficult for her frail self.

Instead, Malcolm walked with Adisa down past the smokehouse, past the garden the enslaved women kept for medicinal herbs and root vegetables, past the old slave cabins, now dilapidated from years of inattention. They crossed a small bridge near the creek, where the cypress trees sagged like weary old men, and reached a secluded area that overlooked the creek's bend. A cottonwood tree stood near the center, the white buds falling like ash.

"This was my mother's favorite spot," Malcolm said to Adisa, surprising her with the tenderness in his voice. "She used to read to me here," he continued.

Adisa did not respond. Her eyes scanned the woods, always alert. She wore a cream shirt that hung off her shoulders, much too big for her svelte body. A hand-me-down dress from her slave friend, Savannah. It hung off her soft shoulders. Her wrists even years later still bore the faint red marks from where she once was shackled during transport. Though her English was poor, she sensed from the intonation of Malcolm's words that he wanted something from her, though she did not fully comprehend the full meaning of his words.

Malcolm took a flask from his coat and handed it to her. "Drink."

She hesitated, then brought it slowly to her lips and sipped the bitter whiskey. It burned her throat, but she did not cough as further testimony to her resolve. He watched her, as always, studying her with that same mix of fascination and authority.

"Do you hate me?" he asked her, still looking at the creek.

"Does a cage bird hate the wind? Or the hand that built the cage?" she responded.

He turned to her slowly. That answer, cryptic and defiant, aroused him more than anything else she ever said. Without another word, he stepped forward and reached for her waist, pulling her into him. She did not resist, but she did not yield either.

The first kiss was not gentle. His desire simmered for years, unspoken. A twisted thread of lust, ownership, curiosity, and guilt. He pressed his lips against her neck, as he inhaled the sweet musky smell of a young slave woman. Still the sweet smell of hibiscus lingered from when older women rubbed into her luscious skin.

He laid her down on the red clay dirt beneath the cottonwood. He had no blanket. The ground was warm and soft. Birds chirped overhead, indifferent witnesses.

He lifted her shift slowly, as if he veiled something special, sacred, and terrible at once. She looked up at the sky, breathing slowly, tears threatened behind her still eyes. Savannah warned her of this day, which explained Adisa's resignation during it.

She just looked up at the sky as she tried to endure the unbearable pain as Master entered her virgin body. Their bodies joined in silence. Malcolm tried to be tender as much as rape can be tender. Because the act itself bores the violence of history. Of conquest. Of chains. Of domination and submission.

And yet at that moment, something flickered. A fleeting illusion of connection, at least on Malcolm's part. She let out a small sound, not of pain, but of something far more complicated. Grief but certainly shame as well. A little bit of defiance and in her own way, her sense of power for one untraceable moment.

When it was over, he laid next to her. His finger grazed her wrist.

"I will give you new clothes. You won't work in the fields." And here was the start of plantation prostitution where the Black slave women's bodies relegated to new clothes or no field work. A tradition the White man perpetuated, this game of domination and denigration of the White man over Blacks. The White man believed everyone, and everything had a price. However, the fallacy of this position was that lack of choices was not domination, but quite simply lack of escape or alternatives or quite simply just rape. Rape of mind, body, and soul like a stain of a scarlet letter.

Adisa turned her head slowly towards him. "I am not your pet."

He blinked. She stood, fixed her shift, and walked back toward the plantation without uttering another word.

Malcolm watched her go, something tight and ancient stirred in him. For the first time, he wondered if he had truly taken her, or if she gave him only what she chose, while she held the rest beyond his reach. That's true[9]. A man may take a woman's body, but it's up to her to surrender her mind, soul, and spirit.

Mistress

Savannah said, "Chile, just grin and bear it. It is the black women's burden and duty to Master." Or so they were taught.

Most slave women understood from the other women's stories as they explained and justified why they had to succumb to the

Master's wishes. They were indoctrinated since childhood, owned chattel without rights, expected not to have feelings and not so human. Which made Master's interest in the slave women more bewildering. To be thought as less than human never quite explained the White man's fascination and attraction for the Black slave women. Is not that beastiality? But it was never about attraction or humanity. Rather, it was about convenience, ownership, and domination, a trait that continued throughout the White man's existence particularly towards Blacks.

Adisa took a long time thinking, "You must understand," she said. In her mind, she thought, "You are not just a man. You are a ledger of crimes. A record and journal of love, survival, and rape."

They called her mistress. But she knew better.

Mistress was a word with silk in its mouth. A word meant for women with a choice. For women whose hearts courted and whose hands kissed in candlelight. As if softness erased chains. But for Adisa? She was chosen, not asked. Dressed in linen, bathed in rose water, her hair braided with care, so she appeared less like property and more like an ornament.

Sometimes, when his hands were warm and his voice was low, she almost believed him. That she somehow was different. Special. But the truth[9] was louder when she was alone.

The other women in the quarters looked at her with eyes that said everything and nothing at the same time. Pity. Resentment. Fear. Some thought she was lifted. Elevated. But they did not know how it felt to sleep in satin sheets covered in sweat and wake up each morning like you either were sick or died the night before. To be trapped in a prison lined with lace and the dank smell of musk.

He said she was beautiful. That she reminded him of someone. His mother, maybe. Or a woman he saw in a painting once in Charleston. She didn't know. She didn't care.

Her beauty, as it was, never did belong to her. It was bought, bartered, and inspected like a gemstone at a market. They said she had Slavic eyes and an African soul. That she was exotic. That she was rare. But birds were still caged. And soul meant little to men who value skin more than spirit.

At night, when he slept beside her, she listened to the frogs outside the window and dreamt of running. Not North. Not even free. Just away. Into a space where no one knew her name, where her body belonged to her, and her silence was not mistaken for consent.

There were brief and cruel moments when she imagined loving him. Not the man, but the possibility of him. What he might be in another time. But then she remembered the faces of the girls who came before her, like Savannah. The ones who cried in the dark. The ones who bore children who looked like their master's and were still sold as cattle.

Mistress. It is a pretty word for an ugly truth[9].

She was not his. Not really.

But until the day came when she reclaimed her name, her voice, and her body, she let him believe what he must. She smiled when she must. She vowed to survive it. She despised him in silence.

Magnolia Tree

The magnolia tree behind the smokehouse was old, older than the "Big House", older than any ledger or overseer that lived. Its thick arms stretched toward the sky like a mother that gathered her children in prayer. It was where Savannah went to think. To weep. To remember. And Adisa knew that if she wanted truth[9], she knew where to find it.

Savannah sat on the low bench carved from oak; her wide frame filled the seat as if the earth itself built it for her. She was a big woman, strong-backed and solid, with skin the color of dark molasses and hair wrapped in a rust-colored cloth that once belonged to her own mother. Her face bore deep creases, not just from time, but from enduring. She held in more pain than any soul should be made to carry. Her eyes, almond-shaped and amber in the sunlight, could both soothe and scold in a single glance.

She gave birth to four children by Master Elijah Wallace, Malcolm's father. All four light-skinned, with eyes too green to come from African blood. Two sold to Louisiana when they were just old enough to walk, like an eight-week-old puppy taken from their mother without any regard for the mother's despair. The other two worked in the fields, unaware the man who owned their backs was also the man who gave them life. Savannah never spoke of it unless asked, but the sorrow hung on her like perfume. You could smell it before she even entered the room.

Adisa stood before her now, silent.

"You gon' speak, or stand there 'til the tree falls?" Savannah asked, not unkindly, as she rocked slowly, peas shells in a basket in her lap.

Adisa sank to the ground, folding herself beside Savannah's knee like a child seeking shelter from a storm. Her voice cracked before the words ever came. Savannah now shucked corn as Adisa approached her.

"He took me to the creek bend yesterday."

Savannah paused mid-shell. Her hands slowed. She did not need to ask who he was.

"I thought...I thought if I just stayed quiet, it would feel like nothin', but I still feel it. Even now. I feel him in my bones, like a sickness that won't pass."

Savannah's eyes did not blink. She simply set the basket down beside her and reached out, cradling Adisa's cheek.

"I know that sickness," she said. "I know it too well."

Adisa swallowed hard. "Did you with the old master...did you ever?

"Love him?" Savannah interrupted; her voice was sharp. "No. Never. Not a day. But I had to pretend like I did. Had to smile when he called me by a name that was not mine. Had to hush my tears and fears when he climbed on top of me, tellin' me I was lucky to be his favorite. Like his winning cards in a table game."

She paused with her eyes fixed on the horizon.

"When my second boy was born, he had the Wallace nose. Narrow. Proud. The missus would not even look at him. Said she would rather drink poison than raise her husband's mistake. They sent him away at six. Just...gone."

Adisa laid her head in Savannah's lap, tears finally fell, slow and hot.

"I do not know who I am no more," she whispered.

"You still you, baby. You still Adisa. You were Adisa before he touched you, and you gon' be Adisa long after he gone. Don't let no White man, no matter how high he sits, take that from you."

"But I feel so dirty..." she deeply sobbed the "ugly cry."

"No. No, chile. You feel used. That ain't the same as dirty. The dirt is on them. It is on their souls, not yours. You are still God's chile. And don't you forget that."

Savannah rocked her gently, humming a low spiritual.

"Nobody knows the trouble I seen, Nobody knows but Jesus..."

Her singing sank into Adisa's skin and soul like balm. For a moment, under the ancient magnolia, two generations of broken but unbowed women sat in stillness, bound by pain, yes, but also by something stronger; the unkillable seed and pride, a strength that carried Black women for generations after. What they called the indomitable spirit.

Wounds

Savannah said once that the worst kind of slavery was not the kind that broke your back. It was the kind that made you doubt your soul had any worth at all.

And for the women in bondage, they went beyond the whip and yoke. They were bodies to be bred, beds to be used, and wombs to be harvested. Not wives. Not mothers in the way the White women ever were. Just currency with a heartbeat.

For every Black man whose name was struck from the ledger and replaced with the price of his limbs, there was a Black woman whose silence was purchased nightly in the master's bed.

Adisa learned that early.

She was thirteen when she arrived from the Gold Coast, motherless and hollowed out from the hold of a ship that reeked of death and desperation. By sixteen, she was sleeping in the "Big House". Not because she wanted to, but because Malcon Wallace decided her skin was too fine for the fields.

And not long after, Mrs. Wallace found out.

Polly Wallace was formerly Polly Mitchell, a skinny birdlike woman with papery white skin and sharp features that made her look perpetually sour. Her beauty had long ago withered under the Southern sun. Frail in body but vicious in spirit, Polly had the air of someone who despised everyone, but especially herself. She never said a word about Adisa and Malcolm, not in public, but she did not need to because of her perpetual scowl. The same Mitchell that would form the second branch of the Mitchell's curse.

She spoke with her eyes and with sudden slaps for no reason. With the way she spilled hot tea on Adisa's hand and called it an "accident." Or how she'd humiliate her in front of the other house staff, pointing out imagined flaws in her stitching or accusing her of stealing lace from her dressing drawer.

When Adisa gave birth to Malcolm's first child, a girl with light eyes and hair the color of dusk, Polly stood in the doorway of the birthing room, her arms folded tightly across her chest. She did not look at the child. She looked at Malcolm.

"She looks like you," Polly said coldly. "How proud you must be," she said smugly to Malcolm.

That same night, Polly insisted Adisa be removed from the Big House. "She is for breeding like a field sow," she hissed. "Let her live with the rest of them heifers."

Malcolm did not argue. Not because he agreed, but because some part of him preferred the distance. It made it easier to lie to himself about what he did.

So, Adisa was sent to the slave quarters. But no distance could erase what was done or what continued.

By the time she was twenty-five, Adisa birthed seven children for Malcolm Wallace. Each time she swore it would be the last time. Each time, her heart cracked a little more.

Each child bore traces of him, though she despised Malcolm. The children never saw her rage, only her enduring love even after each was torn away from her loving bosom. The nose. The hazel eyes. The way they furrowed their brow in thought. And every time she looked at them, she saw the chains that would follow them from cradle to grave, even if they passed for White, even if educated, even if sold to "good" homes. The blood of a slave still ran through their veins. And in the South, blood was destiny.

The other enslaved women whispered behind her back. Some envied her. Some pitied her. But few understood that her position was a prison gilded in suffering.

She had no man of her own. No one dared claim her. Malcolm's shadow loomed too large.

She was neither free nor fully enslaved. Neither mistress nor wife. Not loved. Not safe. Not ever whole.

And as the years passed, Polly aged in bitterness. Though she had children of her own, they served as her punishment. They never amounted to anything because drink and salacious activities occupied their time. Or perhaps it was her shame. But she made sure Adisa suffered from it. she reminded her, every chance she could, that she would always be nothing more than a breeding wench in a house that was never hers.

Still, Adisa endured. Not for Malcolm. Not for Polly. But for her children. For the chance, however small, that one of them might live long enough to find freedom. To speak her name one day without shame.

Lullabies

Adisa used to hum to her children at night, not lullabies, but old songs from the Gold Coast, half remembered from the mouths of women she no longer saw in her dreams.

"This little light of mine, I am gonna let it shine..."

She would hum those songs into their ears while cradling them in her arms as she whispered names from her lost village, stories of spirits in the trees and ancestors who never died. She wanted them to know they came from somewhere before the bondage. Before cotton. Before this seemingly cursed land of red dirt and rusted iron.

But Master Wallace did not care much about the songs. He cared for profit.

By the time Adisa was barely thirty, five of her seven children were sold.

Gone.

Vanished on the back of a cart or shackled behind a wagon, as the screamed her name as White men in boots pulled the reins and rode off into the distance. Her milk barely dried after her youngest daughter was weaned before they took her, claiming she had "the look" to fetch a fine price in Virginia.

Adisa pleaded once. Just once.

"Please, Master. Let me keep this one."

Malcolm would not look at her in the eyes. He muttered, "It's done," and walked out of the quarters, his boots trailed dust and blood behind him.

That night, Savannah sat with Adisa as she rocked in the corner, arms empty, breasts aching.

"You let 'em have your tears, girl," Savannah said, brushing her hair. "But do not let 'em steal your soul."

Of the seven, only Ellen and Bo remained.

Ellen was the quiet one, always watchful like her mother. She inherited Adisa's long limbs and Malcolm's pale eyes. Too light for the quarters, too dark for the Big House. She existed in a cruel in-between world where White folks called her "high yellow" and Black folks whispered that she was "touched by master." But Ellen carried herself like royalty, never arrogant, but aware. She learned to read in secret. Learned to sew with the skill of a French modiste. Polly tried to work Ellen into the ground, but the girl did not break.

Ellen had Malcolm's stubbornness, but Adisa's spine.

Bo was the only one who looked like Adisa's father, as much as she could remember of him. Broad-nosed, deep brown skin, with a fire behind his eyes that scared even the overseers. From the time he was ten, he carried water to the fields, then graduated to pushing plows, and eventually running messages between Wallace's properties. He was clever and dangerous in equal measure. Adisa feared he'd be whipped or hanged long before manhood, but somehow, Bo survived.

He swore to his mother one night, sitting beneath the same magnolia tree she wept under for years, "I ain't never let 'em take me, Ma. I'll die standin' for I live crawlin'."

And he meant it.

The Lineage

It was Ellen who eventually gave birth to a child named Josiah Mitchell, by the brother of Polly Wallace. A frail boy who escaped north during the final years of the Civil War. Josiah became a teacher, then a preacher. He changed his name from Wallace to Madison, to erase the memory of the man who raped his grandmother into motherhood. From Josiah came Nathaniel, and from him John, and from him Andrew.

And then came Malik, the great-great-grandson of Ellen. The inheritor of Adisa's pain and pride. A man haunted by the ghosts of the ones who endured so he could be free.

Malik never knew their names, not at first. But their blood ran hot in his veins every time he faced corruption and cruelty. Every time he stood before men who thought themselves superior in corporate board rooms and whispered truth[9] in rooms that feared it. The fight in him was old but the fight before him was fresh by an understanding and encouragement in the strength and spirit of the Shilohs. Older than bondage. Older than Wallace, Mitchells and the line that traced back to the Al-Abd-al-Dasa and the Dushev. He saw where and sensed their insecurities.

Confederate presence now replaced by White Supremist reiterate about global dominance and the infiltration of immigrants into the country. The fear and lust they held for Black woman and the mistrust of Blacks in general towards Whites. Incapable of seeing their own unique contribution to the animus they perceived or manifested or manufactured to justify their wicked ways.

His sense of frustration and righteousness came from Adisa.

From Bo.

From Ellen.

From a line unbroken by the whip, the noose, or the silence.

The Quarters

The Wallace Plantation quarters were built from rough-hewn pine logs, their roofs sagging under the weight of time, weather, and sorrow. By day, the cabins stood like crooked teeth in the land's mouth. By night, they became sanctuaries of whispered prayers and muffled cries, where memory was both curse and a timeless compass.

Adisa sat near the back of the women's quarter with her knees tucked to her chest, a piece of burlap wrapped around her narrow shoulders. She was still too new to the place; her Swahili tongue a strange music that only deepened the distance between her and the others. The older women whispered in low tones, calling her "jungle girl" or "master's new prize." Yet over time, curiosity softened into care, and judgment bent towards compassion.

A heavy-set woman named Ma Ruth eventually became her protector. Ruth gave birth to eight children, six of whom sold before they could utter her name. Her back bore the keloid map of her punishments; from the numerous times she ran away in search of her children. Each ridge on her back a memory she dared not speak aloud.

'She too young," Ruth would murmur as she rubbed Adisa's back with palm oil. "Too soft, like lamb put in a lion's den. But she got eyes that done seen thunder. That's Africa still in her. Don't let 'em break it."

Adisa nodded quietly, never quite understanding all the words, but feeling the warmth of Ruth's hands and the strength in her sorrow.

The women warned Adisa of the ways of White men, the cold way they touched, the hot ways they looked and punished, the sick way they watched. "You keep your eyes down when Master Mitchell passes," one said. "That man don't just break backs, he breaks minds."

And so, the separation between the Black slave women and men started with the difference in punishment between the two sexes. A source of discipline and separation that became etched in the Black slaves' mind for centuries following, even today. For centuries, Blacks attempted to close that chasm created by the White European slave traders. Their attempts usually thwarted. This tension between the races commenced from the day of capture into the slave castles through the "Middle Passage" and continued today but largely not because of Blacks.

A shadowed memory carved itself into the souls of the enslaved. For Black women, the torment came cloaked in silence: rape and violation masked as a quiet, unending beating. Yet, for Black men, the agony thundered through the fields, bloody and merciless, each lash echoed like war drums of humiliation. The slave master's purpose was not only cruelty but desecration; to strip the Black man of his manhood before the eyes of his woman, to fracture the sacred bond of protection and dignity.

The blows were flesh-deep, but the true[9] strike was intended to be spiritual and eternal: a calculated inscription of inferiority, a wound to the psyche, inflicted like a narcissistic injury, meant to linger like a festering wound across generations in shame and silence. The White slave master's goal was to emasculate the Black slave men before his women. Beatings were physical, but the sense of domination and submission was intended to create an indelible mark of inferiority in Blacks.

The fields were hell. The sun, like an overseer, beat down without mercy, and the whips slicked the silence until the blood screamed. The Black men were prized for their strength but punished for their resistance, real or imagined. They worked harder, whipped longer, and broke faster as intended. The strongest were often put to the most grueling tasks, hauling timber, digging irrigation ditches, building structures they would never own, laying bricks into walls they'd never see finished.

Many of them limped from their labor; their feet blistered, and backs flayed raw. Some bore iron collars around their necks, discipline yokes they called them, meant to keep them from sleeping too comfortably, or running too far. The collars scraped their necks as they rang with every movement. A cruel bell tolling their existence, that left marks on their foreheads, necks, feet, and hands for all to see their bondage.

They were denied the right to protect their wives, women, their daughters, or their dignity. And yet, in their eyes lived a quiet rage that time could not dull. It lived in the way they clenched their fists when no one looked. In the way they prayed for rain not to cool their skin, but to soften the earth for digging holes they imagined as graves for their masters, or sometimes, themselves.

They saw Adisa as something different, not yet broken, not yet bent. Some looked at her with pity, others with longing, and still others with an aching kind of reverence.

"She walks like freedom still in her bones," one of them said.

"Or like she don't know this America gone eat her whole," replied another.

Mitchell Legacy

One man, tall and silent, named Elias Mitchell, often watched her from a distance. He once was a drummer in his homeland, before they took his hands and reshaped them into tools for cotton and cane. When he saw Adisa, he seemed to hear rhythms again, faint, ancient, and defiant as he watched her hips swing from side to side like a sweet slow lullaby. Like a sad omen, rather cryptic in part, was that Elias Mitchell came from Polly Mitchell's family plantation.

Adisa did not speak much, but her presence said enough. She reminded them all what they took, from them, and from themselves. And though she had every reason to collapse into silence, she chose instead to sit each night under the stars, softly humming the lullabies of her people.

It was her way of remembering. And for the men who watched and listened to her hums her in the darkness, who forgot their own tongues and tunes, it was a way they survived.

Except, even the distant memories of the homelands, the African chants, rituals, and traditions that sustained the African in the homeland could never compete with the systemic subjugation of the Black men by the White plantation owners.

Architecture of Dehumanization

The cruelty of the Wallace Plantation was not limited to the lash or the chains. It was something more sinister, more surgical, darker, a deliberate architecture of dehumanization designed not only to break the Black body, but to divide the Black soul. To make those whose souls indeed they broke, to be more susceptible to satanic ways of the devil worshippers.

The slave quarters were more than mere housing. They were laboratories of social dissection and experimentation in cruelty. Black men and women, who once danced as one, prayed as one, lived as one in the lands stolen from, were reshaped by the White slave-owner into mistrustful strangers under the gaze of White power. The power White southerners intended and perceived as legitimate power to leave a lasting mark in the minds of Blacks, if only to keep their souls separated.

What Adisa realized or sensed with little education and understanding she had, was that suffering on the Wallace Plantation was not only physical. It was architecture. It was engineered. Every lash of the whip, every forced breeding, every auction block separation was not just cruelty, it was strategy. A devilish kind. One meant to fracture not only families, but the very fabric of the Black spirit.

The Underground Railroad

The older women whispered this truth[9] in pieces after dark, when the fires dimmed, and the children slept. The beginnings of the "Underground Railroad." The "Underground Railroad" was more than a hidden path through forests and swamps: it was the trembling heartbeat of a people's hope. To the enslaved, it did not merely mean escape, but resurrection. Each whispered direction, each candle flickering in a distant window, each hymn sung low in the fields carried the scent of deliverance. It was the promise that bondage was not eternal, that the lash and the chain were not the final word.

For the Black slave, the "Underground Railroad" was both myth and miracle: an invisible river flowing northward, guided by the stars and guarded by the faith of strangers willing to risk everything. Its stations were not marked by maps but by courage: the trembling hand that passed along food, the silent door opened at the midnight hour, the prayer murmured by a mother as her child was lifted into the dark, bound for freedom.

The importance of this clandestine network lay not only in its power to liberate bodies but in its defiance of a system built on dehumanization. It told the enslaved that they were seen, that their dignity was worth defending, that freedom was not an illusion but a destiny waiting to be claimed. In every mile traveled, in every breath stolen from the hounds of pursuit, the enslaved proclaimed a simple, unshakeable truth[9]: we are not property, we are people, and we will be free.

Within an Inch of Life

Bo always carried a fire too bright for the fields. He would not bow his head quickly enough, nor hold his tongue when Master Wallace's cruelty grew too sharp. The defiance was quiet at first, a stare that lasted a bit too long, a refusal to sing when commanded, but each act of silent rebellion was tinder waiting for a spark. The spark came one sweltering afternoon when Master Wallace, flush with whiskey and rage, demanded that Bo whip another slave for stumbling under the weight of cotton. Bo's hand froze. He would not raise the lash against his own. His refusal rang louder than any shout.

Master Wallace's face darkened like thunderclouds over the fields just over the horizon. "You'll learn what it means to cross me, boy," he hissed, and the order was given for Bo, his own flesh and blood, to be flogged at dawn to an inch of his life.

What a man felt: to raise his hand against his own blood, to drive leather and iron into the flesh of his son until the boy hangs on the edge of breath and an inch of his life? Perhaps he felt nothing at all. Perhaps that was the greater horror. For to beat a child or a young man within an inch of his life was to stand at the altar of cruelty and made a sacrifice of one's own humanity.

The phrase itself was old, carried through centuries, born of the English gallows and debtor's prisons, where punishment stopped just short of the grave. "Within an inch of his life": a measure not of mercy, but of precision. It meant to push a body so near to death that it could hear the rustle of eternity yet deny its passage. It was a sentence designed to remind the victim that his survival was not his own: it was permitted, granted by the hand that struck him down. Almost as if to say, "Boy, I gave you your life, I can take your life."

For a slave father commanded to such a task, the torment doubled. Each blow tore not only flesh but lineage, carving scars into both body and soul. He was forced into the theater of domination, made to perform the master's will upon the very child sired. The whip in his hand or his overseer's hand was not just leather: it was betrayal. It was emasculation. It was the master's cruelest invention: to turn the bond of father and son into an instrument of submission.

And if he wept, his tears burned with shame, for they confessed that his love was powerless before the lash. And if he hardened himself, buried all feeling, then his silence screamed louder than his sobs: that survival sometimes demanded the killing of tenderness, smothered of love, the exile of compassion from the heart.

To beat one's son within an inch of life was not discipline, nor justice. It was ritualized destruction, a performance of supremacy meant to echo through generations. For the master understood a terrible truth[9]: when you force a man to wound his own child, you do not just own his body: you enslave his soul.

"Chile," Ma Ruth would say, rocking slowly in a splintered chair, "They knew what they was doin'. Ain't nothin' accidental 'bout this pain. They bred us like cattle but split us like seeds, so we'd never grow together. Your Bo had to run away. The next time Master took the whip to him surely, he would die."

The plantation was a lab of social dissection. Black men were punished in front of their women and children, stripped naked, whipped until the meat hung off their bones, sometimes even raped themselves, to dissolve the image of protector, of strength, of manhood. But the Black always knew that enslaving a Black man by power not by persuasion was never a sign of a true[9] man or masculinity. In fact, in the deep recesses of the Black woman's mind in the corners of her heart, she always held onto her hopes and dreams for the Black man.

"You see that?" whispered a younger woman named Liddy once, pointing to where Elias collapsed near the barn, blood pooling beneath him. "They don't just beat his back. They tried to erase him from our hearts. Made him look weak to us. Made us hate him for not saving us...even if he can't save himself."

The women were weaponized too, even today, turned into vessels, not for love, but for production. Their bodies used to make more slaves; their wombs reduced to transaction. They were raped by masters, overseers, and in twisted logic, sometimes made to hate the men who could not protect them. And the men, in turn, forced to watch, helpless and ashamed, as the women they loved defiled, resented their own powerlessness, resented the woman who survived the unpreventable. The men retreated into silence or anger. And between them, something sacred broke. Not love, perhaps, but the ability to trust love.

"They broke our harmony," said Ma Ruth one night, as she stared into the flame. "They knew if they could turn us on each other, the chain would hold longer than any shackle."

They even stripped their Gods. Their drums banned. Their names changed. The connection to the homeland, to ancestors, to the divine, all banned and severed. Replaced with sermons that told them slavery was salvation and obedience was holy. What crushed spirit could rise under such weight and lies?

And yet it did and still rises.

Adisa began to hum again, softly, beneath her breath. At first, the women told her to stop, it would bring lashes. But, when the White men were not near, they listened. That song, in a language they did not know but somehow remembered, made their backs straighten. It carried something older than cotton fields. Something freer than horse whips. It was resistance, wrapped in rhythm.

Adisa felt it. The tension. The unspoken divide. So, she hummed the old song from the homeland which served to join them in communion and community.

The women quietly sang as they cared for children born in hardship, instilling a firm resolve in them to face a difficult world.

The Black slave woman's only source of consistent love and comfort for her babies; to feel her soothing gentle strength of hands as she kneaded her love with palm oil into her babies' soft skin. That touch with oil gave the Black child the confidence to understand the true[9] love of a Black woman. The daily ritual of that mother as she applied oil to her child's body made the child more sensual and formidable as a lover, few other races could rival. The real Black man understood and yearned for that touch of oil applied to his body by a Black woman.

Palm Oil

On that night that Elias laid as blood seeped from his body prostrated on the ground before the barn because he suffered from the whipping he received earlier, Adisa passed by him. Adisa stooped down and looked him into his defeated eyes. He did not speak. He only placed his rough, scarred hand over his heart and nodded. Adisa helped him to his feet and brought him back to her cabin. In the cabin, she washed his body down to remove the blood from his tarnished body. Then she applied palm oil to his body, and it was in that moment, Adisa saw it too, what they tried to bury but could not kill. That indomitable African spirit.

Hope.

Despite divisions and demonic systems, their souls remembered their bonds. Even hurt hearts sensed the call of justice and ancient times and ties. Shared pain can foster healing, with time, forgiveness eased suffering. Pain may even forgive the oppressor.

They were scattered as people, yes, but not lost. And, after the Civil War ended, many of the slaves on the Wallace Plantation, Mitchell Plantations, and other area plantations began the long trek North with hopes of better opportunities for a more human life.

The Seed of the Despicables

When the war ended, the guns did not go silent in the hearts of men like Master Malcolm Wallace.

He stood on the veranda of what remained of the Wallace Plantation, as he sipped bourbon, a Confederate flag tattered but still flying above the scorched fields. The war took away his wealth, but not his will. He stared out over the empty slave quarters, silent now but echoing with memories, and vowed aloud to the wind, "The South may have lost the war...but we ain't lost the cause. We will rise again. Not with muskets, but with machinery, with money, and with minds." He screamed as he watched his life's investments leave his land.

That was the seed of what later would be known as one many arms of the Despicables, the "White Trojans." They became a disgruntled White Supremist organization that moved from tobacco and cotton to drugs and other street commerce. A new confederacy born not of rebellion, but of infiltration to control by any means necessary. And after the Civil War they were on the move as many Confederates ran to and settled further in Florida.

Freedom

When word reached the Wallace Plantation that freedom came, Adisa did not believe it at first. None of them did. Freedom, after all, was not anything more than to see the birds fly freely above their heads. A whisper carried by dying men. But this time the chains fell. Not all at once, but one linchpin at a time and not everywhere, but enough to replace despair with hope. For real this time.

Adisa, now in her late twenties, gathered what little she had, mostly sad memories, and walked north with a group of others. Malcolm stood on the porch yelling at them, "You Niggers will be back. Ain't nothing up north for a bunch of coons."

Elias, Adisa, Ellen, and her children were among them. Bo escaped earlier by the "Underground Railroad", settled north, and waited for his family. They all left in silence, never looked back at the house that stole their youth for fear if they chanced a glance might stand still. Again, like Lot fearing to look back against GOD's warning at Sodom and Gomorrah, lest they turned to stone.

Some stayed in Georgia, too old to travel. Others headed west, dreaming of a fresh start in Oklahoma or Kansas. A handful made it to northern cities like Chicago, Detroit, Philadelphia, DC, and New York. There they found jobs but never true freedom. But it still was a thousand times better than plantation life. Some like Adisa and Elias, at first settled in small Black communities or settlements outside Macon, Georgia, until they made their way up further north. They cleared land and tried to carve dignity from dirt. However, when Bo and Ellen started a family, Adisa and Elias moved north to help raise their grandchildren.

During Reconstruction, Blacks began to vote. They ran for office. They preached boldly from the pulpit and freely taught their children to read, once punishable by law. Elias became a deacon. Adisa became a midwife and keeper of stories, the griot of the community. They married in a church made of pinewood, beneath a hand-carved cross, and raised three other children made from their marital bond.

Adisa vowed her children and grandchildren walked with pride even when the road bent low. One of her daughters married a Madison thus where Malik Andrew Madison became, a Mitchell to a Madison.

But the flame of freedom was too bright for men like Malcolm Wallace and those of his station in life. This was not how they intended the world to act. Blacks were intended to be under the White man in every facet of society.

The Despicables Form

Malcolm Wallace and his brethren: dispossessed but not defeated, fled the south for Florida where many confederates settled after defeat in the Civil War. From Florida, they transformed themselves from masters of land into architects of systems. Just as the plantations were laboratories of human behaviors and responses to control, Florida served as a petri dish for further exploitation of human capital. With the help of their Northern industrial partners, they formed banks. Many of these banks helped the plantation owners financed slavery. Others acquired newspapers, and rebuilt plantations as corporations.

They sent their sons and daughters to law schools, West Point, and into political offices. Because access to wealth, capital, and ownership served as well as a barrier to human progress. If the concentration of wealth remained in the White communities, then it would stifle if not control other races' ability to advance. Or if advancement was necessary or unavoidable, then systems were put in place to monitor and control that progress. Today, they refer to it as "institutional racism."

So, these former White slave plantation owners had the ears of power brokers in Washington and Wall Street. They also cornered the market on the proliferation of street commerce with the formation of ethnic enclaves like the Italian, Irish, Jewish, Russian, and reluctantly Black and Brahman mafias. The culmination of these various forces, Wall Street and mafias, established systemic racism. But also the wealth class system known as the lower, middle, and upper classes. The movement of wealth and status among those classes was controlled and predictable as planned. They were also segregated by race. And the embryo for these systems is embodied in the corporations, the fictional version of a person that Satan threatened on earth after his fall from the Kingdom of Heaven.

"We won't beat them with whips," Malcolm once said during a secret gathering in Augusta. "We'll beat them with ledgers. With laws. We'll make the noose invisible and hide behind masks and leave burning crosses on their front lawns as a memory of our power."

They called themselves the Klu Klux Klan, Society for the Southern Order, Opus Dei, Free Mason, and other discreet names. But over time, they all became known together simply as the Despicables. These men relished in their cruelty, greed, and wicked ways to subjugate man in any numerous ways.

They laid the blueprint for "Black Codes." They took over local sheriff offices and state legislatures. Jim Crow was not a relic: it was rebranding. Voting tests. Poll taxes. Lynch mobs. Redlining. These were not accidents. They were weapons of "human dysfunction." The Tea Party morphed into Christian Nationalism to MAGA movements. Many became governors in the south, senators, military commanders, and law enforcement officials who consorted with, hid their Black mistresses and the children they fathered.

Each generation of Wallace descendants carried the charge. They married into other Confederate families, passed down land and legacy, and taught their children to not just preserve the privilege, but to expand it quietly, globally. The Despicables began recruiting not just from the South, but from elite schools, law enforcement academies, corporate boardrooms, political dynasties, and capitalists across the nation. All with the eye towards on a reconstituted brand of White supremacy throughout the US, if not the world. They wore suits instead of gray coats. They smiled at the camera. But their mission was the same. And as their progeny either died or chose a different path in life, it became necessary and imperative to recruit outside the family lineage, just so long as the Despicables had control.

Control. Always managed and planned control.

Adisa's Legacy

Adisa lived long enough to see the turn of the century. She wore spectacles in her old age and braided the hair of her granddaughters with fingers that once picked cotton. She told them stories, not just of pain, but of pride. Of Africa. Of Elias. Of freedom bought not by war but by will.

Her grandsons and granddaughters became teachers, barbers, postal workers, and pastors. One granddaughter, Sarah, would later march with Dr. King in Selma. Another, Jeremiah, would become a Tuskegee airman.

They faced burning crosses and closed doors. They were called everything but the name of Jesus. But they walked forward. Through Emmett Till. Through Bull Connor. Through Malcolm

X and Martin. They marched, participated in "sit-ins," sang, and resisted.

But for every movement, the Despicables moved too. Quietly. Strategically. As America integrated its schools, they fortified their private academies. In those private institutions they instilled and indoctrinated their children in White Supremist ideology. Meanwhile, Black and Brown students fought vigorously to include their history in public education curriculum as southern states moved to eliminate "critical thinking" out of the classroom.

As civil rights were won, the Despicables innovated new forms of oppression like mass incarceration, voter ID laws, and surveillance sponsored by the government and funded by private companies.

They never stopped recruiting. Never stopped building. Never stopped their corruption.

By the time Malik Andrew Madison confronted them, decades later, the Despicables were no longer old White men on porches. They were multinational CEOs. Judges. Senators. Generals, and in law enforcement. They established algorithms inside financial and computer systems. They were ostensibly "neutral' policies with sinister effects.

But, Malik, like Adisa before him, had grit and now memory from Madam Erzebet's stories in his blood. A map etched into his lineage that stretched back through Elias, through Adisa, through the fields of the Wallace Plantation, and across the ocean to the lands where the drums still beat.

He would face them not only with evidence, but with ancestry. Not with courage, but with clarity and in spirit.

Because the story did not start with him. It would not end with them either.

Red Clay

The soil of Georgia bled a color unlike anywhere else on the earth. Deep red, iron-rich, stained the hands, knees, and home of its inhabitants or any child that ever played barefoot in its dust. To outsiders it was just dirt, stubborn and messy, but to those born of it, the red clay carried memories of sweat, blood, and history buried just beneath its surface. The type of unrelenting dirt one could not rid from the house, body and cars.

Farmers cursed it for being hard, unyielding, cracking dry in the summer sun, clumping thick in the winter rains. Yet that same soil birthed cotton and tobacco, fed peach groves and pine forests. Whole empires of Southern wealth carved out of its stubborn breast, fortunes built on the backs of enslaved Africans whose blood mingled with its iron and probably its hue.

Every rainstorm brought the red silt running downhills, led to an uncovered spring or forming a creek, streaked across porches and filled ditches like veins opened in the land itself. It was the color of sacrifice, of old wounds that never quite healed. Generations of sharecroppers bent their backs to it, pulling life from its stingy grip, while the land in turn remembered their names, bound their descendants in an unspoken covenant. As if the land spoke to people that it was always in control.

Throughout his life, Malik often thought of the red Georgia clay. It was part of his education and appreciation of the stock he originated. Every new place he went, he would see the red clay in his mind. It was as if Georgia followed him, its dirt packed into the soles of his shoes of roots he could never shake.

To Malik, the red clay was a paradox that shaped and grounded him. It brought back fond memories of his grandparents. In a strange way, it helped form his value system of wrong and right as if the red clay served as his moral compass.

Grandpa's Love

There is nothing better than the love of a grandpa.

It does not shout. It does not rush. It simply is steady as a rocking chair or like a cruise ship navigating the rocky waters. His hands, worn by time, still knew how to cradle your entire world in a single pat on the back. His laugh, low and rumbling like a summer storm in the distance, could chase away the darkest of clouds. And his eyes, oh those light blue eyes, held stories, warnings, and wisdom he never spoke out loud.

When the world confused you, Grandpa made sense.

When the road got hard, he showed you how to walk it or run on it, one step at a time.

And when you failed? He did not judge. He taught.

Grandpas are time-travelers. They bring the past into the present with a wink and a story to remind you that your roots run deeper than your doubts.

No, there is nothing better than the love of a grandpa.

Because when the rest of the world tries to change you, Grandpa just loves you for who you are, and who you are becoming.

That kind of love wraps around you like a porch breeze in late July, steady, warm, and made of something older than time. It is the kind of love that does not have to be spoken to understand. The kind that lives in the firm grip of a hand, the rustle of worn overalls, the silence between words that still says *I see you, boy. I believe in you.*

But, whenever Malik engaged in big talk, his grandpa Frank said with a chuckle, "Boy, a high mind makes for a soft behind."

And when Malik got older and in college, he would often joke with Malik, "Here comes my educated fool." Noting Malik's book smarts but lack of street sense at times. Malik did not mind because he knew his grandpa's love and guidance sustained him like a refuge in times of troubled waters, like a compass of sorts. It was a deep sense of love that he felt like his grandpa watched over him during difficult times in life.

A life and upbringing so different that the life his ex-wife Monica led.

Georgia Summers

Malik learned that love every summer he was sent down to Georgia with his two brothers and sisters. It was a ritual for the two back-to-back summers his parents sent them to the South to stay with them as they worked two jobs to purchase their first home. Malik's parents would pile the children into their station wagon, each with a shoebox with chicken breast, wing, potato chips, and a piece of pound cake wrapped in foil. The kids were wide-eyed and wild with energy to make the long ride from New Jersey to the open country.

He only understood years later as he got older, why his parents made the kids relieve themselves in glass jars or alongside the highway brush. Although it was in the 1960s, Jim Crow segregation was still rampant in the South so they could not always count on a gas station to let them use the bathroom. His parents usually started the trip in the middle of the night so that the kids could sleep through most of the night before they arrived in Georgia.

And then the roar of excitement, as the children noticed the red clay when they realized Georgia was here. They knew they were close to Grandma Josephine and Grandpa Frank's farm.

That was home, even if it was just for the summer season.

Josephine was a robust, mocha-skinned woman with a soft face and big hands that kneaded dough for her pies and discipline with the same ease. She had no wrinkles, just a lot of wisdom, and her laughter rolled through the house like a song. Whenever Malik told a joke, usually too clever for her age, she would throw back her head and holler, "Oh, that boy tickles me!"

Every single morning, without fail, Malik would hear her voice rising before the roosters:

"Ole Lawdy, thank you for another day." Words he was certain many former Blacks slaves uttered during their morning rise.

Those words soaked into him like sunlight. They were her prayer, her Psalms 91 like shield, her daily survival song.

She used to touch the soles of Malik's bare feet as she passed him sitting in her reclining chair and said, "You are going to have smooth skin just like your grandma." She smiled like she knew something he did not, as if her touch carried pixie dust made for passing down blessings.

But it was his Grandpa Frank who poured himself into Malik like water into a thirsty jug.

Of average height and weight, a man with pale White skin and a nice grade of hair with those searing blue eyes and calloused hands. Frank was both a farmer, a preacher, and could pass as White. By day, he worked on his 500 acres, as he raised cattle, chickens, goats, and hogs while also attended his crop. He earned nothing more than a third-grade education and God-given grit. By Sunday he wore a white suit, dusted off his boots, and stood behind a wooden pulpit in a small, whitewashed church that sat beneath a canopy of oaks. His voice rang through the rafts like thunder when he preached, and the people listened because Frank Hitchcock did not talk to you. He talked to your soul.

Everyone knew Malik was his favorite.

Even the other grandchildren. Even Malik's siblings. Even his own daughter, Malik's mother, who once pulled her father aside and said, "Daddy, you got other grandbabies too, you know."

Frank chuckled and said, "Yeah, but there is just something in that boy."

And maybe there was. Because Malik followed him everywhere, over to Macon to sell cattle, to the auction house, to the tractor repair shop, even out into the pasture to mend fences or birth calves. Every moment was a lesson. Every gesture was affection without apology.

Sunday Church

The Sunday church services were like revivals of the soul. The families of former Black slaves would pack into pews, starched shirts, pressed dresses, shined shoes. Grandma Josephine fanned herself with a paper fan that read Pine Ridge Baptist Church. They would sing hymns until the walls sweated and the tambourine beat like a second heartbeat.

Then there were the family reunions, a sea of cousins, uncles, aunts, folding chairs, a sea of grilled ribs, spade games, lemonade, and drinks. Those days were loud and beautiful, full of legacy in motion.

But Malik's favorite memories were quieter.

On the land, barefoot and free, he and his siblings found adventure in every acre. They splashed around in the creek, always on the lookout for water moccasin snakes that hovered in the creek. They threw stones at wasp's nests, occasionally getting stung so bad two days of rest needed. They never could outrun those wasps. They built forts out of sticks, tracked rabbits in the tall grass, and told ghost stories in the old tobacco shed.

There was both magic and grit in that dirt, and Malik carried it with him even as a man. It stuck to his spirit like red clay to a tire, refused to let him forget where he came from and instilled some of his personal values. Though he did not know it then, his spirit was one of a runaway slave. His ancestors left the plantation: later the corporate plantation, to read and would never return to it no matter the hardships they faced.

Because that love, the grandpa's love, was not just affection.

It was like a spiritual anointing.

And even decades later, when Malik stood in tall rooms filled with power and peril, he knew some part of Grandpa Frank was still there, standing behind him, whispering, "You got something in you, boy." These were the memories that stuck with Malik as he listened to Madam Erzebet spin her yarn of tales. Just like that the red clay of Georgia dissolved from his mind, as if Madam Erzebet snapped her fingers to pull him back from a séance.

The Balance Sheet

"And now the balance must be settled." She peered into Malik's eyes.

The candle between them flickered like it knew what came next.

Malik sat still in the cramped back room of Madam Erzsebet's fortune telling shop in the Village, barely breathing. His body was in Manhattan, but his soul began to drift as the air around him thickened. The old woman's eyes rolled white, and her voice dropped to a whisper thread with thunder.

She gripped his wrist.

"I will show you what was hidden from you."

And then she continued.

He was no longer in the room. The walls melted away. The smell of incense became smoke and iron. He heard the low growl of wagon wheels over red clay.

He was there: Georgia, 1823.

The Mitchell Plantation stretched across fields soaked with slaves' sweat, tears, and blood. Crows perched like sentinels on cotton branches. And in the white manor house, behind Greek columns and blood-polished furniture, sat Master Daniel Mitchell, a cruel White man with a gluttonous eye. The brother of Polly Mitchell Wallace, Malcolm's wife.

He took what he wanted.

And what he wanted was Ellen, Adisa's caramel-skinned slave daughter, not yet 15 on the Wallace Plantation. Every time he went to visit Malcolm Wallace, Ellen caught his eye. She grew even more beautiful since that first day he saw her on the Wallace Plantation when he came to visit Malcolm and Polly Wallace. She was lithe, delicate in stature, but her face carried royalty, cheekbones kissed by Moorish ancestry, hair that curled like ocean waves, eyes deep enough to drown a god.

He summoned her by name. Not with affection, but ownership. She came. She was always made to come.

Over time, Daniel Mitchell laid with her again, not with love, but with lusted possession. He intended to not only brand her as his on the outside, but in her inside with child. By the time he drew his last breath, he sired four children through her womb.

Among them was a boy named Malachi.

Malachi Mitchell would grow into a man of strong shoulders and regal bearing. He spoke little, but when he did, others listened. His skin was the color of sun-warmed cane, and his presence alone defied the yoke.

The Mitchell name, once singular, began to split: like a tree forked by lightning.

Two Branches

From Malachi came a line of descendants who walked with dignity even in chains. Caramel skin. Almond eyes. Thick crowns of hair that coiled like anointed thorns. They were known for their wisdom, their resilience, and their ability to lead without speaking. It was quiet thundering.

Then there was James Mitchell. Malachi's half-brother. Born of Ellen but sired also by Master Malcolm Wallace's brother in las-brother, Sam Mitchell. James was closer to Master Sam Mitchell in blood and temper. His children were fair-skinned, nearly White, with light eyes and ambition laced with hunger. They passed more easily in both skin and sin. This is the Mitchell lineage Monica Mitchell's family originated.

Even on Master Mitchell's plantation, the slaves built a secret world. Food stolen from the "Big House," resold out of hidden, hollowed floorboards. Moonshine brewed in hidden barrels beneath chicken coops. Makeshift juke joints carved out of the deep woods, lit by fireflies and sin, where field hands gambled, danced, and plotted rebellion. They bartered with labor and things stolen from Master's house that others wanted for their enterprise.

It was an underground economy, a criminal network hidden under cotton stalks. During Emancipation, they smuggled votes and bought judges. After Emancipation, it did not die; it metastasized. In segregation, they paid off sheriffs and trafficked labor.

During the Civil Rights era, they wore dashikis in the day and ran numbers at night. And the White woman that ran with them were really spies for the government.

The dark side of the Mitchells learned to profit from every system, even while pretending to be its victims. These Mitchells made a natural ally and recruited for the Despicables who shared the same value that corruption, grift, graft, and undue influence translate into big money.

The Mitchell Divide

As decades passed, the two branches of the Mitchell clan scattered around the country. The heirs of Malachi Mitchell and Elias Mitchell moved north to New York City and New Jersey, settling in Newark, Harlem, Brooklyn, and later Teaneck and Montclair. The descendants of Elias Mitchell as the new Black bastions of the middle class. They became teachers, ministers, city clerks, and musicians. They continued to conduct themselves with quiet strength. These Mitchells kept Psalms 91 in their pockets and still dreamed of deliverance.

The descendants of Malachi Mitchell meanwhile carved out an empire of hustle in Detroit and New York. Bootlegging turned to car theft, turned to racketeering, turned to numbers or "policies", turned to crack, turned to generational grip on the underground economy. From basement barbershops and crooked churches, they spun a web that pulled in politicians, pimps, and pawns.

But blood remembers blood.

And now, they circled again.

The Shilohs and the Despicables as the Elias Mitchell descendants formed an alliance with the Shilohs. The Malachites and the Dushev. As in the righteous and the rogue. The Malachi Mitchells formed alliances with the Despicables.

And standing at the center is you, Malik.

"You are the echo of Elias and Adisa. You are the child of Ellen's pain. You are the one with the curse and the one the curse could not kill. You are the Chosen one not as the Messiah, as a soldier of the Watchtower."

She continued, "Now, two paths, once one, run parallel in Malik's blood."

"One built on dirt and discipline," the gypsy murmured.

"The other on dollars and deception. But both are yours. That is your burden. That is your power and legacy whether on your own or through your children."

The gypsy's voice grew sharper, her grip firmer.

"And your daughter, Jordan, will inherit the blessing and the curse. The only question is which will you feed."

Georgia Soil

But not all Mitchells chose the North.

Some of the Elias Mitchell line, the Shiloh-blooded ones, stayed rooted in Georgia. At first, they were sharecroppers. Picked cotton not for a master now, but for a landlord with the same whip in his eyes and a Bible in his mouth. If Blacks were fortunate, they got assistance under the Freedman Bureau Program which aided freed slaves with food, housing, education, and land transactions. This is not what was intended as "forty acres and a mule" as promised by President Andrew Johnson.

The first of many broken promises made to the former slaves. But the sharecropping system at least put Blacks on the path to landownership.

Over time, they began to buy land, acre by acre, patch by patch. They tilled the earth, built barns, raised crops, and taught their children how to read by lantern light.

They carved freedom out of the red Georgia clay.

By the 1920s, Black Georgians and other southern Blacks, owned small farms. By the 1940s, they were selling produce to local markets. Some sent their children to HBCUs. Others became schoolteachers and midwives. They formed co-ops and farming unions, always careful to stay off the radar of the White men with torches and badges.

Their wealth was not flashy, just steady and clean and out of sight. And through it all, they passed down the old ways. Like your grandparents.

Psalms. Prophecy. Dreams. Watchtower rites. The Shiloh lineage never lost its memory, even when the world tried to bury it.

Long before borders were drawn or flags flown, when empires rose and fell on the backs of warriors and prophets, there existed a secret bloodline born of Moorish and Balkan descent, a tribe divided by fate and spiritual allegiance.

They were known collectively as the *Children of Shiloh*, a people descended from Andalusian Moors who fled the Reconquista in Spain. Many were sold or traded into slavery and made their way during the "Middle Passage" to America. With crosses and swords at their heels, about 100 tribesmen got lost as they traversed the Mediterranean. Unable to reunite with their other tribe men, they found refuge in the hills of the Balkans, where they intermarried with the Slavic Romani. There, in the dense forests of Dobrinje and along the old caravan routes, a new tribe emerged: nomadic, wise, and powerful in spirit. That mixture was seen in your great-great grandmother's countenance.

Among them, two lineages evolved.

The first lineage remained true[9] to the Most High. They called them **Shilohs,** a name taken from the ancient Hebrew prophecy."

"*The scepter shall not depart from Judah, nor a lawgiver from between his feet, until Shiloh come...*"

— (Genesis 49:10).

The Shilohs are Watchers, Seers, and Guardians of divine balance. They moved like shadows, whispering prayers in forgotten tongues, wielded sacred symbols, and preserved the old ways: the ways of light, justice, and spiritual warfare. People entrusted with knowledge of dreams, numbers, stars, and the Word. A tribe bound by evil, protected the innocent, and intervened when darkness rose in the hearts of men. They are gifted.

They served GOD. El Shaddai. Jehovah. The Almighty.

This is the story the old gypsy woman laid on Malik's mind and heart that early morning in her fortune telling shop in the Village. He now understood what he was up against and his role in this continuing saga.

At the end of her story, without warning or help, the candle on the table flickered and then snuffed out. Just as Madam Erzebet transitioned from her stories about the Shiloh to the Despicables.

In the shadows of a street lantern, Madam Erzsebet continued with Malik's ancestral education. It continued with the Dushev who then formed alliance with the Despicables.

The Dushev

The Despicables

"But not all men remained faithful," she winced.

A rogue faction, hungry for power, seduced by secrets they once swore to protect, broke the covenant. They became the *Despicables:* traitors to the Light. These were ones who pledged allegiance to demonic forces in exchange for wealth, influence, and unnatural longevity. They performed rites in caves and unused churches, made pacts with shadows, and sowed deceit through thrones, banks, and boardrooms.

They infiltrated the temples, the courts, then the corporations to conduct the Devil's business on Earth.

While the *Shilohs* protected, the *Despicables* corrupted. Their bloodlines spread into the halls of kings and the chambers of CEOs. They built dynasties, passed secrets through generations, and branded their allegiance in subtle symbols, unseen by the uninitiated but undeniable to the spiritual eye.

They became wolves in priestly robes. CEOs with satanic contracts. Judges with compromised tongues.

Chapter Six
A Cursed Seed

"You shall not bow down to them or serve them; for I the Lord your God am a jealous God, punishing the children for the sin of the parents to the third and fourth generation of those who hate me, but showing love to a thousand generations of those who love me and keep my commandments."

— Exodus 20:5

But the Shilohs and the Despicables shared a tragic link: the Mitchell line.

This bloodline, marked by both promise and peril, passed silently through generations, birthed both saints and serpents. And in the modern age, it found its way into two people:

Malik Andrew Madison, descendant of the Shilohs, Watcher by birthright.

Monica Mitchell, his ex-wife, a descendant of both lines: the Shilohs and Despicables.

Their union was no coincidence. It was a convergence of ancestry and peril.

Their daughter, Jordan, was born at the intersection of these ancient forces. The Dushev curse passed through centuries of betrayal, and an unrepentant sin threatened to take hold of her. In Jordan lived the potential for either redemption or devastation.

The Shiloh elders revealed, through dreams, signs, and scripture, that only a mother could break the curse.

And so, the burden fell upon Monica Mitchell, once known as Monica Madison.

It is her destiny, whether known to her full well or not, to break the generational pact. She must deny the Despicables' dark influence and choose the Light on behalf of her child. This means to sever ties, renounce secret allegiances, and walk away from wealth and ease offered by the Despicables' power.

To break the curse, Monica has to choose sacrifice over status.

To protect Jordan, she must choose faith over darkness.

Now physical combat is replaced by spiritual war as corporate people wage it silently through boardrooms and bedrooms, through court cases and coded contracts. The Shilohs remain in hiding, watching while the Despicables keep building. And Jordan, either a curse or redeemer, is called to reveal the evils of Corporate America, the Despicables' dominion on earth.

Then in 1886, the Despicables caused the great divide between the "haves" and "have nots throughout the world." It commenced when the United States Supreme Court held in *Santa Clara County v. Southern Pacific Railroad Company* that the Fourteenth Amendment "equal protection clause" applied as well to corporations. The Supreme Court opined that corporations, while characterized as fictional persons not like naturalized human persons under the Constitution, the law aka nonetheless considered it as "corporate personhood." This court opinion fulfilled Satan's promise to create his own "person" on earth to wreak havoc in human lives.

It also represented the first seismic movement by the Despicables to tilt the balance of power in its favor, money in the hands of few elite disciples. And, there followed many other political, social and economic movements to solidify power in the Despicables

The Despicables started the "Industrial Revolution" with its initial band of industrialist titans. Then its corruption manifested itself in the incarcerations of many Blacks in prisons; the culmination and combination served as a new brand of slavery.

The final blow to the curse is not one of violence but of truth[9]. When Jordan discovers who she truly is and chooses whom she will serve, the legacy of both tribes may finally be fulfilled.

Or damned.

Malik now understood: before slavery in the US, the corporations, before the crowns, before the crucifixions and false kings, there were the Children of Shiloh.

They came from the south, brown-skinned, sun-kissed warriors of Moorish descent who once held the sciences and scriptures of Al-Abd-Al-Dasa. When the Christians' swords pierced Granada, their bloodlines scattered across the Mediterranean like seeds in the wind. Some fled to North Africa. Others to the Levant. But a chosen few crossed into the Balkan Mountains, where they mingled with Roma: keepers of song, movement, and sacred wanderings.

There, a hidden tribe was born.

They called themselves the Shilohs, those who remembered the covenant of light.

They carried the old knowledge. They walked by dreams, signs, and sacred codes. They were Watchers, ordained to protect the veil between good and evil, to preserve the knowledge of GOD in a world bent towards forgetfulness.

But not all were faithful.

A splinter formed.

Those who craved dominion over others, those seduced by fallen principalities, broke the truth[9]. They consorted with demonic powers, traded prayer for profit, light for luxury, and vision for vanity. They became the Despicables, marked by unclean alliances; their hearts hardened, their hands never clean.

Their mission: to control the Earth from beneath the Heavenly throne.

They planted themselves within kingdoms, courts, and corporations. They whispered into the ears of emperors and now into the ears of CEOs. They built systems, not for justice, but for judgment. They weaponized law, religion, and wealth to create a world that looks righteous but bleeds corruption.

And through it all... the Shilohs endured. Hidden. Watching. Waiting.

But there was a curse, one written in blood.

Long ago, the two tribes, Shiloh and Despicables, were one. The Mitchell bloodline was their shared origin, a river split by a mountain of pride. That blood still runs through descendants today.

Malik Madison was one.

Monica Mitchell, his former wife, is another.

Their child, Jordan, stands on the threshold of the curse.

Born of both lineages, Jordan is the first in 500 years to carry both the Watcher's mantle and the Despicables' temptation. Her soul is the battlefield. Her choices may seal the fate of generations.

Only her mother could break the curse. Only Monica can sever the chain by rejecting the false covenant, renouncing the legacy of darkness, and protecting her daughter from the serpents in her own blood.

This is not a battle of nations.

It is a battle of names, demons, prophecies, spirits, truth[9] and lies.

Wallace. Mitchell. Madison. Shiloh. Dushev. Despicables.

Two tribes. One war. A final reckoning still to come. The Day of Atonement is here.

The Betrayal of the Dushev

"What is done in blood is rarely washed in water. It echoes through generations."

— The Book of Watchers, Verse 7

Long before America's shores knew the weight of the slave ships, before the stars and stripes ever flew, a darker betrayal was born not in Africa but in the Balkans, in the shadowed valleys and forgotten forests of Southeastern Europe.

Two great tribes emerged from the ashes of Al-Andalus and from the scattered Moors: the Shilohs and the Dushev.

Both were once bound by kinship, tradition, and the sacred flame of the Ancients. Together, they carried Moorish blood, Romani rhythms, and spiritual knowledge of the old world. But the ancient alliance seared in the flames which followed as envy crept with the smoke and the subsequent embers. And when the white sails of European ships touched Balkan soil, carrying silver, wine, and muskets, temptation overcame tradition. It was a pattern and practice continued by the Europeans throughout Africa and the Americas, as they plied the indigenous population with bribes, gifts, and left behind bad habits to weaken its people.

And then it became clear to Malik the reason for Madam Erzebet's interest in the Mitchell legacy. It was her Slavic ancestors, The Dushev, whose name would later mean "soulless" in murmured tongues, struck a bargain with European traders.

In exchange for power, coins, and protection, they sold their kin. One hundred souls: men, women, and children of the Shilohs bloodline, were betrayed, bound, and handed over to foreigners.

Among them were the ancestors of Malik Madison and Monica Mitchell.

These Shilohs were branded, chained, and shipped west across the sea to the New World, where they would become property, stripped of name and nation, renamed as Negroes, slaves, beasts.

But blood remembers.

The betrayal ignited a tribal war, not just of people, but of spirits.

The Shilohs cursed the Dushevs.

The Dushev laughed and joined hands with the Despicables, trading their souls for dominion.

From that day forward, the two tribes walked different paths.

The Shilohs spread quietly through the Americas, hidden in plain sight, watching, praying, waiting for the reckoning, the Day of Atonement, if you will.

The Dushev, now entangled with the Despicables, flourished in darkness, evolving into CEOs, politicians, judges, bankers, brokers, and lords of false light.

The war never ended. It became generational. Spiritual. Systemic.

And now, Malik, it is time; the battle returned, not with swords, but with secrets. Not in villages, but in boardrooms. Not through whips, but through contracts. The blood of betrayal and the betrayer meet once more.

Jordan, Malik's daughter, carries in her veins the power to end this war or be consumed by it.

It was 8:00 AM by the time Madam Erzsebet finished her stories about the Al-Abd-Al-Dasa, the Dushevs, the Shilohs, the Despicables and the Mitchells. To say Malik was overwhelmed with thought could never explain his drunken-like stupor as he left Madam Erzsebet. He pulled up Google on his cell phone to check the NJ Transit train Saturday schedule from Penn Station to Asbury Park, NJ. The next train left at 8:25 AM. With a cab ride, he had just enough time to catch the next train.

Reflection

The train hummed like a lullaby as it pulled out of Penn Station at exactly 8:25 AM early Saturday morning. It headed southbound along the Northeast Corridor towards its destination, Asbury Park, New Jersey. Malik slipped into a window seat in the middle of the car. The train was mostly empty except for some young kids going home from a night of reverie, some young and middle-aged women who were either nannies or housekeepers going to tend to the needs of the wealthy on the New Jersey Shore.

His shoulders slumped with the brim of his Yankee baseball cap pulled low over his eyes.

He had not slept.

His fingers still smelled faintly of dust and iron, residue from the gypsy's shop. The kind of meeting that sends both chills and exhilaration of excitement throughout one's body. His mind was still on his clandestine meeting before he met the gypsy. Both provided him with clear instructions, and the gypsy woman was central to his plans.

She assured him that Psalms 91 was the Shilohs' covenant with GOD, although there are others the Despicables are unaware. That scripture provided him with protection in his times of need. Others would come to him in the name of Psalms 91 so that he knew these people were both his shield and sword as he waged war against the Despicables. The details she provided seemed clean.

Except for his mind.

Outside the window, the city began to blur, graffiti-stained tunnels giving way to gray brick warehouses, then stretch after stretch of rusted fencing and commuter silence. He stared through the glass, not seeing anything, just let the rhythm of the tracks lull him to sleep. The smoking brewery of the Anheuser-Busch factory sent smoke that swirled thick into the air, interspersed with the many electric towers that lined the NJ Turnpike. In the distance, Malik saw the airplanes' takeoffs and landings from Newark Liberty International Airport. The train passed slowly over the Pulaski Bridge from Newark to Elizabeth, and the Skyway was not quite full of traveling cars.

The old woman's voice from the storefront rang in his ears like a song half-remembered.

As Malik understood the stories from Madam Erzsebet, 100 Moorish people wandered off from their army towards their trek to conquer Iberia. These 100 Moors, the Al-Abd-al-Dasa, settled and married with the Dushev in Croatia, the Balkans. The Dushev betrayed these unsuspecting souls as they traded them to European slave traders. One of the young women sold was his great-grandmother, Adisa. Adisa later married Elias Mitchell, who came from Polly Wallace's family plantation, the Mitchell Plantation. The Mitchells, also a direct descendant of the Al-Abd-al-Dasa Moors, had two lineages. One became members of the Shiloh, the good line, and the other the Despicables, and its evil empire. Malik was a direct descendant of the Shiloh branch.

"One side of the Mitchell name is marked for light. The other, for shadows."

How the hell did she know about the Mitchells?

The name never felt heavier than now. It was just a name, his grandmother's, his ex-wife's. A common thread, sure, but nothing more. Until now.

"They war through you," she said, "and now through your daughter."

That's what twisted the knife. Jordan.

He reached into his briefcase and pulled out a folded photo of his daughter. It was slightly creased from the way he kept it, always in the inner sleeve of his briefcase. Jordan was eight years old when they separated as she sat on Monica's lap, her arms around her mother's neck, both smiled at the camera. Untouched by the weight of bloodlines, pacts, or betrayals.

But something happened now. He felt it.

The Despicables. The Shilohs. The Dushev. The Mitchells. What was once myth now showed its teeth. The gypsy's warning and prophecy. The strange increase in surveillance; he felt like people were watching him in plain sight, who pretended to be janitors, passersby, executives. The walls even whispered, or so it seemed. Something ancient woke up. He wasn't paranoid, or was he?

The train slid through Newark, then Elizabeth. The light outside was getting brighter, but Malik only felt the pressure building. His world was not falling apart. It unfolded. And he finally began to look at the edges of the design.

He closed his eyes for a moment. Psalms 91 floated up in his chest, not in his voice, but his grandmother's.

"He that dwelleth in the secret place of the Most High shall abide under the shadow of the Almighty..."

He mouthed the words silently as the train rocked gently from side to side beneath him.

The train came to his favorite part of the New Jersey Shore. The section just after Perth Amboy, New Jersey, that signified he left the urban centers of New Jersey to the start of southern New Jersey. The train passed over a rickety bridge, and to his left and right was an expansive section of marshlands similar in appearance to the Florida Everglades, but much smaller. Like the patch of flat marshlands along Highway 75 between Ocala and Gainesville, Florida. Willows and tall grass appeared from the swamplands, as they billowed back and forth in the morning winds. Like the swaying willow was the mark of a Shiloh in response to the battle to unfold. A very soothing part of the hour-and-fifteen-minute ride from Penn Station settled in Malik's mind for the last half of the trip home.

Soon they passed Long Branch as a transfer hub on the NJ Transit southbound line. People began to trickle out of the train: nurses, retirees, teenagers with headphones and sleepy eyes.

Malik stood, slung his briefcase over his shoulder, and stepped off onto the platform at Long Branch for the station parking lot where he left his car. The salty Atlantic air kissed his face as a reminder he was still alive. He watched the train rumbled steadily along the rust-streaked tracks as it curved toward the coast, slicing through swaths of suburban decay and marshy lowlands that whispered secrets from a century past. Malik leaned his forehead against the cool glass of his car window, as he watched the train disappear into the urban sprawl gave way to the long shadows of history. He drove the rest of the way to his home in Asbury Park.

The name struck something in him. It spoke to him when he moved from Chicago and began to look for a home. Almost a two-hour ride to the office by train, sometimes longer by car, was his daily commute from home to work each day. But his zodiac sign of Pisces, the water sign, sang his theme song as he listened to the ocean waves.

Not just a place, but a symbol. An emblem of idealism born in ambition and buried under generations of corruption, disillusionment, and rebirth. Time seemed suspended. The train hissed to a halt, and outside the window, time seemed suspended. There was a strange aura to Asbury Park… a ghost of America's promise dressed in chipped paint and sun-bleached brick.

Asbury Park.

It was once the dream of James A. Bradley, a devout Methodist businessman who carved a town out of swampland in 1871. He envisioned a utopian seaside resort where morals reigned, liquor outlawed, and salvation for sale beneath gilded rooftops. He named it after Bishop Francis Asbury, the first American Methodist bishop. For a moment, Malik imagined Bradley standing on the sand dunes, Bible in one hand, blueprints in the other, as declared dominion over land and soul.

Bradley's vision became reality… or at least, a well-manicured illusion of it. A paradise for New York elites and Philadelphia industrialists. At the turn of the century, Asbury Park, New Jersey, became the crown jewel of the Jersey Shore. Electric trolley lines crisscrossed manicured streets. The boardwalk buzzed with carnival rides, ice cream parlors, and fortune tellers. Grand hotels like the Berkeley-Carteret loomed like fortresses along the coast. And yet, as Malik understood so well, beneath every utopia was a shadow.

Segregation was a silent architect in Asbury Park's rise. Black families pushed to the West Side of town to Springwood Avenue, where they built a vibrant cultural life out of what little they received. Clubs like the Uptown, the Cuban Club, and the Elks Lodge exploded with the sound of jazz, rhythm and blues, gospel, and soul. Legends like Billie Holiday and Count Basie walked these cracked sidewalks. But those same streets one day burned.

Malik knew what came next. The story echoed in so many Black communities across America.

By July 1970, decades of racial tension, economic neglect, and police brutality erupted in riot. Springwood Avenue, once a proud Black business corridor, reduced to charred ruins. Buildings burned, dreams turned to ash, and the promise of integration withered in the smoke. The city never fully recovered. White flight turned Asbury into a hollowed-out relic. Grand hotels became flophouses. Crime overtook the boardwalk. The elegant façade cracked, and behind it, Malik recognized the fingerprints of the Despicables.

It was no coincidence. These collapses weren't merely urban decay, they were orchestrated acts of economic warfare. Strip the resources. Gut the businesses. Replace culture with crime. Then wait. Wait until the property values collapsed, the people displaced, and the land was ripe for redevelopment… for conquest.

But like all things touched by divine breath, Asbury Park refused to die.

In the early 2000s, artists, musicians, and members of the LGBTQ+ community began to rebuild.

The Stone Pony, the rock temple that birthed to Bruce Springsteen, Southside Johnny, and the Asbury Sound, reopened its doors. New restaurants, art galleries, and condos sprouted like shoots from a scorched field. The city once again became a haven for dreamers. The New York City and Philadelphia "gay elite", aka the "gay mafia," poured thousands of dollars into Asbury Park. They opened art boutiques, Chelsea-style lounges like the Watermark, eclectic restaurants, and brought a childlike promise of elegance once again to Asbury Park. On the weekends, the gay elite traveled from Manhattan and Philadelphia to gaze and gawk at the "hot" straight daddies that enjoyed the beach close to the gay section. Over time, it became a game each weekend to rank and place each hot daddy that seemed to parade before the lustful gay men.

The gays did not just respond to the call. They multiplied and brought with them that urban swag and grandeur. The vamp of a drag queen and the masculinity of an MMA fighter with all genres in between. It made for a fun and glorious environment.

One Saturday mid-afternoon as Malik walked the refurbished boardwalk after he left the beach, he overheard one young gay man say to a "hot" Asbury Park police officer, "I bet you stop traffic." The gang of young men laughed heartily as the hot police officer smiled back. That was the vibe in Asbury Park, NJ, where everyone tried to accept the other. For the most part, it clicked.

Yet still Malik saw the other side. Gentrification in disguise. The same cycle, washed in more appealing colors.

He closed his eyes. Asbury Park wasn't just a stop on a map. It was an American parable.

A city born in righteousness, exploited by avarice, divided by racism, sacrificed by policy, and now resurrected for profit. In it, he saw the pattern. The same pattern he saw at PAINCO. The same one whispered by the gypsy. A spiritual war encoded into economics and real estate deeds, into train lines and voting districts. Asbury Park merely was one of the early battlegrounds.

The train ride jolted him wide awake. Malik walked out the station to his parked car. He drove home and then sat in front of his house as he continued with his thoughts about the history of the place churning in his mind. It was no accident that the Despicables operated along such fault lines. They preyed on sacred spaces. And this city was sacred ground. Not because it was pure. But because it had been broken and rebuilt by the hands of the faithful, again.

Like Malik himself.

But nothing about his life was normal anymore.

Something was set in motion, and the tracks did not lead back to safety. Only forward into some type of spiritual war.

Chapter Seven
Silos

"For by wise guidance you can wage your war, and in abundance of counselors there is victory."

— Proverbs 24:6

This is how you know a Despicable. They lie. They cheat. They steal. A denial of a lie means they cheat and steal. If they say they don't cheat, then they steal and lie. If they protest when faced with a theft, then it means they lie and cheat. If they say nothing in response to an accusation, it means they lie, cheat and steal. Today, they refer to this behavior as "gaslighting."

The Despicables scoured the corporate landscape as they looked for unwitting recruits, victims or targets, or individuals open to their entreaties. They covered both ends of the personality spectrum and conjured whatever vibe the situation required. Some were affable. Often agreeable, or sometimes just downright mean, simply because it truly was their nature, and eventually their true self almost certainly emerged during a relationship or interaction. Regardless, they really held indifference to their target or victim. Communication was simply a means to an end. Sometimes it was the summer intern or the wife of a senior executive, the son, daughter, friend or associate of a manager, or another executive who was a "wannabe" who fell under their rapture. It really did not matter to the Despicables because people were expendable so long as the person fulfilled their nefarious purposes. And after they did the dirty deed or deeds, the Despicables had no further use for the individuals, or they were forever captured in their wicked web, forever doing their bidding.

The Despicables

It was almost cult-like. For the Despicables were wicked people. In this way, they showed no mercy, or discrimination, or affection for anyone; provided the person carried out their sinister plans. Cruelty was the Despicables' signature. Dysfunction was their strategy. Gaslighting was the technique to show the signature and strategy. No one escaped the wrath of the Despicables, even children. But the Despicables held a special objection to women.

Women did not escape the grasps of the Despicables either, who often used them to blackmail the unsuspecting man as they left the stench of their despicable cologne behind. Like Black slaves, White women also were simply vessels for the Despicables' pleasure. And so too women in business met the ire of the Despicables' wrath as much and often more so than the men in their meetings. The Despicables viewed and treated women as chattel. Their elevation to positions of power within the organization was more show than substance. For a man was behind the throne of women in business. Their only role was to gain leverage and to satisfy the appearance of equality when in fact nothing was further from the truth[9].

They taught their disciples: "You have to have a little larceny in one's heart to conduct business." This was not just some pithy motto but rather embodied a belief system so entrenched in the psyche of the Despicables to move from folklore to reality. Like acid. Like an oath. If you did not agree, if you did not act like you agreed, you not only failed but perished. You just didn't move out. You were discredited inside and outside the cocoon that once was your sanctuary. You were labeled as not a "team player" or labeled "difficult to work with" if you rejected or resisted their proposals. Most times they simply destroyed you if they had no further use for the target. They "blacklisted you."

Malik knew this to be true because he witnessed it firsthand. And every time someone at PAINCO disappeared without warning, every time a position was suddenly restructured, it was preceded by a firm tap on the shoulder. He saw this unfold countless times. Or after a period, the former executive wound up employed by a competitor. Soon thereafter, the caravan followed. The caravan of liars, cheaters and thieves would slowly trickle one, two or three from PAINCO to the new company to complete their dastardly deeds.

Malik was promoted to Senior Counsel, Legal Department, PAINCO concurrently with his transfer from the company's Chicago office to its Manhattan regional office. It was a director level position just one level below the coveted Vice President. As justification for the transfer, he was told it showcased his exceptional legal mind and displayed his talents in litigation, contract drafting and government relations. The promotion allowed him to make major contributions to the company's growth objectives. It seemed like an offer he could not refuse.

Warnings

Gino Colucci stepped into Malik's office without knocking, and slammed a manila folder down on his desk. Gino always approached Malik the way an oncoming storm entered a valley: calm on the surface but with pressure that dropped and everything suddenly still.

Gino was a portly 5'9", 180 pounds of Italian sausage with a balding and receding hairline. He always sported a perpetual tan which later Malik discovered was mostly spray painted on his face. Always nattily dressed in his tailored suits. Always genuinely insincere.

Malik looked up from the flowchart spread across his desk. A dozen corporate logos connected by arrows and shell companies stared back at him. At the center: PAINCO. The Pan American Insurance Company. A hydra with a thousand heads located throughout the world.

Gino smiled the kind of smile that made men nervous. He wore a crisp charcoal suit, slim-cut and expensive. No tie. The first two buttons of his black shirt opened, revealed a thin gold chain and the top edge of a tattoo that peeked out of his collarbone. It looked like a serpent or a sword. Malik was not sure.

"Mind if I come in?" Gino asked, already halfway through the door.

"You are already in," Malik said coolly.

Gino closed the door behind him without a sound. "I heard you have been asking questions."

Malik leaned back in his chair. "That's my job to ask questions. Is that a problem?"

"Not yet."

"Which is it…not yet…to ask questions or there is a problem?" Malik replied, as placed his hands flat on the top of his desk.

Gino walked to the edge of the desk, picked up a red stress ball, and squeezed it thoughtfully. "But let me give you some friendly advice. Questions are like grenades. They don't always wait for you to throw them before they go off."

Malik said nothing. "So, he is telling me this place is a landmine," Malik thought.

Gino dropped the ball and smiled again. "I like you, M. You have a clean look. Sharp mind. People like you usually do well here, if they don't go looking for things that aren't theirs to find."

Malik folded his hands. "And what exactly isn't mine?"

Gino did not answer. He turned instead to the window and looked over the skyline. "You ever wonder how a company like PAINCO grows so fast, so clean? We cover more ground than most governments. Cross more borders than the CIA. And yet," he turned back to Malik, "we never had a single federal investigation stick."

He said it so proudly as if an investigation itself is not an indictment of sorts.

Malik felt the weight of the moment. This was not small talk.

"You ever hear of a tribe called Dushev?" Gino asked suddenly.

Malik's face twitched. The name struck something ancient inside him. "How did he know about the Shilohs and the Dushevs?" Malik thought as he tried to mask his concern. This indeed was a game of poker at PAINCO one mastered quickly or failed miserably.

"Of course not," Gino said, reading him. "Most people haven't. But they are real. Old blood. Older than these skyscrapers, older than this city. You ever get the sense your life is not yours? Like you were, born into something?"

Malik stood slowly. "You came here to tell me something. Say it."

Gino's smile faded. "You are on a path, Malik. A dangerous one. There are things in this world bigger than you, bigger than all of us. The Shilohs, the Dushev, the Despicables. These are not bedtime stories. They are power structures."

"Whose side are you on?" Malik asked.

Gino looked him dead in the eye. "I am on the side that survives and wins."

He stepped closer, his voice low. "You are playing in dangerous currents that go back centuries. Tribes. Blood. Betrayal. You want to find the truth°? Fine. But just remember not everyone wants it found."

"I just want to make sure I cover all matters," Malik responded.

Then he turned and walked out, just as silently as he entered.

It was clear from the file that Gino slammed on Malik's desk was a test. He reviewed the file, and it was apparent Malik was drawn and mired in PAINCO's dangerous web of corporate corruption. Another offshore company structure was presented in the file and not in compliance with corporate governance standards and even the law.

Malik felt like he was caught between a rock and a hard place. Failure to do as instructed risked danger to him and possibly his entire family. He would bide his time, until he could figure out a way out of this entangled web of deception, secrecy and corruption. How could he successfully remain neutral was still an open question. Malik racked his brain for ways he could slow down the process, to hinder the project assigned to him by Gino or not do it at all. Time was not on his side as the board of directors meeting to sign the resolution to incorporate the offshore company approached soon.

And then there was the matter of Doug Venier, who knocked on Malik's office door not soon after Gino's unannounced visit. Doug was six feet two inches of lean, muscular, aristocratic-looking man. Distinguished and handsome in a White European way. Doug looked like he came from money. And, he made no effort to hide it. The pampered look. The overly confident demeanor and the insincerity he projected. An entitlement mentality, some said.

Doug was the type of person that made everyone feel uncomfortable, like Gino. He smiled too easily. Wore silk ties knotted with surgical precision. Graceful with an edge as if he could handle himself in a street brawl. Never raised his voice and somehow always got what he wanted. Doug ran the Risk Management Department, and Malik was assigned as his legal counsel.

However, though it was clear that Doug held a high position within the PAINCO organization, he did not appear on any organization chart that Malik saw. No direct reports and no dotted or solid line reporting relationship to anyone in the company, just powerful influence. And somehow, Malik was assigned to him as his legal counsel. "But why?" he wondered.

Doug came to drop another manila folder on Malik's desk.

"Malik, I have a small favor to ask you," Doug said with that dreaded Cheshire cat smile all came to detest. The contract inside the folder stated: "Consulting Transfer – Internal Vendor Shell." It sounded like standard financial jargon, but Malik got tense as he looked it over quickly. He became irritated.

The vendor did not exist. The address was a law firm in Luxembourg that looped back to a private company incorporated in Las Vegas, Nevada. The State of Nevada, Business Licensing Division, Secretary of State, did not require the identification of company officers and directors in its incorporation documents. This allowed for the hiding of the identity of the true owners and officers of a company. It was often the "most favored nation" state of incorporation for companies and individuals who kept things "close to the vest."

And the identity of the prospective company's officers and directors were not provided in the contract before Malik. The signature on the incorporation documents did not match the digital signatures in the chain of custody for corporation formation.

Company standards required the company's compliance with the many standards for corporate governance, internal accounting and more importantly, insurance company laws and regulations. Insurance holding company laws are very onerous and highly regulated.

"This is not compliant with company policy or the law." Malik looked up at Doug.

"There are several misrepresentations in the documents which make their filing difficult," Malik added.

Doug chuckled. "Aw, Malik. Just make it happen. Do your magic and get this approved by the State of Nevada. It's very important to PAINCO this company exists," he added.

Malik did not sign off on the file. Instead, he pushed back on Doug. He said that he needed time to review the file. That he would get back to him by the end of the week. This seemed to satisfy Doug, at least for the moment. He needed to buy some time.

Doug said, "One week, Malik. That's it. Be a team player." Then just like that, he exited Malik's office.

Malik stood alone in the office, the city lights blinking behind him like a nervous system. He looked back at the flowchart on his desk. The red lines, offshore accounts, and untraceable trusts overwhelmed him. He racked his brain for all possible solutions to extricate himself from this morass.

And in the center: PAINCO.

Suddenly, it did not feel like a chart anymore.

It looked like a map.

A battlefield.

Malik worked at PAINCO long enough that he knew something was not right. But now, he finally saw it.

They were everywhere, like an octopus with a zillion tentacles, able to reach out and snatch something away.

The Despicables.

They did not wear horns or capes. They did not breathe fire or chant in Latin. No, they wore thousand-dollar suits, custom-made shoes from Milan, Rolex watches that set off enough bling that caught enough light that distracted you while they slid the knife in your back.

They smiled too wide, over-inflated, spoke too calmly and laughed when no one said anything funny. These were the Despicables.

And they always watched.

Their offices, cold and sterile, lined with minimalist furniture and abstract art that masked surveillance and coded messages. Every corner of the 39th floor was curated for illusion: beauty over truth[9], and control over clarity.

PAINCO's leader, John Irolla, CEO, though he approached the company's mandatory retirement age, gave no signs his departure was imminent. A short, nerdy-looking man who surrounded himself with other short men, all of whom bowed to his expansive ego. How Irolla became CEO was where legends were made. Some say it was the eighth wonder of the world.

Doug Venier, ran the risk team as a command unit, was not in the business of preventing loss. He was in the business who decided, who burned and got paid.

The Despicables

He never raised his voice. He did not need to. The Despicables had that certain knack where a single look cleared the room. People obeyed them the way animals obey a scent: instinctively, silently, and without question. These men were hunters.

Others were scavengers who picked the remaining meat left on the bone by the hunter. And at the bottom of the food chain were the maggots who really did the dirty work that ensured the remains of the carcass had completely disappeared. And these individuals enjoyed the "clean up" because the closer to the bone, the sweeter the blood. The last two were people in IT programming, software development and financial accounting.

It became more fact than folklore, that the public viewed financial service companies such as insurance companies along with pharmaceutical companies as villains who engaged in shady businesses. However, artificial intelligence because of its anonymity only enhanced the status of insurers as villains. More corporations incorporated it in their business models from logistics to customer support.

Inside corporations, the Despicables became silent mercenaries, hiding within an industry. Like two separate silos existing simultaneously but with different purposes. With the proliferation of artificial intelligence, the Despicables found a silent army and a new way to penetrate and re-engineer the insurance market. The dark silo of a corporation was comprised of the Despicables, who spent centuries that infiltrated different industries. It perpetrated its darkness throughout the world. Its reach and influence extended to law enforcement, law firms, and every other facet of society.

Its reach and mission were generational, with purported ties to the old Confederacy now reconstituted to various White Supremacist groups. Forces who joined with corporate types to move the Despicables' agenda forward. The Confederates never accepted the outcome of their civil war loss to the north. These were evil and a calculated lot. Some said they did not evolve as a human species. Other said the Despicables were the aliens from another world we search for, as they operated right before our very eyes.

They operated in the comfort of mysteries. And now they wore Brooks Brothers shoes, Armani suits, and carried company key cards instead of rifles. They bought board of directors' seats as they purchased significant blocks of company stock to gain a foothold if not control over the targeted company. The board of directors' seats typically represented the "White Hat" silo within a corporation, but now some of these positions were occupied by the Despicables to gain control over these publicly traded companies. Other times the Despicables operated without board of director oversight.

Across from them in a parallel universe were the "White Hats" who battled them for control and influence in corporations. Sometimes the "White Hats" were secretly placed Shilohs. Idealists, guardians, compliance officers, and typically attorney who served as warriors. Internal auditors with a conscience who served as prospective and potential "whistleblowers". They fought against the Despicables' grift, graft, corruption and undue influence, often in vain. Because once the Despicables targeted something, they operated like parasites, sucking the very blood and life from the corporate organism. By the time shareholders' derivative lawsuits were filed or the government initiated an investigation, the Despicables were long gone. Someone was always left to hold the bag. They had "cooked the books." This possibly happened in many publicly traded companies when you consider the demise of Sears, Xerox, Enron, Kmart and other corporations that fell by the wayside. Many believe it happened because of corporate greed and corruption.

Slowly, subtly, they placed their soldiers in key places in departments of an organization. A system of "gaslighting" that was replicated in any industry or company the Despicables targeted. They deployed accounting practices, compliance standards and corporate subterfuge designed to delay, linger and wait from detection of financial improprieties long after the pirates left the company.

Then there was Gino Colucci, who smiled too often, too bright, laughter too full for the occasion. He played the affable fool, told off-color jokes in break rooms, and made everyone believe he was just a good old boy from Illinois. But Malik saw the real Gino. The eyes that went dead when he thought no one watched. The way he made calls from the 42nd floor at night with the lights off. The sudden appearance of offshore accounts tied to his name that no one at compliance flagged because they were too afraid.

The Despicables did not fire people. They made them disappear in a variety of ways. One day your email just stopped working. Your badge would not scan. Your nameplate was gone. Your company cell phone stopped working. Suddenly, nobody talked about or to you ever again.

You were not just terminated. You were erased. Its tentacles reached in all segments of society from unions to the three credit bureaus to the major credit card issuers to the government. Suddenly, you hit a wall where prior to your employment with a Despicable organization you were once respected, revered, and doors opened to you, now closed. And they controlled hundreds of companies trading on the New York Stock Exchange. Had contacts with the higher echelons of American corporate life and governments.

Their power was not written in memos or minutes. It felt, in the chill of the conference room, in the silence when someone asked the wrong question. Like in the way junior analysts flinched when summoned to "private meetings." In that way, your telephone calls suddenly were not returned.

Malik used to think PAINCO was just another multinational corporation. Now he knew better.

PAINCO was a citadel. One of many temples to the Despicables.

They used the company to launder control, to sanitize evil in spreadsheets and PowerPoint decks. On paper, they sold life insurance and other financial security products. They insured corruption and avoided paying claims because of that corruption. Protected power. Insulated sin. They did not just underwrite policies; they wrote people's fates.

And Malik was trapped in the middle.

A Shiloh among snakes.

A watcher, as in a lamb in a lion's den.

An endangered man in a glass fortress of evil. A pimple on a "rump's ass."

Especially when truth[9] starts cracking the foundation.

The fact of the matter: Malik was preoccupied with the last six months as things revealed themselves to him within and about PAINCO. It was late as he sat at the table behind his large mahogany desk as the night lamp peered out the window at the Manhattan skyline before him. He had a lot on his mind that competed with and conflicted the thoughts that swirled in his head. His world lacked trust and was replaced with danger suddenly.

From the moment Gino and Doug last stepped into his office with their veiled threats, everything changed for Malik. And then the gaslighting accelerated quickly. He sensed it before their last meeting, but it was readily apparent following. It probably went on all along and Malik was not fully aware.

It started subtly. Almost dismissible. The cursor on his laptop moved by itself, it slid across the screen like a lazy serpent, blinked in and out of code. At first, Malik thought it was a glitch. A delayed input. Maybe an update was synced in the background. But then it started typing. Just one word. "STOP." These were no freak actions but appeared very purposeful.

Over time, Malik got greater clarity about the gaslighting. It was a result of a software patch. A software patch sent through an email or text message on his cell phone by the oppressor. By opening the email, text or answering a cell phone call, which was often referred to as a "Potential Spam," allowed third-party access to his personal electronics. The software patch enabled its sender to open the recorder, camera and microphone functions on cell phones, laptops and other handheld devices.

Sometimes, they would call or send an email from a similar number or name in a target's contact list; which, if answered, sent through the software patch that opened the "windows of the soul" of the target. Or the software patch, wherever it originated, might disable it to cause the cell phone to recharge slowly, if at all. The Despicables had any number of electronic means to put a target or victim under their surveillance. And they were not upset if the victim or target knew it happened. In fact, there were those who believed the Despicables wanted detection: to let their target know they were watched, to cause stress, doubt and fear. The weakest among them fell victim to illness, suicide and submission.

It was a quiet secret within PAINCO that one young Black man in the Procurement Department was so terrorized by the Despicables that he took his own life. The pressure he faced and was under, so insurmountable in his mind that death seemed easier than to endure the constant harassment by the Despicables as they attempted to procure him for their evil purposes. Except, Malik was no longer a young man, but a seasoned and gifted man with a thorough understanding of his daunting task.

"STOP."

His emails were monitored more at the office and at home. A colleague in IT told him his login credentials were pinging on terminals that Malik never touched. Human Resources flagged his vacation schedule, claiming an error in his accrued days. He found out around tax filing time that PAINCO failed to change his tax withholding state from Illinois to New Jersey. The worst was that Malik received an unmarked and unidentified envelope with no return address. Inside the envelope were a series of articles about the death of a "whistleblower" at some US company in Hong Kong.

The message was clear. Though it did nothing to dissuade Malik from the task before him.

The Despicables showed their hand. And they were inside PAINCO and everywhere. Not just a few bad actors, but a structure: like a second silo or shadow department within the corporation. They operated as separate people and tribes, like different types of beings, except artificial intelligence over the internet served as their cloak of clothing. A budding syndicate or cartel that operated outside but alongside the visible corporation. Like a malignant tumor that grew without the harvester's knowledge. And people like Doug and Gino were not visible employees. They were handlers. They had invisible soldiers who operated over the internet through social media networks like Facebook, Instagram, TikTok, BlueSky, Telegram, etc., whose singular purpose was to harass, intimidate and scare selected targets: individuals who represented a threat to the Despicables' kingdom.

These operatives functioned as rogue enforcers; more akin to a freelance militia or domestic extremists; unleashing chaos on unsuspecting individuals to coerce compliance with the Despicables' agenda. Their victims were often people of color, who bore the brunt of this orchestrated terror. It was as if the Despicables wielded the internet as a digital disguise, a modern-day hood, while the relentless harassment they deployed etched itself into the psyche of their targets like a burning cross.

Deliverance

Six months before his trip to Budapest and Prague via Zurich, Berlin, Amsterdam and Barcelona and his return, Malik awoke to a package outside the door to his home. Inside the box was a burner cell inside a padded pouch. Inside the envelope was fifty thousand dollars in small denominations. He opened the box in his home office as he sat at his desk before the computer screen. The screen glowed cold in the dark.

Another envelope was also in the box. He opened it.

One message.

No signature.

No thread.

Budapest, December 10, 2019

47.49801 north, 19.03991 east.

An airplane ticket, passports with a different name with his photo affixed to it.

He entered the coordinates into Google Maps, which led him to a precise location on the Pest side of Budapest at the Intercontinental Hotel, a sleek modern fortress of glass and silence facing the water directly across from Castle Hill. A perfect vantage point. A place for eyes.

Malik stared at the cell phone for what seemed like hours that evening, as he paced his bedroom floor in his socks. Then it occurred to him as he stared out his bedroom window at his perfectly coiffed yard, with his breath fogging the window. The game is back on.

The Despicables were in motion, and someone, somewhere, chose him as a piece on the board game again. That was his signal to move.

The next morning, Malik took a cab to the lower east side of Manhattan, where he entered a crumbling four-story brownstone with a dented steel mailbox that read: "K. Szorba – Travel Services." A small Hungarian flag decal flaked off the side of the door. It was in this travel service that the old gypsy woman told him the man inside would arrange his travel arrangements. She told him, the man was an agent for secret Hungarian intelligence: an offshoot long presumed to be defunct. The gypsy came through as Madam Erzsebet assured him as she pointed her crooked finger at him.

"Trust me," she said.

Behind a warped oak desk sat a narrow-faced man in his sixties, with slicked-back hair and unsettling stillness.

He never spoke his name. It was not necessary for this particular transaction.

Malik simply said, "Psalms 91." He continued, "I received a text. Budapest. December 10. The message instructed me to see you."

The man did not respond immediately. Instead, he opened a large black ledger and flipped to a blank page. Then he reached for a beige rotary telephone at the far end of the desk. The numbers clicked with each rotation. The entire scene seemed like

Malik was back in communist Hungary with the old telephone and the crusted room they conducted business in.

He waited. Then on the third ring, the number connected.

In a voice as thick and sour as day-old wine that sat opened too long, a man on the other end said, "Arai sisa, I have your travel arrangements."

Malik let go of his breath. He did not think he needed a code name, but just in case, his nickname from childhood would do. "M&M" aka Malik Andrew Madison.

"Where do I go?" he asked quietly.

There was a pause. Then the voice replied deliberately, "You are to report to 1115 Memory Blvd., NYC. Two o'clock PM. No later." The man said abruptly with a thick eastern European accent.

Then the line went dead.

Malik looked at the Hungarian man behind the desk. "Is that it?" he asked.

But the man was already tearing a ticket voucher from a leather binder. He slid it across his desk, along with a new phone, some passports for his return trip, and a pair of thin leather gloves.

"No metal, no conversations during the flights. Do not draw any attention to yourself whatsoever," he warned.

"He'll be holding the 'Economist.'" He looked up with his blue eyes suddenly glazed and said, "Do not speak first."

Malik nodded, took the passports, folded the tickets and placed the bundle in his briefcase without saying a word. As he stepped into the street, the winter wind hit him in the face like a speeding train without a warning.

The sun was out, but the darkness settled in his mind. Somehow the contrast between the two felt gray.

1115 Memory Blvd.

At precisely 1:56 PM, Malik stood directly across from 1115 Memory Blvd., NYC. Before him stood a rather nondescript limestone building, nestled next to a shuttered Polish deli and a Russian social club with soot-stained windows. The building bore no signage, no visible entrance buzzer, no apparent security camera; just a metal black front door, and a single brass address plate screwed loosely into the wall.

Malik did not cross the street immediately.

Instead, he observed the front of the building for a couple of seconds. He pulled his coat collar up behind his neck and his Kangol hat towards the front of his face. A delivery man slouched past. A young woman pushed a stroller with a toddler as if she was the nanny.

Malik pretended to ignore her. It was not a particularly busy street, though there were several cars parked on the street. Just not a lot of pedestrian traffic for a busy Manhattan street. All seemingly routine except for Malik's presence.

However, everything about Malik's instincts and his very existence buzzed with tension. His veins felt like electric wires frying from pressure overload. The place was a hole, like a place that housed government employees or ghosts.

At exactly 2:00 PM, Malik stepped across the cracked asphalt, pulled on the leather gloves so as not to leave any fingerprints along his circuitous path. He knocked twice on the black door with the edge of his knuckles.

Silence.

Then a soft click. The door opened itself. He stepped in.

The hallway inside was dim, lit only by a banker's green shade lamp sitting on a desk table. The pungent smell of sulfur, like freshly struck matches or gunpowder, traveled in the hallway. The wallpaper was yellowish and somewhat stunk, twisting at the edges, and a dusty staircase rose toward a second floor veiled in shade in the hallway.

A man stood at the end of the hallway, back turned. He wore a tailored blue suit and a beige wool overcoat. He was someone who waited for no one. As Malik approached, the man turned halfway and extended a gloved hand without directly looking at him. Tucked into his overcoat pocket, was a rolled copy of the "Economist."

"Psalms 91," Malik said. Inside was a single hotel key, a thumb drive, and a folded piece of paper with a Budapest address written on it in pencil.

Sas utca 2, V. District, Room 609

Dec. 11, 22:00 hours.

The man finally spoke, after he received his signal from Malik. His English was perfect, clean, and dry like cold gin.

"You'll be met. Don't speak unless prompted and even then, hesitate, unless prompted. You know the code word. If you see the man, leave immediately. If you see a feather on your hotel desk and the hoot of an owl during your journey, then it is safe to continue."

Malik nodded.

Then the man stepped around him and disappeared out the door without another word.

Chapter Eight
Budapest

"When a stranger sojourns with you in your land, you shall not do him wrong. You shall treat the stranger who sojourns with you as the native among you, and you shall love him as yourself, for you were strangers in the land of Egypt: I AM YOUR LORD."

— Leviticus 19:33-34

Malik boarded the plane at LaGuardia Airport on a cold Thursday winter night. His body was calm but his mind stormed. Most of the flights from NYC to Europe occurred in the early evening so that the traveler arrived in Europe in the next early morning hours.

The flight was overnight: New York LaGuardia Airport for a flight first through Zurich on Lufthansa Airlines, a six-hour layover, then another flight on Swiss Air to Prague. The total hours of the trip were close to 16 hours, so he had plenty of time to think further about the history the old gypsy woman laid on his mind. The route ostensibly was not chosen for convenience but for obscurity.

He wore a gray hoodie under a tailored overcoat, jeans, and black sneakers. It was late Fall when he took the flight, His carry-on was light: just a laptop, a leather-bound notebook, and an encrypted flash drive he kept zipped inside the lining of his bag. Everything else he needed, like additional clothing was already waiting in Europe, arranged by contacts he trusted, for now.

Too many eyes watched him in the States. He needed time to breathe and to think. He needed answers as his long conversation, or more like recitation by the old gypsy woman, scrambled his mind.

The engines roared as Malik's flight ascended over New York, as it sliced into the night sky over NYC, then Boston, to the English Channel like a scalpel across velvet. A direct flight to Budapest was not the approach to his adventure, so the gypsy's agent booked his travels through Zurich, Switzerland, a six-hour layover that he initially considered an inconvenience. But now, it felt like a necessary detour.

He dozed briefly on the flight, which was a nice diversion and unusual as a nervous flier, lulled by the cabin hum of the soft whiz of the engines and the distant clink of ice in glasses. The descent into Switzerland was smooth, the sky over Zurich painted in slate gray. The moment the wheels kissed down in Zurich, he felt the stark difference. The plane landed like it touched down on polished marble: silent, immaculate, an indifferent type of efficiency.

It was barely 6:15 AM local time when the plane landed, but the airport buzzed like midafternoon. Zurich was a major European hub for many destinations throughout the continent. Zurich Airport, or Flughafen Zürich, was modern and spotless: a cathedral built with efficiency as the Swiss were well known for their precise timing, structure and organization. But Malik was not interested to wait at the terminal surrounded by overpriced coffee and luxury shops. He had six hours until his next flight to Prague.

His curiosity tugged harder than caution, plus the free time enabled him to see if anyone followed him during this first leg of his trip. Malik passed through customs with ease, his US passport scanned, stamped, and returned without a single question.

He swung his carry-on luggage over his shoulder as he searched for the train from the airport to the City of Zurich.

Still, he felt watched.

He stepped into the terminal, changed a hundred euros to Swiss francs. He purchased a ticket from the SBB kiosk and descended into the sleek gliding tunnels of the Zürich S-Bahn. It was about a 20-minute ride on the S-Bahn train into the city.

Twenty minutes later, he emerged from the Bahnhofstrasse station into the gray morning mist of downtown Zürich. The morning chill slapped him in the face as he exited Zurich Hauptbahnhof. The city rose before him like a dream rendered in stone: clean, geometric, and restrained. It felt much like it was the first time he traveled to Europe during college when he visited Amsterdam: rather mystical, whimsical and fantastical. It was a strange balance of old-world grace and sterile perfection. Cobbled streets met glass towers. Romanesque arches stood next to modern banks.

What immediately struck him was the order. The stillness. Even the pigeons seemed to strut more gracefully here. The streets were wide and pristine, bordered with ornate stone buildings, each one a quiet monument to history and discipline. The architecture carried stories of medieval Gothic, stitched together by cobblestone paths and sharp rooflines.

It was beautiful. But cold. Not just the temperature, but the spirit and people of the place.

People moved with mechanical precision. Eyes averted. Smiles rare. Conversations hushed. The Swiss were fluent in neutrality. And though many spoke German, French, Italian and English, Malik noticed something strange: whenever he asked for directions in English, people hesitated, just long enough to make him feel unwelcomed.

Yes, they spoke English. But no, they did not want to speak it. At first, Malik thought he imagined it. He stopped a well-dressed couple in their forties to ask for directions to Lake Zurich, and though they seemed to understand his English, they responded in clipped German and moved on. Another man, a banker type with a briefcase and a scarf, simply looked at him, shrugged, and kept walking.

He wandered the Old Town, Altstadt, where timber-framed buildings leaned like old friends, their eaves nearly touching over the narrow, winding lanes. Flower boxes spilled with crimson geraniums from the windowsills. Churches like Grossmünster and Fraumünster rose above the city with stoic grace, their towers stretched like silent sentinels over the Limmat River.

He walked through Bahnhofstrasse, Zurich's famed luxury shopping street, past banks that did not just store money, but for which the gypsy arranged a large deposit in a Swiss bank in the event he needed discreet sums of money during the journey. These banks not only stored and traded money, but they also contained hundreds of years of secrets, money and history. Yet for all its beauty, there was something closeted about Zurich.

French. German. Swiss German. Italian. Even Spanish. Yes, they spoke English. But, no, they did not speak it.

"This place is not just a city," Malik thought. "It's a vault."

He ducked into a narrow side street, where a small café offered warmth and espresso. He sat by the window, he sipped slowly, as he scanned faces in the crowd.

"Everyone looks like they are hiding something," he murmured to himself.

He thought about the gypsy woman and the things she laid on his mind. The words of Madam Erzsébet consumed the space in

Malik's mind. Gino. About PAINCO. Everything had new meaning, and all became surreal, layered in dank mirth. He pondered the explanation provided by the gypsy woman about why she helped him.

Her explanation was that her family was once part of the Dushev back in Hungary. It was her people that sold the 100 people of the Al-Abd-a-Dasa tribe to the Europeans. The tribe that Malik's great-great grandmother Adisa fell into the slave traders', then slaveowners', hands. The same hands that transported her as a slave to America. This and other transactions by the Dushev placed an eternal strain and stain of immorality as the early vestiges of the guilt of human trafficking by the Balkans. And it was her burden to cancel that debt to the devil and to set the course right for those 100 Al-Abd-a-Dasa tribespeople's descendants traded to the Europeans.

Throughout history, the Swiss were known for their neutrality during war; in fact, their position towards wars often avoided both attack and participation. However, while the Swiss did not directly participate in wars and even in the African slave trade, they most certainly participated and benefited from its financing and laundering of profits from war and the slave trading industry.

Because of its clandestine history, Zurich made the conspiracy and the stories the gypsy woman told sound real. Tangible. Like this was where it all funneled: money, influence, deception, secrecy and corruption. This was where the Despicables, who were comprised of the progeny of the Dushev, and the slave owners" descendants of the Mitchells, Wallace, etc. and then the Italian, Jewish, Irish, Black, Russian and gay mafias, banked and hid their sins in offshore accounts.

They even laundered money through the Catholic Church, then the Protestants, Baptists, and even the Pentecostals. These religious institutions later coalesced and operated under the single moniker "Evangelicals" or "Christian Nationalists." Wherever and whenever the Despicables could offload large amounts of cash, they did. For the concept of mass criminal enterprise originated in Europe and was refined in the Americas but still found its way into the secret banking society of the Swiss and other banking institutions throughout the continents.

By noon, Malik made his way back to the airport. His phone vibrated once with a blocked number. He did not answer it because he already knew the game.

Inside the terminal, he moved through security again, this time glancing at every uniformed face, every camera overhead.

A man in a black suit with an earpiece seemed to watch him for a second too long.

Another passenger bumped him too hard in the corridor, then said "Shiloh" just loud enough for Malik to hear.

He turned.

The man was gone.

When the Swiss Air plane lifted off, Malik felt a strange sensation. Not fear. Not excitement. Weightlessness. But not as if a burden was lifted, but that he flailed aimlessly in the wind.

He stared out the window as the Swiss countryside gave way to clouds. He opened his notebook and scribbled something the gypsy said in New York:

"You walk with ghosts. And soon...they will speak."

Budapest was waiting.

And the answers were no longer behind desks or emails or encrypted drives. The answers lay ahead of him. He did his espionage research the evening before he stumbled upon Madam Erzsébet that early Saturday morning. The man he met told him how to complete the task he planned. He was a former Israeli Mossad agent with a treasure trove of information about clandestine operations. He found the former Mossad intelligence agent from a news reporting television producer friend. As an excuse for the introduction, Malik told his friend he wanted research for a screenplay he composed. It was Madam Erzsébet who put the rest of the plans in motion.

All the information he compiled represented old blood in hidden lands. The truth[9] followed him across the ocean.

Prague

Malik stepped onto the platform at Praha hlavní nádraží, Prague's main train station, just after dusk. The sky was bruised purple, and the city glowed with a quiet, golden melancholy.

He wore a long navy coat this time and switched from his foldable leather carry-on bag to a small black duffel bag. He carried it over his shoulder. No luggage tags. No traceable cards. He paid in cash. Always in cash now.

Outside the station, Prague breathed like a poem carved in stone. Baroque cathedrals. Gothic spires. Narrow cobblestone alleys where the past groaned at your back. It was beautiful, mystical as the large ancient sun dial clock glistened in the darkness that fell. But the city was not safe. The medieval Pražský castle from the 1200s stood in the distance, high above the hill.

The red ceramic rooftop tiles inside the castle seemed to run endlessly along the castle's landscape. Malik would save a visit to the castle for another trip as he was tired from his day's travel.

During WWII, unlike other European nations like France, England and Hungary, the then Swiss, Swedish, Danish, Finnish and Czechoslovakia voluntarily surrendered to the Nazis to preserve their rich-in-history medieval architecture. Most of the latter nations still maintained their old medieval charm. The architecture itself seemed to define the meek demeanor of the Czech people. The Czechs were more like the Swiss than Hungarian, than Spanish, than German. Like the Swiss, the Czechs wanted to preserve their culture, architecture and way of life. So, the Czechs capitulated to the German demands during WWII. The architecture in Prague was incredibly preserved and absolutely astounded visitors because of their complicity with the Germans.

He hailed a taxi and gave the driver the address of a small pension tucked in a side street near Mala Street, the old quarter.

The driver said nothing during the entire ride.

That was fine. Malik did not want to have a conversation. He needed rest, and time to think further.

By 9 PM, he was in his room. The pension was modest: aged walls, a worn velvet chair, a radio that only played one Czech station. Malik sat at the desk and opened his notebook. He drew a line across a blank page, then names beneath it.

Venier, Colucci, Irolla.

He paused. Then he wrote one more:

Aldridge.

He tapped the pen against the paper.

"One of them flipped. Or all of them."

He wrote more names on the list until it totaled 12 people.

His eyes drifted to the window.

Across the street, in the shadow of a church tower, a figure stood still too long. Not smoking. Not checking the phone. Just standing. Watching.

Malik clicked the desk lamp off. He left the pension an hour later, walking south toward Charles Bridge. Tourists thinned out, left behind violinists, lovers, and wanderers such as himself. The Vltava River shimmered under the arches like oil and light.

He felt a tug on his coat.

An old Romani man, gray-bearded, wrapped in patched clothes, looked up at him with eyes that knew too much.

"Psalms 91. Your name is not safe here," he said in broken English. "They are looking. They watch from places that do not cast shadows."

Malik stiffened. "Who sent you?"

"Shiloh," the man whispered. "You must go south. Tonight." He grabbed Malik's hand and placed a token with a crescent moon seal affixed on it.

Malik looked down at the token. When he looked up again, the man was gone.

He quickly returned to the pension to retrieve his personal effects.

Malik took a bus early the next morning from Prague heading to Budapest. The bus pulled out of Florenc Station in Prague just at dawn. Malik sat in the back, window seat, hood up, headphones in, but no music playing.

He wanted to be invisible.

He needed to observe. An impossible task as the only Black among a trove of White people.

The coach was nearly full of travelers, students, and migrant workers. Nobody paid attention to the tall Black man in the last row. That was the point. They chose the bus over the train or flight: less surveillance, no customs scrutiny, fewer databases to ping. Just motion, shadows, and time to think again.

He leaned his head against the glass.

He watched the city shrink behind him, those regal rooftops, Gothic churches, red clay tiles that sat like crown jewels on old-world architecture. Prague gave him more eyes than answers. He moved as instructed by the Shilohs.

"Budapest," he said to himself.

The Czech countryside blurred into rolling fields and stone villages, then gave way to the misted woods of Moravia. Somewhere along the way, a pale boy two rows up snapped a photo of Malik. He tried to make it discreet and failed in his mission. He was Black, a novelty in the Baltics. He understood their curiosity as the cars slowed as their occupants stared at him through half-rolled windows. To them, he was a strange novelty in their midst.

Malik stared at him until the boy looked away.

They still watched.

He closed his eyes and drifted, not asleep, but somewhere in between.

That place where memories become mirrors. Where déjà vu seemed like cinematography.

He saw the gypsy woman's face again. He saw the man in Prague who whispered "Shiloh."

He saw Jordan, as she stood by a window back home, her hand pressed to the glass like she could feel the storm formed across the ocean.

The bus stopped at the Czech-Slovak border. The road was flanked by gray outposts and sagging pine trees. A checkpoint loomed ahead: concrete booths, steel barriers and a row of stern-faced uniformed officers border guards in forest green. It was here that the bus offloaded its passengers for customs checks before it continued its last leg of the journey into Budapest. Inside the bus, the air was tense. The passengers offloaded and made their way to customs checkpoints.

The expressions of the customs guards who checked passports, did so without much words. Malik switched to the one of the five passports provided to him by the Hungarian man at the travel services. His face was clean-shaven, symmetrical, and classically European. His features were fine, like cut glass, fair-skinned beauty Prague men and women was known. The men were lean, sharp-jawed; the women, porcelain-featured, with soft blonde hair and eyes the color of winter skies.

Prague was polite, cold, but elegant and classy, modern and urban. A city of artists and bankers. Cafés and cathedrals. The "Paris of Central Europe," they called it.

But its beauty was precise, controlled, and curated.

Malik felt it. Admired it, even. The people that adorned and populated Prague were some of the most beautiful people he ever saw. But he never once felt welcome in it.

Eyes lingered too long. Smiles came with questions behind them. And every conversation in English felt like a negotiation.

Malik approached the Hungarian custom station. The guard extended his hand to accept Malik's passport. Malik handed his over, eyes forward. One of them studied him longer than others.

"American?" the guard asked.

"Yes," Malik replied, calm but steady and ready.

"Where are you going?"

"Visiting friends. Budapest."

The guard nodded, with a quiet smirk, stamped it, and moved on. Malik nodded, took it back, but did not relax.

But Malik saw it.

A second officer took a quick photo of his passport on a handheld device.

He was being flagged.

The bus rolled on.

As they crossed into Hungary, the shift was instant.

The landscape flattened. The houses grew humbler. The faces at the roadside became rounder, darker, more weathered.

Slavic. Hard-lived. Quiet.

Where the Czechs walked like peacocks with credit cards, the Hungarians moved like ghosts with debts.

The eyes were soft but sad, the heaviness of history etched into their brows, as if the soil itself remembered every invasion, every winter, every betrayal. Whereas the Czechs willingly submitted to the Nazi invasion of their nation to preserve their rich architecture, particularly in the city of Prague, the Hungarians waged a fierce resistance against the Germans during WWII. The city of Budapest paid a heavy price for their defense against

German invasion. This eventually led to the country's surrender to the Nazis and communism.

Budapest wasn't the "Paris" of anything. It was the "Gulag of Eastern Europe," grander than most realized, older than most remembered, but touched by a melancholy that never left.

Malik noticed it immediately.

In Prague, people looked at him with curiosity, or concealed suspicions. The closer an ethnic person got to the Soviet Union, the more pernicious nature of the "isms" felt: communism, racism, elitism, sexism, etc., roared their ugly heads.

In Hungary. While the curiosity of the Czechs made Malik feel safe this was not the case in Hungary.

He leaned his head back against the glass and watched the signs change into different languages. His own reflection stared back at him: Black, foreign, marked by a bloodline that stretched from the slave ports to spreadsheets, boardrooms and now battlefields.

"They do not see me. But something does." He thought to himself.

The pendant in his pocket, the one the Romani man in Prague pressed into his hand, warmed faintly.

Malik closed his eyes. When he awoke, they arrived in Budapest.

Malik wandered alone beneath the amber glow of Budapest's lit lanterns. It was dusk when he decided to wander the city a bit.

Pest, the flat eastern side, was busy in silence.

The streets buzzed not with people, but with their presence.

Broad avenues lined with art nouveau façades whispered the stories of bankers and ballerinas, revolutionaries, and rats. Government buildings towered like monuments to lies. Statues of saints and generals loomed over parks that once hid resistance fighters.

Malik passed Andrássy Avenue, where designer stores sat like smug ghosts above basements that once held secrets. Above, the spires of St. Stephen's Basilica pierced the night sky, a holy dagger beneath a heaven that had not answered in centuries.

The sidewalks were clean. The air was sharp. But something in Pest felt staged.

Like a city dressed for judgment, hoping no one would ask too many questions.

He passed a café where an old man mumbled to himself in Hungarian, clutching a newspaper and a cheap espresso. A police car cruised by slowly, its lights off but engine humming. A camera followed him from a lamppost, then swiveled away.

Everyone saw him.

No one acknowledged him.

When he reached the Danube again, the waters looked black and endless. A slow-moving vein of history separating not just land, but time.

He stood at the foot of the Chain Bridge, looking back at Pest.

And forward to Buda.

He crossed.

Each step felt heavier.

Each lion at the bridgehead watched without moving, as if guarding not the city, but the truth[9] beneath it.

Buda rose from the hills, older and quieter. It did not shout like Pest. It murmured.

He climbed narrow, cobbled lanes toward Castle Hill, past ivy-covered lamps. Gaslight flickered across the Fisherman's Bastion, where turrets stood like white fingers pointing back through time. Beyond that, Matthias Church glowed, its tiled roof glistening like a crown in exile.

Everything here felt slower.

Heavier.

Wiser.

This was not a city of ambition; it was a city of memory.

He passed a Romani woman sweeping her steps in the dark. She looked up at him briefly and nodded, not as if she knew him, but as if she always expected him.

He nodded back.

Malik reached a terrace that overlooked the whole of Budapest. The Danube shimmered beneath him like a silver thread sewing two worlds together.

Buda, the keeper of the past.

Pest, the illusion of the present.

And in between, him.

A man born of both bloodlines. Of fields and files. Of prophets and predators. Of Mitchells and madness.

Ana waited. And the road not finished with him yet.

The night air in Budapest was colder than Malik expected.

A biting cold, not just in temperature, but in spirit. The kind that seemed woven into the stone. The Danube sliced the city in two like a black mirror, its surface reflecting centuries of war, grief, and buried memory.

Malik stood at the foot of the Széchenyi Chain Bridge, where two stone lions guarded each other like ancient sentinels. Tourists were gone. Even the street performers vanished. Only a few yellow streetlamps buzzed in the mist.

He checked the time.

11:03 PM.

She said: "Come to the bridge where the lions sleep. Cross it by foot. Do not speak to anyone. I will find you." Then she hung up abruptly.

He adjusted the strap of his bag and stepped onto the bridge.

The river glimmered below, indifferent. The silence was holy.

Halfway across, he stopped.

Not footsteps. Not noise.

But presence.

She stepped from the darkness, as if the shadows shaped her.

Ana.

She wore a long black coat, high collar, and boots that made no sound against the stone. Her hair, thick and coiled like river roots, was pulled back with a silver clasp shaped like a crescent moon. Her eyes: gray-green, ancient, burning with quiet fire, locked onto him before a word was spoken.

Malik's breath caught up with his mind.

He saw her in his dreams.

Felt her in his prayers he did not remember.

"Ana," he said, his voice low, almost reverent.

She nodded. "Malik."

She said his name as though it was a key, something sacred and forgotten, just now turned.

For a moment, neither spoke.

The wind moved around them, but not between them.

"You are late," she said finally.

"I had to come the long way."

"They know you are here," she said flatly.

"They knew since Zurich. They knew since Prague. They tracked your aura, not your phone. You shine, Malik. Too brightly."

"So, I noticed. It's been the story of my life," he replied dryly.

She stepped closer. No smile. No hesitation.

"I waited a long time for this meeting. My mother told me I would find you. In a city of blood. On a bridge of lions."

"You are Shiloh," he said as more of a statement and not a question.

"The last born of the Balkans. The only one who remembers the whole song."

She reached into her coat and pulled something wrapped in deep crimson cloth. She unwrapped it with care, revealing an object unlike anything he ever saw.

A seal.

Circular like the earth with various continents etched into markings. Down the center of the etched world globe were two ornate daggers, one on top of the other to form a single cross. The daggers were clad in gold, rubies, sapphires and diamonds. It was the ancient seal of the Shilohs.

In the language of the Watchers, it read: "Psalms 91."

Ana pressed it into his hand.

"This belonged to Adisa's family tribe from the Moors when they entered the Balkans many centuries ago. Your great-great grandmother Adisa's tribe. She left it behind when she was captured and sold to America."

Malik stared at it, his heart hammered.

"What do I do with it?"

"Remember."

"Remember what?"

Ana stepped even closer. Her voice dropped.

"That you are not just a man. You are the prophecy made flesh. The last light in a dying order."

"And Jordan?"

"She is the doorway. If they corrupt her, if they twist her, they win."

"Who's they?"

"You know their name."

Malik clenched his jaw.

"The Despicables."

Ana nodded slowly.

"And worse. The Dushev now walk among them. Your blood's betrayers. The ones who sold your ancestors into chains now walk freely in suits and government. They know your line returned. And they are afraid."

A rumble sounded in the distance: subtle but distinct. A black SUV crept along the bridge; headlights turned off.

Ana did not flinch.

"We have to go."

"Where?"

"To where your line was born, and where it must rise again."

She turned and walked across the bridge towards Buda. They were to meet early the next morning.

Back at the pension, Malik reflected on his arrival in Budapest. Malik's arrival in Budapest was unannounced, unconditional, and deliberate. The trip was booked through a secondary passport issued by the gypsy, through an intermediary in Budapest. The entire trip to Budapest took almost 24 hours.

The city sat under brooding skies. In fact, one might describe Budapest as one big gray blob of a city from its grayish-looking people, buildings, and food.

Even the air in Budapest felt clandestine. Hearing. Watchful. Being a Black man from the US made him stand out like a tribal native. And the people treated and reacted to him as one.

From the moment he stepped off the bus, Malik felt as though the city studied him. Budapest had the grim elegance of a place that saw too many wars and invasions. It was as if the city was painted in the shades of gray and ghost memory.

On the Buda side, the hills rose gently towards the citadels, moss-covered and bulky, like foreign sentinels. Stone staircases spiraled up into crumbly watchtowers where pigeons roosted in bullet-riddled walls. The iron cannons still perched over the hills as if the cannons stood watch the oncoming marauders into Budapest.

Malik walked these narrow paths past old monasteries; the Danube River currents flowed in green silence. The air carried the smell of rain and history.

Across the Széchenyi Chain Bridge, Pest unfolded like a theater worn from use: flat bureaucratic government buildings with baroque façades. The buildings stood side by side with heavy concrete slabs. Everything bore the scars of two emperors: the Habsburg grandeur and the Communist chalk-white exteriors. One could see, feel, and hear the Soviet influence in Budapest.

The people's faces were round and unsmiling. People walked quietly with shoulders curled inward as if broken in spirit, eyes darted like ping-pong balls to detect notice. Malik was not immune to such looks and notices. This was his impression of the city that first morning when he arrived in Budapest as he traversed Buda and Pest to get a lay of the land. Yes, Budapest was not a city of diversity, but a city defined by the absence and fear of it.

The people of Budapest were not so classically beautiful. Not in a cinematic way or sense. Their features were broad, coarse, and dressed in muted colors. Thick brows, deep-set eyes, olive, or hazel. Hair uniformly dark and jet black or dusty brown, and stiff, always seemed unkempt. Almost like a curtain that swallowed their looks. An ethnic flatness that revealed a Balkan entanglement and Slavic blend. But not in the classic beauty like the people of Prague. One could tell the distinct difference between the ethnic nations once crossing the border from Prague to Budapest.

Malik felt a growing discomfort in Budapest: not fear, but worse, like a burden. There was no welcome in the city. Its people were closed to outsiders, especially darker ones. He did not feel welcome in Budapest. Its sordid history told the full story.

In earlier centuries, the Hungarians served as the first line of defense against the dark-skinned Moors' invasion from Africa into Europe, as the people fought fiercely to repel the onslaught of vicious Moorish attacks. This feeling embedded over centuries a cold distrust of dark-skinned people in the city to cause a cold, distant glance from its residents he passed in the streets.

He stayed in the Gellért Hills under the name Johnny Appleseed, in a nondescript pension that smelled of mildew and old tobacco. From his window, he saw the twin spires of a grayish white mausoleum nestled in the hillside. It was like something from an ancient tale: ornate and sorrowful, crowned by angels who stopped caring for the city.

He walked away from it the next morning as he waited to meet Ana, as he imagined bones beneath it wrapped in silk and rot and torture. Even that next morning following his initial meeting with her, Budapest never was warm. The sun felt strained, diffused behind a constant gauze of cloud haze. Rain came without warning: a slow drizzle that lasted hours, soaked into the cobblestone pavement and chilled Malik's resolve. Even the light was suspect: gray in the morning, gray in the evening, as though time itself stopped and stripped the city of its color and life.

But Malik came not for beauty or even sightseeing or even protection. Budapest was simply a means to an end. A pass-through stop to get to his protection. He came for clarity and for a strategy.

The Despicables: Gino, Doug, and John among others like the board of PAINCO, the secret shadow operatives, tightened their noose around their "pet." And they cast a wide net to catch him, or so they thought. Budapest, in its gray austerity, gave Malik the emotional cover and fortitude to scheme. There, no one asked any questions. No one cared about his thoughts. It was as if the people were wary of independent thought. This city, almost like Zurich, was a place where secrecy was built on clandestine matters which often resulted in torture or death.

The Road to Dobrinje

The morning after the late-night meeting on the Chain Bridge, Ana pulled up in front of the pension in Pest just after dawn. The sky was still pale, the city quiet, as if it held its breath. The city of Budapest disappeared.

Her car idled like a beast with hunger.

It was a 1965 Škoda Felicia convertible, jet black, well-kept, the kind of car that looked like it belonged to another time. Its chrome accents glinted in the soft Budapest light, and the license plates partially obscured by a dangled strip of black cloth, on purpose.

Malik stood by the curb with his duffel bag.

Ana did not honk.

He opened the passenger door and slid in. The leather was cold. The scent inside was a mix of sandalwood, lavender, and oil. An amulet hung from the rearview mirror: a crescent moon over a star carved from obsidian.

She did not speak as they pulled away from the city.

She drove with both hands on the wheel, her posture straight, eyes fixed. She did not need a GPS. She knew the road like she knew the story: by heart.

They passed through the outskirts of southern Hungary, where the villages sat like forgotten thoughts along narrow roads. Red-tiled roofs, hay carts, old men drinking brandy at breakfast, wild dogs pacing the edges of fields. Life moved slower here, but the land remembered faster.

"Why this way?" Malik asked finally, watching as they turned onto a gravel road that wound between forest and field.

"The highways are watched," she said.

"And this road belongs to our people. Always has."

The engine rumbled low as it dipped into a valley flanked by dark pines and rustling poplars. Occasionally, Ana would point without looking:

"That grove? A Shiloh child was born there during the war."

"That chapel? Burned twice. We rebuilt it each time."

"That barn? Dushev hid weapons inside during the last purge. We never forget."

Malik listened. The road began to feel more like a trail of memory than a path on a map.

They crossed the Drava River midmorning, a rusted border checkpoint abandoned since the fall of Yugoslavia. No guards. No paperwork. Just faded flags and ghosts.

"We are in Croatia now," she said.

"So, this is the Balkans."

"This is the wound that never healed."

As the kilometers passed, their silence became its own language.

Eventually, Malik broke it.

"Have you always known who I was?"

Ana did not answer right away. Then:

"I knew what you carried. Not who you were. Not until last night."

"What do I carry?"

She looked at him for a long moment before she returned to the road.

"You carry the covenant and the curse. You carry blood that both betrayed and was betrayed. You are a crossroads, Malik. That is why the Despicables want to collapse you."

"Collapse me?"

"Make you doubt. Break you in half. Turn you into a shadow of yourself before Jordan ever finds the light. To convert you to their side."

"What if I fail?"

She did not look at him, but her voice softened.

"Then she's lost. And so are we."

Ana drove deliberately, as if she carried precious cargo. Malik watched her from the rearview mirror.

The car was a 1965 Škoda 1000 MB sedan, its engine low and steady like a quiet throb, the kind of car built before speed mattered. It growled across the Hungarian backroads with the elegance of a war widow: worn, graceful, and impossible to ignore.

They did not speak for the rest of the trip.

Ana kept one hand on the wheel, the other on the window frame as if to hold the window in place. Her long, slender, smooth fingers drummed the glass. Her blue eyes never left the road. Her hair spilled out of her coat collar, catching the early morning sunlight that occasionally broke through the leafless trees.

Malik glanced at her now and then, tried not to let her calm fool him. He was in a foreign country and conditioned himself to trust no one and to rely on his instincts about what little information was available to him in the situation.

She was too quiet. Too composed.

The road south out of Hungary took them through Moravian farmland, where the land was dry and flat, but the villages leaned in as if they listened to their travels. Stone fences ran along the ditches. Laundry hung motionless on frozen lines. Smoke rose from the chimneys like unspoken prayers.

Malik reached into his bag for a map.

"I know the way," she said softly. And she did.

They passed through Brno by dusk, the city's cathedral silhouetted against the amber sky. From there, she avoided the major highways, turned east into smaller roads: military supply routes from the Cold War days, now long forgotten by Google Maps and border patrols alike.

The sedan climbed steadily into the foothills, its engine groaned, caused a momentary pause for concern in Malik. A look of frustration appeared on Malik's face.

He could see Ana looked at him from the rearview mirror as Malik appeared in her view.

"Do not worry. I rebuilt the engine myself." She smiled sweetly at Malik. "From the engine to the upholstery. I trust this car more than I trust most people."

Malik believed her only from the precision of her walk, her confident words, and actions. Though it still felt like a lie.

They crossed into Slovenia under cover of night: no checkpoint, just a wandering backroad with moss-covered, mildew- and frost-laden pine trees leaned in from either side. The stars blinked through the branches above them. Somewhere nearby, an owl hooted.

In a spiritual sense, owls often symbolize wisdom, intuition, and transformation. They are seen as messengers from the spiritual world, to guide individuals to trust their inner wisdom and pay attention to hidden truths[9]. The significance of the sight of an owl has great godly significance for the Shilohs. It means that GOD or the ancient ones guide those under their protection.

Malik certainly found and believed it was his spiritual ancestors' hands that played a role in his trip to the Balkans. This knowledge or belief afforded him some comfort and a feeling of protection while on his journey.

And then the landscape changed again once they entered Croatia.

It was almost imperceptible, not a line, but a shift; the road turned to gravel. The woods grew thicker. The night deeper. The only light was the dull yellowish glow of the sedan's headlights cutting through the dark like a blade.

"You sure about this place?" Malik asked, finally again he broke the silence between them.

Ana nodded. "Dobrinje is where men go to be forgotten. And for now, that's exactly what you need." She said with her cat-like smile across her face.

Dobrinje was asleep if it ever truly woke up. The stone houses sat low and dark against the hills; the chimneys curled with smoke, in sharp contrast with the frost and wood ash. He could smell sage burning from the many chimney stacks. A dog barked once in the distance, then fell silent.

The smell of sage also gave Malik some additional assurance. Sage had spiritual significance as a symbol of purification, healing, and again spiritual connection. The smoke from the sage served as a ritual of sorts because it was believed to clear negative energy and restored harmony in spaces, places and among people who smelled it. A negative reaction to its sweet, pungent smell by an individual, warned those in their midst that the person may carry evil spirits. The smoke believed to carry unwanted evil energies to the person's nose to create a more balanced and safer environment for those in the person's midst.

It was a ritual that the Black slaves picked up from the Native Indians in their company. Sage smelled constantly in the plantation slave quarters along with the gospel.

By late afternoon, the trees began to thin, and the mountains softened into rolling hills. A stone sign covered in ivy read: Dobrinje - 2 km.

The car slowed as they entered the village. Ana killed the engine. The car shut down as if it waited to exhale. Then Ana restarted the car, and they slowly moved forward.

They stopped once again for a brief moment, surveying the landscape.

Malik looked over at her. "Thank you."

She did not turn. Just said, "Remember Psalms 91 and do not get caught."

"How was it possible for a Black man to blend into a totally White society without drawing attention?" Malik thought to himself. But this was exactly what he paid for, among other services.

Then Ana stepped out of the car and walked away into the chilly morning mist. He followed her.

It was smaller than Malik expected. Maybe thirty homes, most stone, some painted in fading pastels. Children played near a crumbling fountain. A woman hung wet sheets from a balcony. An old man whittled something beneath a walnut tree.

Everyone turned as they passed.

Not with fear. Not with suspicion.

With recognition.

Malik sat up straighter.

"They know?"

"They feel." Ana said. "You are not the first to return. But you might be the last."

She parked the car beside a moss-covered stone wall. Beyond it, a house half-swallowed by vines: old but strong. The windows were shuttered. The front door was carved with symbols: some Moorish, some Slavic, some older than language.

However, Malik felt the townspeople looked through the slats of the shuttered windows.

They returned to the car and the engine sputtered again as they crested a final ridge, and then below, the village of Groščče.

A wide, shallow valley bathed in the dawn frost and bruised light; Groščče was more crossroads than a town.

A few shingled homes huddled in the mist, smoke curled from their chimneys, like they tried to breathe themselves awake. The air was sharp and metallic. Somewhere, a rooster crowed.

Again, another spiritual sign of a rooster's crow. In spiritual contexts, a rooster's crow may symbolize new beginnings, vigilance, protection, and even repentance. It can mean the end of darkness and the start of a new day, both literally and figuratively. Though Malik had nothing to repent as his mission was certain: to create an environment even far across the oceans to destroy the Despicables. Of that he was clear and resolute.

The road sloped into Groščče like a forgotten dried river.

Ana guided the car with one hand, like a samurai and his sword. The tires skidded slightly in the wet red clay, and the Škoda coughed once more, then cut off entirely as it rolled the last thirty feet on its own motion before stopping in front of a weathered wooden sign.

They made it.

"Welcome home," she said quietly.

Malik stepped out.

The air smelled of earth, smoke, and sage.

And somewhere in the distance, a bell tolled once: deep, hollow, and ancient.

Malik stepped out into the cold, his boots crunching against a layer of frost. In Dobrinje, the dirt was red clay. Not like the dull rust of forgotten ruins, but a living, breathing crimson that clung to the soles of Malik's shoes as if to remind him he was trespassing on ancient ground. As in his summer memories of the Georgia red clay. The clay was heavy, rich with iron, and stained by centuries of rain and blood. Farmers spoke of it as both a blessing and a curse.

Like Georgia red clay: hard to till but nourished when broken open. Malik felt its weight as he walked, as though every step tied him deeper into the marrow of the Al-Abd-Al-Dasa, Dushevs', Shilohs', and Despicables' histories. More so embedded into the legends of the Shiloh whose bones, perhaps, still whispered beneath the surface. The soil was not just earth; it served as memories for him.

Thousands of miles away, Georgia, USA, told another story. There, too, it bled red under the Southern sun, a constant reminder of a land both fertile and unforgiving. The clay shaped the foundation of homes, stained the clothes of the laborers, and bore witness to centuries of toil. Enslaved Africans once pressed their hands into that same soil, carved out lives under conditions designed to break them. Later generations, children played in it, sculpted small castles and warriors, unaware that they molded history with every touch.

What struck Malik was not the difference, but the kinship between the two red earths. One belonged to the old world, the other the new, yet both spoke the same language of endurance and identity. The red clay was a bond across continents, a natural scripture that testified to struggle, resilience, and the continuity of hope and spirit.

Standing in Dobrinje, Malik scooped the soil into his palms and felt Georgia in it: the weight of ancestral chains, the grit of survival, the stubborn refusal of the land itself to be erased. Both soils told him the same truth[9]: empires rose and fell, but the earth remembered. And in that remembrance lies both warning and promise. Though the silence here was not empty, it was saturated with memories of ghosts of whispered disappearances.

Malik looked at Ana as she pulled her coat collar up around her neck against the biting wind.

"Three kilometers," she said.

Ana nodded. "On foot from here. We do not bring cars into Dobrinje. Too many questions. Too many eyes."

Malik was reassured. It was obvious Ana did this before and was now a seasoned professional. What secrets and stories her adventures held. If only he had the time, inclination, and permission to ask. But this was a "Don't Ask, don't tell" transaction.

They walked the rest of the way under a rising sun like a wound slowly healing.

And they disappeared into the trees. Malik knew the real journey was just beginning. It did not start with him. Nor would it end with him.

The drive from Budapest to Dobrinje was not an easy one. All total, it took 10 hours of constant driving to get to their destination. Ana had a 5-gallon can of gasoline in the trunk of her car, so they did not have to stop along the way for gas. She drove without GPS like a nomad in the desert following the North Star.

The last 3 kilometers of walking drained Malik. They arrived at their destination.

Malik was exhausted after an almost nonstop ten-hour trip from Budapest to Dobrinje in a small antiquated foreign sedan through backroads. As Malik settled into another dark apartment in Dobrinje, his mind drifted as he laid down on the wrought iron bed. His mind wandered to thoughts about Denai and then to the wicked morass he found himself in at PAINCO.

"Business trip," he told her over the cell phone while he looked out of their patio door at the yard. He put his passports in his briefcase. Just a five-day trip, but he would be out of the country. It was all she needed to hear. She learned over the past year not to ask too many questions.

Ever since they executed their plan, she learned not to press for too many details. Malik counseled her about plausible deniability.

After everything, the legal mess at PAINCO, the secret settlements, the headlines that almost happened, Denai learned to read between the lines from his silence. She knew when something was above her clearance or on a "need to know basis" or not part of her plan.

"Call me when you land," were her final words before they hung up.

Among the team members was Kendall, who was employed in the mailroom at PAINCO. While Kendall diligently managed the logistics of mail distribution within the company, he also pursued his passion for music production in his personal time. He communicated lyrics to friends online and, during work hours, was responsible for sorting correspondence addressed to specific individuals at PAINCO.

Jordan was more cold, distant, and calculating, much like her mother. The looks of a fashion model. The intellect of an Ivy League graduate like her father and the street smarts of a boss lady in the Mexican cartel like her mother. But mostly, Jordan showed grace she revered in her stepmother, Denai. Denai served as her company mentor while Jordan worked in PAINCO as a Senior Vice President, Corporate Relations, PAINCO. The company was none the wiser about the truth Denai's and Jordan's relationship.

And this made sense as Jordan refined her game from 4 years in the Peace Corps, where she traveled through Europe, Central, Latin and South America to learn every variety of the Spanish language there was. It gave her an added sophistication and served as many a topic of conversation at notable events. Monica got Jordan the job with PAINCO through whatever sources, but the fact Jordan went by Jordan Mitchell allowed Jordan to withhold her connection to Malik.

Jordan was placed in an extremely sensitive position as in Corporate Relations on special assignment to PAINCO's CEO, John Irolla. It was the reason Jordan was aware of the suicide of the young man in the Procurement Department that committed suicide because of the unfair pressure he was placed under by his superior. Pressures to violate his core values and fundamental principles, all to further the Despicables' agenda of grift, graft, corruption, and undue influence. Jordan managed the settlement agreement outside of Legal between PAINCO and the young widow with two infants of the young dead man.

She had direct access to all the activities of John Irolla and PAINCO. She maintained his calendar and meeting schedules. Each family member had a very distinct and discreet role to play in uncovering and exposing the Despicables' evil plans and operation. Although by far, Malik had the largest piece of that puzzle because he understood the entirety of the relationships between PAINCO, the Despicables and their worldwide counter-intelligence operations. He was the unofficial puppet master pulling the various strings in this staged drama. He reflected once again.

The Caravan

It began, as most things in corporate America do, with resignation: both the emotional state and literal resignations.

The press releases were always glossy and sterile: "After eight years of dedicated service, we thank Executive Vice President Alvarez for his leadership and wish him well with the next chapter in his life." There never was any real mention of the reason for the departure. No mention of closed-door meetings. No mention of the rumors that followed. No mention of the quiet panic in the eyes of those who stayed behind.

But Malik noticed the pattern.

At PAINCO, the Pan American Insurance Company, turnover at the top was not random; it was rhythmic. Executives never simply left. They migrated, though at times some sat on the sidelines for a bit due to non-compete clauses, or as punishment. Most likely to get them back in line or if they knew too much or were forced to succumb to the direction of the Despicables. They held something over their heads until they complied with orders. Often, these victims' finances remained at risk without sustained employment; they were forced to dip into savings to survive as the Despicables tightened the noose around the neck until the target begged for mercy.

Human Trafficking

Most people think of human trafficking in terms of young immigrant boys and girls transported in freight containers against their will and forced into labor. While this is true, human trafficking also occurs in corporations at the executive and board of directors' levels. Such activities are not viewed as human trafficking since the impacted individuals are highly compensated. While compensation, or the lack thereof, is one of the elements of human trafficking, the fact of compensation does not lessen the burdens of human trafficking.

People's movement, place, and restriction of movements by corruption and undue influence still constitutes human trafficking. Nothing was more painfully apparent within PAINCO as he studied the corporate structure and watched activities played out internally and externally. Jordan, in fact, gained an upfront view of these movements better than anyone at PAINCO, including her father.

They migrated. And often not alone.

Within months of a senior leader's departure, often under duress, or vague "retirement" terms or "new opportunities," a wave would follow over a span of time. Sometimes a year to two years of the executive's separation from PAINCO the company rumor mill discussed the departure. Analysts, assistant vice presidents, treasurers, managers, actuaries, risk officers, even HR partners and contract compliance attorneys. A caravan of former PAINCO operatives pollinated or populated other insurance companies like clockwork, embedded themselves in the new firm like "sleeper cells."

It was corporate colonization of grift, graft, corruption, and undue influence, both externally and internally of the company.

They rarely called attention to themselves other than the announcement of their new positions at the targeted company. They did not wear pins or flash signs. But the moment they arrived; company policies and strategies began to shift. Internal controls tightened around data access, particularly employees' and clients' profiles. Legal departments became more isolated, more autonomous, harder to penetrate. Human resource departments restructured as "bad cops" to centralize background vetting and performance data. Treasury accounts rerouted through obscure subsidiaries, often located in Luxembourg, Guernsey, or Delaware.

For the Despicables to keep the machine well oiled, new recruits within the organization were found. Pressure and undue influence applied to individuals they compromised. It was the only way their network and operations could flourish on a global scale. To lie, cheat, and steal was their virtue.

But Malik saw it for what it was: vertical and horizontal integration of a corporate intelligence operation to mask its underground ties and networks of pirates cascading the corporate landscape for new victims. They committed "Piracy Over the Cyberseas" where the second silo within the corporation used the internet for multiple criminal purposes; from mere harassment to outright online theft. The company executives turned a blind eye to such activities if they were not directly involved themselves.

At the center of each migration, there was always one constant: an attorney with some connection or allegiance to Gino.

Usually, some mid-level manager in PAINCO's Legal Division got a promotion to the executive ranks at the new company, rewarded for allegiance to the Despicables. Or because the person put to a further test to see if they were worthy. Quiet. Methodical. Highly competent but never drawing full attention. They did not lead; they observed. These attorneys were embedded alongside the executive and shadowed them, but Malik suspected it was the other way around.

He grew particularly suspicious after the departure of a senior executive named Myron Castillo, who took a top job at Syner-Trust, a mid-sized insurer on the West Coast. Within six months, four former PAINCO staff members joined him, including a senior finance manager, VP Operations, a compliance liaison, and an attorney named Alessandra Bell.

Human trafficking, even at the highest echelons of life and in corporate America.

Not in the crude, street-corner way the news and movies portrayed it. This was elite-level, systematized, boardroom-sanctioned exploitation, corruption, embezzlement, and corporate gamesmanship. Almost like a professional sports team where the key players are paid a lot of money, but it was really the team owners that made all the money and traded them at will. And player trades occurred within or at the end of each contract period because many senior executives were retained under employment contracts of sorts. The fact these individuals are highly compensated does not change the fact about the transactional nature of their employment. Coupled with employment conditions under some type of undue influence does not make it any less than it is: human trafficking.

Chapter Nine
Human Trafficking

"For our struggle is not against flesh and blood, but against the rulers, against the authorities, against the powers of this dark world and against the spiritual forces of evil in the heavenly realms."

— Ephesians 6:12

But the human trafficking at PAINCO did not just extend to the corporate ranks; it seemed to Malik it went outside the company as well. Through affiliated shell companies and insurance claim practices or manipulation, PAINCO executives allegedly created a network that trafficked human beings under the guise of "medical transport," "international risk repatriation," and even "employee assistance relocation." Malik found redacted invoices tied to private air charter services in Eastern Europe, in Southeast Asia, and parts of the Caribbean: services listed under wellness programs, survivor recovery, or executive protection. There was a myriad of ways and designations to obfuscate the true nature of the human trafficking operations of the Despicables.

But the passengers were not always executives.

They were property.

Young women and men flagged as "undocumented independents" or "undocumented immigrants" somehow hid, separated from their parents along the long trek from both domestic and foreign homes. Then they were turned into forged employee records, as migrants, hotel workers, landscapers, and any other convenient labor occupation. Children coded under medical case IDs and eligible for government assistance which almost never made it into their pockets. Foreign nationals listed as subcontractors with zero earnings history, shuffled between subsidiaries like inventory.

This network and its operations did not just generate billions in illicit profits; it also forged extortion and kept those who participated in the "game." Senior officials at all levels, departments of government and corporations were compromised and controlled to keep the Despicables relevant. Some just invited to "private retreats" and filmed snorting white powdery stuff or in delicate situations with young boys and girls.

And always, wherever the operation extended, there followed the caravan of former PAINCO employees, like parasites looking for a new host.

Malik began to map the patterns, creating a sprawling chart with yarn and pins, like a detective in a dim-lit garage. The spiderweb was vast, stretched across six countries, even into the Vatican, three federal agencies, over two dozen insurance companies and law firms.

Gino was not just a company strategist in the legal department of PAINCO. He was a handler. His job was not only to grow the Despicables, but to guard their secrets. His method was always the same: he placed one of his own at every nexus: a lawyer, a mole, a second set of eyes, a conduit for the flow of money in and out of an organization as in money laundering.

PAINCO installed many South Asian Indians in executive-level positions, and at least two sat on its board of directors. India is known for its support of a society that reveres its "caste system." The level of corruption in India among government officials is unrivaled. A study by Transparency International stated that 62% of India's population paid a bribe to a government official. In 2010, a report about India indicated that between 1948 to 2008, $462 billion was lost in the Indian economy due to illicit financial activities.

Many of the families and funds associated with these transactions made their way to other nations. And their values about corruption got transmitted as well, suggested Indians as prime targets for Despicable recruitment as they made their way into corporate America. This was both in the boardroom where Indians now had enough money to control shares in publicly traded companies and to influence the placement of associates throughout the targeted companies. PAINCO appeared to be one.

In his preliminary research, Malik observed that earlier iterations of organized crime, traditionally characterized as Italian, Polish, Jewish, Black, Russian or even gay mafias, rarely operated in isolation. These groups frequently established cartels, each contributing specific expertise or resources to joint operations and shared in the proceeds. Over time, the underground economy evolved into a more sophisticated, corporate-style entity that functioned within legally gray areas. At the top of this network were key figures, referred to as the "Despicables," who exerted considerable influence across society, undermining economies, governments, and individuals.

Human trafficking was just one of many ugly ways the Despicables continued their degradation of human life and society.

Malik believed that Alessandra Bell, and others like her, were not just former employees. They were watchdogs reporting directly to Gino: logging conversations, flagging whistleblowers, identifying threats.

That meant Malik's movements, his own questions, were under surveillance. But the question was always by which organization: the Despicables or the Shilohs? A combination of both at different points of time.

It also meant something far worse:

PAINCO was not a corporation infiltrated by the Despicables. PAINCO was a Despicables construct, like other insurers.

Its very structure: an international network of subsidiaries, off-shore trusts, indemnity pools, and "special risk" divisions, designed for obfuscation, not oversight.

And Malik, now realized the full scope, understood he was not just exposing corporate corruption.

He waged war against an ancient empire.

Christian Nationalism

And all the above is couched within the context of Christian Nationalism. A movement more so than a religion that used scripture to misinterpret GOD's view. They used the Word to justify slavery, human trafficking, child sex trafficking, grift, graft, corruption and undue influence over human beings. The Bible is replete with verses which speak against slavery and human trafficking. But those that rely on the Old Testament find virtue in slavery, human trafficking and sex abuse, even of young children. These were Malik's thoughts the night after his trip to Europe and would occupy his inner thoughts upon his return to work.

Chapter Ten
The Barn

"Fight for your brothers, your sons, your daughters, your wives, and your home."

— Nehemiah 4:14

Malik paused at the edge of the field; his eyes darted from side to side while still fixed on the structure before him. The barn looked as though it was abandoned to time itself, its walls bowed inward, its timber scarred with age, its roof patched and broken. Vines crept along one side, and the red clay earth beneath it was littered with shards of stone and brittle straw. He took in every detail, scanning the shadows around its perimeter, the slant of the hills beyond, and the dirt road that wound back towards the village.

His legs finally moved after the adrenaline kicked in, slow and heavy, carried him towards the barn doors. He approached slowly, each step deliberate, his boots crunched on the red clay. When he reached the barn door, its weathered boards groaned against his touch. He pushed it open just far enough to slip inside, then halted. The barn smelled of dust and earth, the stale breath of a structure long forgotten. That smell he recalled from his summers at his grandparents' farm in Georgia. His eyes quickly swept across the space: the sagging rafters, the broken ladders, the scatter of old hay. He noted the dark corners where someone might hide, the wide gaps in the walls where the wind rattled through.

Above, a yawning gap in the roof let in a shaft of early morning light. It fell in a column that reached the barn floor like a holy beam, scattering motes of dust that danced in the air. Malik stepped into it instinctively, tilting his face upward as the warmth of the sun washed over him. For a moment, he looked less like a man preparing a deadly bargain and more like a figure waiting for ascension, an angel poised between earth and heaven.

But inside, his heart trembled with unease. The weight of what he was about to do pressed against his conscience and raced within his heart. Was this covenant righteous? Or was it merely vengeance dressed in necessity? His thoughts circled and then steadied on the scripture he carried like armor since the beginning of his journey: Psalms 91. He recited the words silently, almost like a breath: "He that dwelleth in the secret place of the Most High shall abide under the shadow of the Almighty." At the end of the day, Malik concluded: "There is nothing softer than a pillow, then a clear conscience of the mind."

Malik drew strength from it. He believed, with a fervor that burned through his doubt, that God justified what was to come. He was not choosing bloodshed for its own sake. He was preparing the hedge of protection for his family, the last shield against the Despicables. And if it served a higher purpose, then so be it. And if the plan demanded such a covenant, it was not his own making but theirs, chosen by their corruption, demanded by their violence.

The sunlight lingered on his shoulders as if heaven itself bore witness. Malik exhaled, squared his stance, and waited for the man he came to meet.

What he was about to do went against the moral fiber of his being; it shook him to the core of his spiritual self, and it still caused him to question his values. Except, he reconciled in his mind; he justified his actions as necessary to protect his family. And if it served a greater purpose, that his mission was indeed God's covenant to the Shilohs in Psalms 91, then Malik was just the messenger, as a soldier of GOD, to carry out GOD's judgment on the Despicables. Like the Despicables, Malik believed he simply offered his target a choice. If they did nothing, then there would be no resulting action; however, if they came against his family, only then would the next steps be necessary. In this sense, the argument is: "I did not do it; you did it."

Malik had arrived at the barn about 30 minutes before the meeting. Ana had pointed out the barn to him when she left him last night. Malik looked around to make sure no one was around. Seeing no one on the outside of the barn, he opened the barn door and entered it.

He quickly surveyed the room and saw no one. The early dawn sunlight just began to appear through a wide hole in the barn's roof. Malik stood in the light as if he was an angel of mercy awaiting his ascension into heaven.

Then the barn doors yawned when they opened. Their eyes met. He was a ruggedly Eastern European handsome man in his late 30s, about 6'2", with a lean, athletic, muscular build around 190 lbs. His hair was deep black and slicked back with gel. His coat collar stood upright against the back of his head with a black, thick turtleneck sweater beneath his coat. He wore jeans, rider boots and black leather gloves. The shades that covered his eyes prevented Malik from looking into his soul, if such a man even possessed one.

Malik threw the leather satchel onto the ground in between them. The assassin stooped and his fingers reached inside the satchel for a moment, as though weighing not only its contents but the cost of what it represented. He had not yet lifted it. Instead, he took off his shades and revealed his pale blue eyes.

"You understand," he said slowly, his voice carrying the gravitas of an oath, "once I accept this money, there is no return. Do you have the list of names?"

Malik nodded and reached into the inside of his coat pocket. He retrieved an envelope with 12 names listed on it with relevant personal information about each: name, address, telephone numbers, email addresses, etc. He had identified these names as Despicables from his hours of research about the Despicables' international operations. He walked slowly forward and handed the assassin the envelope.

"These names become chains. Each one is a life tied to your own. If you fail, they fail. If you disappear, they vanish. There will be no mercy, no hesitation," he said directly into Malik's eyes.

Malik's chest tightened, but his face betrayed nothing. The dim morning light carved harsh shadows across their features, sharpening their jawlines, making their eyes burn darker and more resolute. A silent pact formed between them.

"This is what I require," Malik replied.

"The Despicables thrive on fear. They must learn that it cuts both ways. If I am lost, let them inherit my silence in blood," Malik said.

The assassin, for the moment, studied him with unsettling stillness. His weathered skin, marked with fine scars and the roughness of a man who lived too long in the company of death, caught the faint light. He seemed both ancient and ageless, as though his face was carved out of the same earth that surrounded Dobrinje.

"You speak like a man already dead," the assassin murmured.

Malik's lips twitched into a faint, humorless smile. "Perhaps I am, because the old me certainly feels dead. But even a dying man has a wish and can write the terms of his own legacy."

The assassin leaned forward, folded his arms across his chest. He stood about five feet from Malik. "I have worked for men of wealth, men of power, even men who believed they commanded God. They all came to me thinking themselves untouchable. You are different. You bring me names not for greed, nor for conquest, but only for the protection of your bloodline." He paused, his gaze softening ever so slightly. "That is dangerous, because it makes you both stronger, and more vulnerable, than they will ever be."

Malik felt the words pierce deeper than he wanted to admit. He clenched his hands to steady himself, feeling the grit of red clay still clinging to his skin from his walk through the fields. "Strength and vulnerability are the same coin, just on opposite sides of it. My family is my weakness, yes, but they are also the reason I will never yield."

The assassin finally lifted the satchel. His knuckles tightened around the leather strap. "Then our pact is sealed. The list is scripture, as you called it. Should the Despicables take you, I will banish their names into silence."

He stepped backwards, his shadow stretching across the barn wall like a specter. The pigeons overhead rustled as if stirred by their words. Malik stepped forward, his eyes following the assassin's every movement.

"Tell me," Malik asked at last, his voice low, "do you ever regret it? The lives you take?"

The assassin froze at the threshold of the barn's door, his back to Malik. For a heartbeat, the barn seemed to hold its breath.

Then he spoke, his tone neither proud nor ashamed, merely factual.

"Regret is for men who believe they have a choice." He turned his head slightly, just enough for Malik to glimpse the profile of his hardened face. "I do not kill for revenge. I kill for balance. Today you brought balance. Pray you never need to see it delivered."

With that, he slipped into the early morning, the barn door creaking behind him.

Malik waited in the barn for about fifteen minutes after the assassin left. As he stepped outside, the red clay again crunched under his boots. The clay smelled the same here as it did in Georgia: rich, iron-laden, unyielding. It clung to him, staining the soles of his boots just as memory stained the soul. He thought of the men and women in Georgia who labored in silence, their sweat absorbed into the red soil that never forgot. He thought of his ancestors, the Shiloh bloodline, who hid in these lands and carried secrets across generations.

For the first time since arriving in Dobrinje, Malik felt the strands of his life: the personal, the ancestral or spiritual, and the political truths, all woven tightly together. He had not simply purchased an assassin. He had set into motion a covenant of survival, a curse against his and the world's enemies, and a promise that his bloodline would not die unnoticed.

Yet beneath his resolve, a tremor of unease still lingered. He was not blind to what he had done. A list of names now floated like ghosts between him and his conscience. Each one carried the potential for blood, for justice confused with retribution, for a cycle that might never end. And still, he told himself, this was not vengeance; it was preparation. It was the insurance of a man who refused to let fear dictate his family's fate.

He stood on the red clay path, staring out across the valley where the hills dissolved into shadow. His fists clenched at his sides. The assassin's words echoed in him: "Pray you never need to see it delivered."

Malik whispered into the morning dew; his voice barely audible but nevertheless still carried by the wind. "Balance paid, then. So be it."

And with that, he walked away from the barn, the red clay swallowing his footprints, leaving only the heavy silence of Dobrinje to remember the covenant made within.

Turbulence

"In the world you will have tribulation. But take heart; I have overcome the world."

— John 16:33

Malik sat in the window seat of the American Airlines flight as it departed from Amsterdam to New York. The morning fog over Schiphol Airport delayed the departure, and now the skies over the English Channel looked like they were boiling. Gray, ominous clouds roiled like an ancient wrath. He had taken a train from Dobrinje to Amsterdam for his flight back to New York City.

He traced his fingers across the fake Hungarian passport that got him this far. It was the last of the documents provided by Madam Erzsébet, the enigmatic agent who operated more like a sorceress than a smuggler. Malik slid it back into his coat pocket and exhaled slowly. The journey from Dobrinje to Berlin, then to Amsterdam, was tense and quiet. He left Europe behind. But something wasn't done with him. It was an uneventful train ride through the Croatian countryside into Hungary, the Czech Republic to Germany.

On his flight home, he stared out the window as the clouds thickened.

In his mind, Madam Erzsébet's parting words returned:

"The Despicables are not men. They are bloodlines. Thrones. Beasts that feed on time. They wear nations like cloaks and corporations like skin. But they can be unmasked. And you, Malik, were born to do it."

He closed his eyes, the hum of the engines providing a thin veil for the war that raged inside him. Questions swirled, each more damning than the last.

How did he, a Black man from Asbury Park, end up married to a Mitchell?

How did he rise so quickly at PAINCO?

Had every move, every mentor, every merger been part of their plan?

Was Denai... in on it? Was his favorite aunt, who kept a perpetual stash of cash hidden in her bra, and whose husband, his uncle worked part time at night and in the evenings in a Bed-Stuy bodega, part of his trap?

Then it hit.

A sudden, sickening lurch.

It is often said that in the instant before a tragic death, a person's entire life rushes before them—moment after moment flickering like slides in an old-fashioned projector. These snapshots become an urgent accounting of choices made, deeds done, and the legacy one leaves behind. In that suspended heartbeat, the soul weighs its own journey and wonders which figure waits beyond the veil: Satan at the Gates of Hell, or St. Peter at Heaven's Gate.

Malik thought to himself, "Is this GOD's verdict for his life after what he just arranged with the assassin, or the Despicables' reckoned with him for his transgressions against them?"

The aircraft dropped like a stone, 2,000 feet in seconds. Malik gripped his armrest tightly as the plane violently tilted from side to side like a seesaw. They were over the English Channel, just 3 hours away from Newark Airport. He was already a nervous flyer; this severe turbulence caused tremendous stress as his heartbeat raced. His heart thumped out of his chest with each jolt of the plane.

Gasps and screams filled the cabin. Suitcases and barf bags flew from the overhead bins. A mother clutched her child. The flight attendants fell to their knees, crawled for balance as the lights flickered.

Malik gripped the armrest until his knuckles went pale. But it wasn't the fall that terrified him. It was the fear of drowning just as Madam Erzebet asked him the first night they met in her Village shop.

The Vision

It was the revelation she said to him. The gypsy woman asked him if he ever dreamed of drowning.

His vision blurred. Whether from lack of oxygen or the will of God, he didn't know. But suddenly he wasn't on the plane.

He was beneath it, seemingly he had an out-of-body experience.

Somewhere deep, deeper than bunkers or boardrooms.

A vast stone chamber opened before him, lit only by torchlight and the eerie glow of a circular table made of obsidian. Twelve men sat cloaked in black robes. Their faces were a blur, shifted like reflections on disturbed water.

And behind them stood others.

Taller. Inhuman. Ancient.

Figures with eyes like coals and teeth like scrolls. Their presence pierced the veil of time.

"We are not new," one hissed. "We are Babylon. We are Rome. We are Wall Street. We are Vatican. We are Empire. We are Legion."

Their fingers drummed in rhythm. A symbol burned into the air: a serpent wrapped around a globe, impaled it with a golden sword.

Malik tried to speak, cursed them, but his mouth was both parched and sealed.

Then another voice thundered… this one brighter, female, eternal. "And yet I shall overturn their table. Their feast shall rot. Their riches shall melt. For I have raised one born of many tongues, of many tribes. And he shall see their end."

It was the voice of the Shiloh woman. Or maybe Ana. Or maybe God. "You were never meant to serve them, Malik. You were meant to judge them."

And just like that, he was back.

Seat 14A. The plane levelled out after four minutes of the most violent turbulence Malik ever experienced.

The captain's voice crackled overhead:

"Ladies and gentlemen, sorry for that unexpected turbulence. We've stabilized at 33,000 feet. Expect smooth sailing into New York. Estimated arrival: four hours."

The passengers applauded weakly.

Malik didn't move.

His pulse slowed, but his eyes burned. He wasn't the same man who boarded this flight.

He no longer just escaped Europe.

He was flying home to war.

Return to Work

When Malik returned to work at PAINCO, nothing changed. Doug Venier continued with his unusual demands. And Gino's overbearing and constant presence had no limit.

Malik remained weary from his journey, burdened by what awaited him. The significance of his discoveries and plans often felt overwhelming, left him to wonder, "God, why me?" Though he never found a clear answer, he understood his mission's purpose was simply to act, not to question. This is what is meant by faith.

Nevertheless, he realized the quiet migration of former PAINCO executives, the gaslighting, the embedded legal operative. The ghost trails of human trafficking invoices. The overarching electronic surveillance of his every move and whereabouts, consumed him. He had not slept for 36 hours. He stared at his dual monitors, spreadsheets open with offshore wire transfers and a web of corporate names generated by AI: meaningless, soulless, and camouflaged from clarity without a complete understanding of the picture.

Chapter Eleven
Board Games

"For our struggle is not against flesh and blood, but against the rulers, against the authorities, against the powers of this dark world and against the spiritual forces of evil in the heavenly realms."

— Ephesians 6:12

"When two elephants fight, it's only the grass that gets hurt."

— African Proverb

But, what if the two elephants are fighting on sinking sand? Will one elephant perish in the sand?

This was the thought in Malik's mind as he saw the letter which appeared in the fax machine in his office.

Then the fax machine beeped. A beep that pierced the hollowness in his soul.

Once common but now rarely used, the fax machine at PAINCO, housed in a glass and steel tower, typically reserved for formal, confidential, or government notices to avoid internet detection. Malik seldom used it, but this fax came from the New York Department of Insurance and included an attachment. The top right corner featured text in all caps.

Genesis

NOTICE OF STAKE INCREASE AND INTEREST: GENESIS FINANCIAL GROUP INC.

Pursuant to NY Regulation 1520.2, Section 8.

He unfolded the fax. The language was sterile and boiler plate. But one line detonated like a bomb.

Genesis Financial Group, Inc. intends to increase its ownership stake in Pan American Insurance Company from its existing 4.3% to 8%, effective immediately upon regulatory approval.

Malik's hands went cold.

Genesis?

Eight percent?

Wait...Genesis, who?

He scrambled to his laptop on the office desk and opened to Bloomberg Terminal. He typed in the ticker.

GENESIS FINANCIAL GROUP, INC. Assets under Management: $140 Trillion.

One.

Hundred.

Forty.

Trillion.

Dollars.

With a T.

It was not a typo. Genesis was more than just a large company; it was enigmatic and operated largely unnoticed, spending little on public advertising. Its clients were major institutional investors and governments, not everyday consumers. And this fact was seldom known by the average person: that above the Allstate, State Farm, Progressive, Amazon, Microsoft, Berkshire Hathaway, Tesla, Citibank, Wells Fargo and other financial institutions, there were layers of a handful of larger companies with far greater assets than these Fortune 100 companies. These were just American financial titans: the Rothschilds, BlackRock, Blackstone, Wellington Wealth Management, Fisher Investments, etc., which control and dominate the financial markets, and many said, nation states. They wielded a broad range of economic, social and political power across the world. These companies operated in the darkness, rarely advertised by trade name or their services.

This was Darwinism distorted and dressed up as capitalism. It was never about the true "survival of the fittest." Instead, it resembled a darker trickle-down theory, where dysfunction, corruption, and despair cascaded downhill like soiled and poisonous water which flowed to its lowest levels. It spoke volumes of the "powers combined, shrouded in secrecy." Suddenly, Malik realized the gravity of the situation: Genesis embodied "survival of the fittest."

It spoke volumes about the "darkness" of principalities and power warned as written in Ephesians 6:12: unforeseen darkness, the demonic forces waged by the so-called "corporate persons" and by nations themselves against the fragility of the human soul. Truly the spawn of Satan.

It was really a trickle-up theory, not simply economic. It was a socio-political-economic, and spiritual: a war of principalities waging war over the world. The hierarchy was brutally clear: the homeless and the poor at the base, then the middle class and the wealthy, above them the oligarchies and multinational corporations: entities now granted the legal fictional identity of "personhood," and finally, the nations on earth, with the US, China, Russia and the European Union enthroned at the perceived summit.

And yet, in this contentious contest of powers, in this theory of warring entities and false gods, one immutable truth remained: above them all: above the corporations, above the nations, above the oligarchies, sat the Most High God, whom the mighty so often ignored.

And it fitted the reference to Genesis, which lacked a clear headquarters; its board members obscured but influential, and its executives rarely appeared publicly, instead attended exclusive global forums like Davos Summit and the UN Peace Initiatives. These modern-day "robber barons" remained unknown to the public. Malik was unaware that Genesis held a stake in PAINCO, let alone that it quietly increased its investment.

He rocked back in his chair; it nearly tipped over.

Just then, his office door creaked open. His assistant poked her head in, breathless.

"Malik...you might want to get up to the executive suite," she said plaintively but calmly, as if she saw this drama unfold before.

"Why?" he asked.

"Because all hell is breaking loose," she responded.

By the time Malik got upstairs to the 50th floor, the air was electric.

Heads snapped in every direction. Executives who never spoke outside their silos were now huddled in tight, whispered clusters. Officers from Risk, Treasury, and Corporate Strategy flooded into the executive boardroom like into a war room. The general counsel sprinted past him without making eye contact.

A few of the younger staffers looked excited. Most just looked terrified.

It was not just that Genesis was large. It was that nobody saw it coming.

The Despicables

Those at the top of the pyramid, PAINCO's old guard, moved quickly and silently, eyes grim, faces unreadable. Their energy was not that as a surprise; it was of recognition, as if they knew this moment would come one day.

And that terrified Malik even more. Because if there were larger companies than Fortune 500 corporations, what havoc and control could these behemoth corporations wreak on the world? Can they control the social agenda of nations? Could they return the world to an old-world order? Where women were subjugated to homes, immigrants illegally deported, a return to child and Black slave labor?

The second- and third-tier vice presidents, directors, and senior managers realized they were mere pawns. Anxiety grew as they wondered if Genesis's takeover meant they would be replaced, restructured, downsized, or absorbed.

Someone asked out loud what Genesis wanted? Another mumbled something about it as a "custodian of sovereign and inter-generational capital." Malik knew what that meant: old money. The kind that predated the United States. The kind whose families never appeared on the Forbes lists but owned the companies that were.

But there were other whispers as well, darker ones. Genesis did not buy. It consumed.

They didn't file lawsuits. People disappeared.

They were like Vatican finance, but with even fewer morals.

Then the voice of reason, someone with far more experience than most in the room, spoke up. It was John Irolla, CEO of PAINCO, who imparted the voice of reason.

"No... no. They want something from us. Or want us to do something. This is a move for a board seat, if not control over the company. Our company is structured such that its value is more attractive than selling us or breaking us up. There is something more subtle at play here," he said to the nervous room. The general counsel was instructed to make a telephone call to the Genesis general counsel to determine exactly what Genesis's intentions and interests in PAINCO were. In the meantime, Irolla would make telephone calls to the various board members to alert them of this notice. It was all hands-on-deck now.

Back in his office, Malik reviewed the stake disclosure again. It was signed by a compliance officer whose name did not even register in online databases. A ghost. He looked back at the corporate family tree of Genesis subsidiaries: shell after shell, holding company after trust, each with names that sounded biblical, alchemical, or arcane.

The Web

He realized, with a deep chill, that Genesis very well might be the parent of the Despicables. Or at least the vault in which their power was stored.

PAINCO, in all its darkness, just might be its pawn.

Malik's mind raced.

If Genesis acquired an 8% stake, they would likely seek representation on the board. Its interest could be just as simple as a desire to drive the PAINCO stock price up or a dissatisfaction with the current stock price. Should they obtain board control, this allowed them access to internal information such as client lists, policyholder databases, whistleblower reports, and details of ongoing investigations.

Malik picked up the phone and dialed the one person he trusted in Legal, as much as one could trust anyone among a den of thieves. But no one answered.

He opened the encrypted folder on his desk. He reread the names of missing foreign nationals, the encrypted charter flights, and the surveillance files.

It all made a sinister kind of sense now.

PAINCO was never at the top of the chain.

Genesis was the hand behind the curtain. The invisible cathedral. The Vatican of finance. The source cup from which the Despicables drank.

Then it struck him. Those executive migrations from PAINCO were not random after all. The caravan did not just leave PAINCO. It was placed. They were sleeper cells, seeding the private sector with loyalists. The moment Genesis took control of a firm, the caravan reversed course. PAINCO operatives became Genesis agents in disguise.

And the lawyers, the ones Malik thought were spies for Gino, were more than that. They were priests of a financial religion. Their scripture was regulatory code. Their sacraments were Non-Disclosure Agreements and shell companies. Their God was control and the idolatry of money.

And Malik was added to their watch list, but for what purpose?

The Despicables never feared God. They feared exposure.

From the outset, it was understood that religion often functioned to exercise power rather than solely to foster faith. This influence enabled the shaping of societal morals, pursuit of wealth, alleviation of guilt, suppression of dissent, legitimization of leadership, and exclusion of adversaries, all under the justification of divine authority.

Some did what they always did.

They infiltrated to rape, pillage, and plunder the weakest and unsuspecting among us.

They infiltrated religions, homes and office spaces using electronic surveillance technology rather than traditional contact, leveraged computers, the internet, and AI to access people's secrets and ambitions. Disguised as clergy, they created a covert communication ministry where predators blended in behind expensive attire and ritual roles.

Democracy and religion were replaced by systems governed by codes and algorithms, leading to widespread corruption, grift, graft, and undue influences.

That was not to say the Despicables did not move through the Church's hierarchy, for surely, they did. They just did not influence and inculcate doctrine; they just appointed gatekeepers. Gatekeepers in terms of computer networks, IP addresses, and cable lines.

Scripture as a Sword

These were Malik's thoughts upon further contemplation of Genesis and PAINCO. The irony was that historical records revealed that at one time PAINCO insured slaves before Reconstruction.

The Despicables did not just tolerate the Bible; they weaponized and funded its scriptures into everyday human life. Suffering and cruelty were their brand.

Genesis 9: they saw Noah's curse on Ham as racial justification for the enslavement of Black bodies.

In Leviticus and Exodus: they clung to passages that permitted slavery and the selling of daughters as servants, claiming divine endorsement of bondage.

The Despicables

They quoted Deuteronomy 20 to justify genocide, Joshua to legitimize conquest and Numbers to frame children as spoils of war.

From Old Testament verses without inclusion and consideration of the New Testament, they carved an unholy alliance and doctrine.

That slavery was not only permissible, but it was also sacred.

That domination over weaker peoples was prophetic fulfillment and some sort of ordained manifest destiny.

Children were seen not as angels to safeguard, but as vessels to be broken and initiated.

These beliefs did not stay in the dark but only remained in remission until one realized their manifest destiny.

These principles either were excluded or included wrongly in the "Black Slave Bible."

Churches, particularly during confessionals, were frequently used as places of refuge by individuals who sought cover.

There, victims whispered trauma through screams, only to have their pain cataloged, not healed. Bishops took detailed notes. Priests reassigned the guilty. The abuse did not stop. It scaled.

The Despicables operated like a virus, moving clergy from one diocese to another, always upstream, always hidden by sacrament and immunity. Allegations were buried in Latin documents no layperson could read. Investigations were handed over to "internal review boards" composed of the very men responsible for the crimes.

And at the center of it all was a chilling truth[9].

The Despicables maintained that the mistreatment of children served both as a means of control and as part of certain rituals.

Desecration was designed to shatter innocence, that bound the soul in trauma, and created psychological dependence, ensured the child would either grow into a compliant servant or a shattered witness incapable of testifying.

These rituals, Malik would later uncover, were not confined only to the Church. They were echoed in secret societies, elite boarding schools, and "re-education retreats" sponsored by global nonprofits with ties to the Genesis Group.

But the Vatican was their cathedral. Its Swiss Guard its battalion and the Jesuits its mercenaries. Assassins. A walled fortress of unaccountability.

Malik once found a ledger in PAINCO's deep archives labeled "Tithes." It was disguised as a donation log; millions transferred annually to tax-exempt organizations that bore names like Sancta Domus, the Society of the Lamb, and Pax Lux Holdings. Beneath the surface, these were not charities. They were laundering operations. Catholic bishops absconded with church funds only to build themselves large estates on the oceans.

PAINCO's largest "clerical risk mitigation" insurance payouts were linked to settlements in Ireland, Boston, Buenos Aires, and sub-Saharan Africa, involving coordinated cover-ups.

A Cloaked Covenant

The Despicables' infestation of the Church was not merely institutionalized. It was spiritual as well. They replaced the image of Christ with the image of control. They turned the Holy See into a throne of treachery, deceit, and secrecy.

The Despicables

In a restricted Vatican vault known only to a few, a centuries-old letter sat beneath glass, written in a cipher by an unnamed cardinal during the Inquisition. In it, the cardinal warned:

"There is a hand among us that touches no altar but commands everyone. Its ring is not of Peter but of Caesar. Its doctrine is not of Christ, but Mammon."

The hand was the Despicables.

Their reach stretched to televangelist empires. To tax-free megachurches, where prosperity was promised in exchange for silence. They taught that poverty was a result of disobedience, and that power was a gift to be hoarded by the righteous.

Malik understood now: religion was not immune from corruption. It was its oldest host.

And if the Despicables infiltrated the Church, then the war he fought was confirmed as not financial or political, but spiritual as the old gypsy woman warned him.

The sum of all these various and nefarious activities was akin to the "Tower of Babel," destined to crumble down from GOD's dominion from the weight of the affront to the Most High.

Oyster Bay

The air in Oyster Bay felt wrong. Even before Malik stepped out of the car, his spirit registered the pressure. He spent close to two hours in mind-boggling traffic from his office on the Long Island Expressway to Cross Island Parkway to Southern State Parkway to get to Oyster Bay. Traffic on a Friday evening during the summer was abysmal, as people traveled to the Long Island shores like the Hamptons, Sag Harbor and Fire Island to name a few of the favored attractions and weekend homes.

It would be well after midnight when Malik returned to his home in Asbury Park, NJ.

"Why in the hell would Gino have a meeting on Long Island on a Friday?" thought Malik as he navigated the heavy traffic, even at 7 PM that Friday.

He knew why. "Gino lives to be contrary, and plus he lives on the Island." Malik sighed.

Malik really resented that Gino imposed a meeting on him without much explanation as to why his appearance was needed or without much notice. But Gino positioned the request or demand in such a way Malik didn't believe he could refuse him.

It was not just the towering sycamores shrouded in the fog that clung to the coastal trees, some covered with moss, that were ominous. The unnatural stillness, the weight of the unseen, like a breath held too long.

As he adjusted his collar and approached the large estate before him, the heat in July, not the weather itself, but angst, gripped his chest.

"LORD," he muttered, "where have you brought me?"

The circumstances he found himself in felt unnatural, so spiritually volatile, that Malik swore he had walked straight into the fiery furnace. He hoped he would emerge from that furnace like Shadrach, Meshach and Abednego.

Only this was not Babylon. It was Long Island, NY, and the fire was not lit by kings and idols. It was powered by corporate darkness consisting of greed, ambition and disguised as spiritual rituals, masqueraded as executive strategy which were only attempts to be God-like.

Malik walked down the winding stone path towards the white mansion. The kind of property shielded from the naked eye and Google Maps. It sat on a cliff above the Long Island Sound, modern and monolithic. A legacy without speaking its name.

He had researched the address, but it was owned by some company without even a registered agent, which he found strange.

Waiting at the door was a man in a charcoal gray suit with no necktie, no warmth, and eyes that did not blink.

"Mr. Madison," he said, not asking. "Right this way."

Inside, the estate was quiet, almost too quiet for a meeting. The atmosphere stale with aged wood, old books, and fresh tales. No one greeted him. No one smiled. The man led him down the walkway lit by candle sconces, not electric bulbs. He passed oil portraits of men who had long since died, yet somehow still looked.

Finally, he arrived.

A great room, circular like the "Oval Office," with vaulted ceilings and a single stone carved into the shape of a seven-point star.

Around it sat twelve people. Gino sat at the southernmost point, flanked by Doug Venier and a woman. Malik did not recognize her. She radiated power. No one stood. No one spoke.

A chair waited for him in the center of the star as if he appeared before an Inquisition.

Each attendee began to speak in turn, offering names without warmth, only designations in a grand design. Malik realized what this was: not a usual business meeting, but a cartel. Present at the meeting were:

- Gino Colucci, Executive Vice President, PAINCO
- Doug Venier, Vice President, Strategic Risk Management, PAINCO
- Marion S. Raynor, President, MOLDAVU INTERNATIONAL LTD.

- Alan Prentiss, Senior Partner, Strathmore and Swan
- Jasmine Rizall, Vice President, Global Trust Bank
- Lt. Marco D'Agostino, NYPD, Organized Crime Bureau
- Anna Marie LeClair, National Home Security System
- Clifton Barnes, Central Cable Network Inc.
- Jerome "Black Ice" Santiago, Miami street gang known as "Ice Ice"
- Nathan Wright, Project Manager, Long Island Electric Company
- Bo Johnson, Head of the White Supremist group "Enemies of Revenge"
- Various other insurance companies representing the cities of Houston, San Diego and Atlanta.

Malik felt like he was at a United Nations Summit or more like in the center of a pack of hungry and salivating wolves.

Malik sat in the seat meant for him, at the head of the table, though he clearly understood he was not in charge. His placement at the table only caused salivation from a pack of wolves waiting for the hunt to start.

The conversations cloaked in euphemisms. They did not talk about sex trafficking but spoke of "human commerce." They did not mention drugs but rather discussed "synthetic demand-based risk markets." "Blackmail" became "compliance leverage." Pornography was "content streaming portfolio."

Clearly this meeting and Malik's purpose for attendance was to seduce him as well as to introduce him to PAINCO's underground business. A business fraught with as many illicit activities to call for extermination of the infestation. It also now explained the high rates of return generated by some PAINCO affiliates and their divisions in a low-interest environment. Further, it also showed the tremendous pressure publicly traded companies were under to create shareholder value, especially in a company and industry with negative growth. Or perhaps, Malik was too charitable in his view and simply refused to accept the pervasive practice and resignation of "white-collar crime" in corporate America. Insurance companies certainly were the leaders of the pack in this race to corruption.

The Corruption of Insurance

Insurance business by its very nature and existence lent itself to corruption. The entire business model was predicated on a practice to delay, linger, wait and then deny claims. Policy language was very much like the "policy" or numbers racket that once flourished in the urban centers of the US. Underwriting guidelines and claim practices were designed to avoid liability. In this sense, it bred an environment of greed, grift, graft, corruption and other undue influences. And it tended to be a heavy cash-flow operation attracting unsavory characters who perspired from the prospects of getting at that cash or washing large sums of money through insurance companies.

Regardless of the cynical nature of the insurance business, Malik was not fooled by what he saw or heard. This meeting clearly was a cartel. A clean one to the outside world, but its insides were as dirty as a pig at slop time. No designer or tailored suit with polished shoes or "lipstick" would ever make this pig pretty.

Every genre: gay, Cuban, Italian, Jewish, Irish, Black and women of the organized crime world was represented at this meeting. And these same types occupied positions in the executive towers of many publicly traded companies. Most people viewed the dirty part of organized crime as "street commerce," but that was back in the old days. Italian mob families and some White Supremist families sent their children to Ivy League colleges and universities to penetrate the corporate executive ranks and boardrooms. These various organized crime families formed cartels with one family specializing in a particular skill set needed by a different ethnic cartel. The same loose paradigm organized crime applied to street commerce. The Confederates fled further south to Florida and vowed that one day the "south would rise again."

Bankers, gang leaders, lawyers, law enforcement officials, tech and utility companies were all part of the cartel. Each provided a particular legitimate specialty and served as distribution for various factions waited for their cut of the profits from both street commerce. It was a strategy of détente achieved among the various crime families and affiliates formed into cartels. And from time to time, things might get off track and that's when a big company like Genesis came along to "gin up" the soldiers.

And this was probably replicated in other industries, including film and entertainment, as well. Regardless of the mix, Whites were at the apex of the Despicables who, in addition to their economic interests and domination, had a social agenda far more diabolical than sheer greed. The entire matter conveyed a certain level of invincibility about it. And one supposed to some extent there was a certain truth[9] as it had gone on for centuries.

Then came the seminal question in Malik's mind:

"How do they move all that cash?"

The second question was, "How do I extricate myself from this situation which now appears to place me at the point of no return?" After all, they didn't bring me to this meeting to show me their dirty washing without me somehow carrying the laundry basket to the washing machine."

Allen Prentiss addressed the question. He was outside counsel for PAINCO. Malik had dealt with him once on a big acquisition by PAINCO.

"We have structured sovereign equity vehicles in Abu Dhabi and Singapore as compliant debt as index swap corridors, all underwritten for reinvestment under partnership entreaties. These swaps occur contemporaneously with the withdrawal of PAINCO Florida," he spoke.

This served as a "EUREKA!" moment for Malik as he was working on the paperwork for the company's Florida company wind-down with the Florida Department of Financial Services. The offshore money flowed to PAINCO, and Florida administered the withdrawal, and the liquidated assets went into some "black hole" and were divided up among the impatient vultures.

When the meeting ended, most filtered out through the quaint side doors well hidden by canopies of large trees.

Ms. Raynor approached Malik. He was familiar with the name, having seen her name associated with Moldavu Ltd. She looked at him with a frigid woman's look for a very long moment.

"Mr. Madison, let me save you some time and wondering," she said to him. "Gino Colucci will never leave you."

Malik didn't blink and simply offered her a bewildered look. He only met her gaze with a quizzical look.

"You think it is about your legal mind? Your pedigree? It is not. You were selected. Whether you willingly or not participate, you are in the architecture now."

She turned and disappeared. And this was generally how the Despicables caught others in their deplorable web of corruption, deceit and greed. They provided you with dangerous information which cornered the individual into a choice of complicity or endangerment.

Malik left through the front door. Alone. Well after everyone else left the estate. In the distance, the Long Island Sound roared as if it read his mind.

As he approached his car, out of the darkness the man he met with before he saw the gypsy, stepped towards him. He didn't even know his name. Malik handed him a thumb drive. They departed each other without uttering a single word.

He drove onto the Southern State Parkway heading home. Malik's mind was weary from the many different thoughts that filled his head.

A dark sedan, hugging the edges of visibility, followed behind him. Exactly one-eighth of a mile back.

It never sped up. Never changed lanes; it just followed Malik. He adjusted his rear-view mirror. Tapped his brakes. The car behind him slowed down a bit.

Malik reached for his cell phone and held it over his right shoulder. He drove his car with his left hand, maintaining the speed limit. Click. Click. The flash went off twice, momentarily blending and lighting the darkness behind him.

The reaction was simultaneous and immediate. The sedan behind him quickly jerked. Brakes. And three miles later, the car exited the Southern State Parkway.

It was almost certainly the sedan that followed him throughout this year-long ordeal.

He did not head directly home that night. He gripped his steering wheel tighter. Rest would not be his companion that night. He needed clarity of explanation. He entered the car's GPS navigation system an address in the Village.

The Despicables

There were truths[9] that needed sharing. Loyalties that required testing. And a family that needed to understand the danger. This was no longer simply a corporate scandal, but war.

Chapter Twelve
The Other Watchtower

"Pride goes before destruction."

— Proverbs 16:18

The gypsy woman waited for him. She knew Malik would come again. He had to come to fully understand the battle, the reasons for the battle, and why him?

He rang the doorbell. The old gypsy woman opened the front door to her shop. It was 2 AM, but she was still awake. It did not seem as if she ever slept from what Malik saw from the two other times they met. He immediately followed her into the back of her shop. He took his usual place in the chair before her table as she hobbled around him to her chair on the other side.

Once again, before Malik could open his mouth, she spoke.

Hidden Ones

"Long before they were called the Despicables, they were known simply as the 'Hidden Ones.' They emerged in the courts of empires, behind the papal thrones in Rome, in the shadows of the pyramids, and in the merchant banking world. Conversations in low murmurs in the ears of kings, poisoning the wells of consciousness. They were not a nation or race, not a secret kingdom, but rather a belief: that power should be concentrated, imminent, elusive, and absolute.

They started the lie that man can be God, not to elevate him, but to enslave him, by any means necessary.

But with every darkness, there is light.

The Despicables

The Shilohs were born not in a palace, but in a flight scattered across deserts, forests, and mountains. Exiled children who got lost as they conquered Europe, particularly Iberia. These 100 Moorish people were mystics and found their way into the Balkans, then Slavic seers, and gentle warriors. After the fall of the Al-Abd al Dasa in 1492, the Catholic crown erupted through Iberia. It started with the Inquisition. That's when the Despicables infiltrated the very Church that pretended to protect people.

It was not that the Despicables believed in God. Far from it, but they saw people's faith in God and the Church yet another opportunity to exert control over them. The fact that the Church through its priests influenced altar boys represented yet another way for the Despicables to broaden its evil throughout the world.

The Despicables long understood that true power was not seized solely through wealth and politics, but through the desecration and manipulation of faith. Over centuries, they crept into the sanctuaries of every major religion, to turn pulpits into platforms of control. They funded bishops, installed cardinals, and whispered into the ears of popes, rabbis, imams, and preachers alike. Scripture was no longer sacred; it was strategic. They turned the gospel of liberation into sermons of submission, teaching the enslaved to pray for deliverance in the next life while as they quietly endorsed their oppression in this one. Beneath the stained glass and behind holy altars, the Despicables reigned: defiling confessionals, laundering their sins through tithes, and cloaking their corruption as investments stitched with gold. In this way, their dealings with the Church were strictly transactional no matter how much money the Despicables washed through the churches.

False Prophets

Today, they call it Christian Nationalism, which is not a religion, but rather a perverse spiritual movement that thrives on cruelty and racial separatism. This primarily is the work of the various White Supremist extremist groups who preach hatred, misogyny, homophobia, and discrimination against every other people who are not considered the White race.

But before this, over time, the Despicables developed computers, the internet, social media networks, artificial intelligence, and cloud sourcing to cause catastrophes throughout the world. Their success in these technologies emboldened them in their belief the Despicables represented God on earth, if even there was a GOD. They began to undermine the churches, revealing hypocrisy, corruption, and sin in the churches. They pointed to their advances in technology as evidence no God in heaven existed. Invasions into people's privacy, artificial intelligence, and cloud sourcing were the Despicables' tools and became normative behavior, among many others, as evidence these tech titans were indeed gods on earth. These technologies allowed them to perpetuate these myths. Its purpose was to pick off a portion of the population to cause doubt in their faith in a heavenly GOD. Except, the Shilohs understood their master plan from the beginning of man's history. It was more about business than faith for the Despicables unless that blind faith believed in their goals.

The old gypsy woman took a long sip from her teacup and continued. Except the Despicables were more than false prophets. They were the devil incarnate and the "person" that Satan threatened God he would create on earth.

Malik listened intently to the old woman; the throbbing in his head increased from information overload.

She continued, "The Despicables are so mistaken. All that happens in this world is according to GOD's plan. It is precisely their technologies that will destroy the world, if they are not stopped. Like the Tower of Babel, they will fail from the weight of their audacity. And that's where you play a role, Malik: to stop the Despicables."

She looked deep into Malik's eyes as if she saw into the windows of his soul. She grabbed both of his wrists with her wrinkled veiny hands.

"You are Shiloh and the Chosen One; not as in the Messiah but as a worthy warrior, a valiant soldier, if you will," she smirked as if to challenge his doubt of her statement.

Malik stammered, "But…but…but…why me? I never asked for any of this. How do you know I am the 'Chosen One?'"

The gypsy leaned back in her chair. The fire was dying low, sparks breaking loose from the burning logs and spiraling upward as if they too longed for heaven. Then Madam Erzebet leaned forward, her shawl draped like a shadow, her eyes bright with a strange light. Malik sat still as if not to break the trance, but aware enough to sense that her words were not hers alone, but pulled from something older, deeper, perhaps eternal.

"When the Watchers fell," she whispered in a raspy voice, "most chose dominion, their towers, their thrones, their idols of gold, silver, dollars, coins, and blood. They became the fathers of corruption, the architects of an empire. But one; only one; refused the oath of darkness. He descended from the high place, not to sit with kings nor to whisper into the ears of merchants, but to walk among the broken, among the hunted, among the despised."

Her voice lowered with more earnest and inflection, so Malik leaned closer to hear every word.

"He walked with the Moors as they fled across the seas. He wandered with Roma, cast from every gate. He cloaked himself among the forgotten, and from them was born a hidden people:

the Shiloh. A bloodline not chosen by nations but by heaven's last defector, the one who would not bow down to corruption. Through them endurance was preserved, cunning was sharpened, and compassion for the oppressed carried like a sacred fire."

Malik shifted uneasily. He wanted to dismiss it as folklore, another fireside story told to frighten or to inspire him. Yet the air around them seemed to hold its breath as if to test his intellect. The stones of the ruined watchtower moaned softly in the wind, as if they remembered.

"You are Shiloh. According to the ancient covenants Shilohs had with God, the Chosen One would be born to take down Satan's spawn: the Despicables. The Chosen One is a man with a crescent-shaped birthmark on the inside of his left leg, just right of the knee."

Malik thought, "I have the same birthmark in the exact location. But I cannot be the Chosen One?".

According to the Shilohs' covenant with God, a man with a crescent-shaped birthmark was a person of great spiritual wisdom and intuition. Your path is one of spiritual awareness. The Chosen One is called upon to break generational curses.

His thoughts immediately turned to Jordan. He thought it was Monica's mission to break the generational curse her family brought into their lives.

The gypsy woman sensed his doubt and understood his question without Malik speaking the words.

"When a descendant of Adisa married a Mitchell descendant, that was the sign the separated tribes of the Al-Abd al Dasa must be made whole again to break the evil spell of the Dushevs and the Despicables. Your first wife's ancestral family is also part of the Al-Abd al Dasa who intermarried with the Dushevs. Together we must break the curse and destroy the Despicables to restore the Shilohs to their rightful place, the true Watchtower here on earth."

However, what was missing from the gypsy's story about the spiritual battle between the Shilohs and the Despicables was that greed, power, blasphemy, and corruption were derivatives of pride. Unbridled pride inevitably led to failure and/or destruction. How could he be assured that it was not the Shiloh's own pride that was destined to failure?

"Why are you telling me this?" he asked finally, his voice rough.

The woman's gaze cut into him, unblinking and resolute.

"Because it is not a story, Malik Madison. It is blood. Your blood. You are that line. The Shilohs did not vanish, though the Despicables hunted them across kingdoms and ages. Their seed endured. And in you the Watcher's gift runs hot, though you do not yet know its powers."

Malik shook his head. "I'm just a man; caught in a game too large for him. A pawn in a war of corporations and cabals. My family pays for my choices. That is all."

Her lips curved into something between a smile and a sneer.

"That is what they want you to believe: that you are small, that you are accidental. But the Despicables know better; they know the Shiloh bloodline remains their shadow, the unforeseen hand that can unmake their towers. That is why they will stop at nothing to break you, Malik. They fear you though they cannot shake you, if you remain steadfast and unflappable because it's your gift they want. They want to either compromise or destroy you. That is the test they presented to you last night in Oyster Bay."

The fire hissed, a log collapsed into ash. Malik felt a shiver crawl up his spine. He thought of the turbulence over the English Channel, the storm that seemed almost alive. He thought of Ana's warnings, Madam Erzebet's riddles, the assassin's cold oath in Croatia. Was it all converging toward this? Toward him?

"How do you know I am the Chosen One?" he asked plaintively.

Crescent Moon

"The story told throughout Shiloh generations is that the Chosen One would carry a very distinct birthmark as a sign of his worth. That birthmark is a crescent-shaped moon on the inside of his left leg near and just below the knee on the thigh." She smiled warmly at him as if to reassure him of her words.

"Wait…I have a crescent-shaped moon birthmark on my left leg just outside the inner knee above my thigh," he gasped.

Madam Erzebet's smile broadened. "Yes, I know; I saw it the first night you entered my shop as you sat down. It's the same birthmark the man who sent you to me saw as well. That's how we know you are the Chosen One. It's the same birthmark that probably the Despicables noticed as well."

Malik's heart and brain thundered with multiple thoughts as they competed to determine which got attention first from the information overload shared by Madam Erzebet.

"If this is true… then what am I supposed to do with it?" his voice dropped to a whisper.

The old woman's eyes softened, though her tone remained unyielding.1

"You must continue to watch. You must wait. And when their towers reach for heaven higher than Babel; you must strike. Not for yourself, not even for your family, but for the generations that will be enslaved if you do nothing. You are not the end of the story, Malik. You are simply the hinge upon which it turns."

Malik peered into the fire, and for a heartbeat he thought he saw faces moving in the flames: ancestors, exiles, warriors, martyrs; all watching him. He clenched his fists, torn between denial and destiny: chosen not by men, but by heaven as the last defector.

Chapter Thirteen
Signs

"And the seventh angel poured out his vial into the air; and there came a great voice out of the temple of heaven, from the throne, saying, It is done."

— Revelation 16:17

After his visit with Madam Erzebet, Malik now had a complete understanding of the depth of the Despicables' evil reign on earth. The Despicables built their empires on concrete and code, on finance and fear. They created digital towers to surveil nations and engineered markets that could collapse governments with the flick of a keyboard. But for all their intelligence and innovation, they remained blind to the oldest language of all: the earth groaning under their wickedness. The voice of GOD as he spoke to the world through storms.

The Breath of the Bound

"The Lord is slow to anger but great in power; the Lord will not leave the guilty unpunished. His way is the whirlwind and the storm, and the clouds are the dust of his feet."

— Nahum 1:3

They said the hurricanes came from the sea. In fact, they did; the storm started off the eastern coast of Africa in the Atlantic Ocean.

But the sea was long haunted.

It carried the breath of the bound, those torn from the motherland, shackled in iron, swallowed by waves and sorrow.

Their cries once muffled beneath the decks of greed, now rose in the wind.

Each storm was a sermon. Each flood a written psalm of justice. Each tornado a scripture. Each hurricane a day of judgment. Each earthquake a covenant with God. These are the voices of God.

They were sacred echoes from the Middle Passage

They were the groaning of creation, the testimony of the tortured, the breath of the bound reclaiming the land.

The spiritual reckoning invoked by the hurricanes thus became a judgment not against the lands it ravaged but upon the financial institutions that still, today, in various ways, prioritized profit over justice, denying relief and perpetuating harm. As for insurance companies.

Hurricane Katrina stood as a modern parable, a living incarnation of the sacred reckoning of the mass worldwide corruption wrought by financial institutions. While Hurricane Katrina's storm surge broke through the levees surrounding New Orleans, flooding 80% of the city, its flooding did not discriminate. History already did so. Racial geography, imposed by centuries of redlining, history, exclusion, slavery, Jim Crow segregation laws and environmental harms intended as further injustice, meant the Black and Brown communities. These communities bore the brunt of devastation. In the Lower 9th Ward, New Orleans majority Black neighborhoods were disproportionately submerged while the White wealthy above-sea-level communities were largely spared or experienced lesser storm surge impacts. This constituted environmental redlining.

The raging waters thus traced the scarred map of injustice; each flooded home a testimony to the continued legacy of inequality. As the immediate response was tepid and then somewhat waned, further patterns repeated: federal response in the form of FEMA disaster and recovery relief, failed to reach the Black victims with equity. Thus, the natural disaster served as a multiplier of injustice; a further insult to injury to the "Middle Passage," an enduring fury, and in a biblical sense, the continuation of institutional sin against the Black slaves.

The language and meaning of catastrophes, if put in biblical context and as prophecy, risked making the secular sacred. Hurricanes represented the thunderous breath of those who died at sea or the dead bodies tossed at sea as the African slaves gave ancient prophecy for the meaning of catastrophes.

Malik now understood fully the irony, arrogance, and stupidity of the Despicables who failed to see and heed the signs from God about the sins of the world. Floods now swallowed cities and rural areas of the United States in seasons that once brought harvest. Hurricanes arrived with such frequency as to forecast warnings, spinning faster, forming wider, striking harder, and leaving regions uninhabitable. It was as if his African ancestors blew vengeful formidable winds as hurricanes to the southern coast as a reminder to the Despicables of the treachery they wreaked on the African slaves. For their lack of humanity. Fires swept across continents like biblical judgments and United States, Australia, California, the Amazon were all choked with smoke.

Earthquakes split the ground where children had just played. Famine, plague, and pestilence returned like ancient ghosts, and the seas boiled from plastic and decay.

And still, the Despicables laughed.

To them, these disasters were insurance claims and relief contracts. And a further opportunity to exact their special brand of cruelty to deny, linger, and wait on the payment of claims following some type of catastrophic event during the most stressful time of people's lives. A broken promise contained as language in a policy as one big collective gaslighting experience. Opportunities to acquire land at discount to displace the weak and poor. They called it the new normal. They called it climate change when it was convenient for them to state so. They convened forums and created white papers, but never asked the only question that mattered:

What if this was not the randomness of nature… but the wrath of God?

"Vengeance was mine, said the Lord."

— Romans 12;19.

They dismissed the Watchers' warnings, ridiculed the seers and prophets, and dared to play God and mocked the true and living One.

Malik saw it now, clearer than ever. The spiritual war wasn't just being fought in boardrooms and data centers. It was also inscribed in every flood zone, every drought-stricken farm, every fire-scorched mountain, life and health insurance policy, and annuity. In every federal government bill that cut funding for FEMA.

The Despicables built towers to monitor the skies, but none high enough to see the hand that moved the storm.

They created satellites to map the oceans, but none that could measure the depth of GOD's fury. None that erased the sins of slavery,

And when the earth cried out, they heard only static.

Malik had his marching orders. The battle continued.

Chapter Fourteen
Family Matters

"The eternal is a refuge, and underneath are the everlasting arms."

— Deuteronomy 33:27

Asbury Park, New Jersey

The Despicables' greedy hands were in every sector of the economy. Malik saw their imprint and influence everywhere. There was no way to escape their reach and influence.

Malik felt their constant presence, and everyone in his town was suspected. His thoughts returned to the rebirth of Asbury Park, New Jersey. It rested along the ragged edge of the Atlantic Ocean, where the salt air carried stories as old as the tide. In its earliest days, Asbury Park was a shining jewel of the Jersey Shore. It boasted elegant Victorian hotels, horse-drawn boardwalks, and a grand carousel that spun in rhythm as the turf rose of Asbury.

Disinvestment, redlining, and White flight hollowed the once-thriving resort town. The elegant hotels fell into disrepair, the boardwalk rotted underfoot, and Springwood Avenue: the lifeline of Black culture; was reduced to rubble and memory. For decades, the city was a portrait of urban decay, its grand past a ghost behind boarded-up windows and broken glass.

But like the tide that defined it, Asbury Park would not stay down.

Yet amid the surf culture and gentrification, the soul of Asbury Park remained contested. Developers pushed eastward, while the west side: the heart of Black history in the city fought to en-sure its stories weren't buried beneath new condos. The ghosts of Springwood still hummed in the air, asking to be heard.

Today, Asbury Park was a city of contradiction; resurrected but restless, historic yet in transition. It was a place where the waves still crashed against time, and where the dreams of the past sought justice in the present or delayed to the future.

Malik sat on the front porch of their house as he contemplated past events and upcoming plans following the Oyster Bay meeting. After the meeting, he left believing he had three options. He could involuntarily continue to do the Despicables' corrupt bidding; be terminated, most likely as "unalived," or take down the Despicables. He went for option 3 because clearly, he and his family were in imminent danger as the vice grip tightened.

Malik knew he must extricate and protect his family from the Despicables, from the "Mitchell curse," and at the same time take down the Despicables. Thus, the reason he summoned his family home.

He sat on the front porch and waited for his family members' arrival. Denai and Kendall were scheduled to arrive by early evening. There was no telling when Monica and Jordan would arrive, although probably separately. Jordan scheduled a meet-ing in the company's Manhattan office and took the corporate jet from Chicago to a regional airport in New Jersey. Monica was less specific about her travel plans.

The Atlantic mist rolled in from the shore like a ghostly veil, casting a gray silence over the weathered porch of their Asbury Park house.

Malik sat at the head of the reclaimed oak dining table, his fin-gers steepled beneath his chin. The house was quiet, but tension churned the air like a brewing storm. The entire family convened together under one roof around 8 PM. Malik summarized the Oyster Bay meeting. He left out the ancient history details about the Dushevs, Mitchells, Shilohs, and Despicables for the children's sake. However, in separate conversations he provided Denai and Monica with the fascinating history and his European adventures.

To his right sat Denai, regal in her poise, her honey-toned skin glowing in the candlelight, legs crossed, eyes sharp. Across from her was Monica, shorter, still beautiful in that way that defied time: petite, intense, a miniature tempest in heels. Jordan, their daughter, leaned slightly forward in her chair, observant and uneasy, her Mitchell last name shielding her at PAINCO but no longer hiding the truth[9]. Kendall sat by the window, arms crossed, watching his father with both loyalty and caution.

They were all there. It was years since the entire family gathered under one roof. During those infrequent family gatherings, the days and nights were fraught with discourse and tension as Denai and Monica jockeyed for the "Queen Bee" status in the house. The children just watched them dumbfounded by the acrimony both mothers had towards the other. At least on this auspicious occasion, for once, they weren't at each other's throats. At least, not yet.

Pawns

"I didn't think I'd live to see the day when the five of us would sit at the same table," Malik muttered, half to himself.

Monica smirked. "Desperation makes for strange bedfellows."

Denai's jaw clenched. "Let's not romanticize this. We're here because the Despicables are real, and they've targeted all of us: through our work, our family, our memories."

Jordan nodded. "They use me, Daddy. Irolla had me dig through audit trails. He thought I was just identifying wasteful policyholder payouts. But now I know: those payments weren't wasteful. They were intentional siphons. Human trafficking fronts. Dummy claimants. AI-replicated identities."

Kendall leaned in. "They approached me too. Not directly. Through recruiters. Offering me crazy sums to join a crypto startup backed by Genesis Financial. But when I traced the shell companies, I saw the same patterns. The same black-box accounts, the same slush funds."

Malik exhaled, slowly. "I know. Genesis is making a move on PAINCO. They want to gut it from the inside. Turn our policies into pipelines for profit. They want our cash reserves They see us as either pawns; or threats."

"Then we stop being pawns," Monica said flatly. "We take back control of our lives."

"From a trillion-dollar Hydra?" Denai snapped. "These aren't crooked board members or rogue traders. These are entities embedded in churches, governments, NGOs, even the Vatican."

"Yes," Malik replied. "But they forgot one thing. They left a family scarred; but alive. And each of us has something they didn't count on."

He stood. "Monica has the dirt. Jordan has the access. Kendall has the code. Denai has eyes on the inside. And me? I have nothing left to lose but my family."

Monica reached into her leather case and slid a folder across the table. "Here are the passwords to two offshore accounts registered to Genesis subsidiaries. Trace those payments and you'll find the contracts for mercenaries and hit squads. I want immunity."

Denai rolled her eyes. "You'll get redemption, Monica. That's what you said you wanted."

At its most basic level, Monica was a creature of instinct and habit. Her most instinctual response to any conflict was survival. As the net tightened around the Despicables, she realized her chances were raised of getting caught by law enforcement, rivals, or internal cartel suspicions. She also realized her time as a trusted "mule" might come to an abrupt, untimely death. Helping Jordan to break the Mitchell curse was her only pathway to her and her daughter's salvation. Even still, Monica's story was not only about doing the right thing, but in her world, negotiating a spectrum of moral ambiguity.

Her position of money laundering and moving large sums of money for the Russian mafia was not only one about psychological trauma but like a slow-motion suffocation. She dreamed of a life unbundled by coded phone calls and too many close-called getaways.

It was not that Monica was so jaded she had no compassion and empathy for others. She certainly loved her daughter Jordan in some benign way. Except, her empathy in this way was one where she felt conflicted empathy between her own self-preservation and others. However, Monica recognized in the present moment she possessed information about the critical nodes of the Despicables' criminal operations: trusted lieutenants, laundering routes, and the logistics behind cash movements. Monica's ability to monitor these critical pathways enabled them to map and expose the weak points in the structures.

Denai could watch how the money from Monica's networks worked its way into the PAINCO books. And Malik could see the ultimate company designation for those funds.

Jordan would monitor Irolla's activities by phone, emails, scheduled meetings, and take notes on who and how he met with the Despicables within PAINCO.

Kendall would retrieve the mail that centered around their plans to make sure no one within the company had any advance warning of the approaching tsunami. By the time the Despicables got wind of what just occurred, the damage would be done and their demise fully set in motion.

"Forgiveness without a path to redemption," Malik said, "is a vacuous promise to God."

He looked at each of them in turn.

"We do this together. Or not at all. Tonight, we are not exes or rivals or estranged siblings. We are a frontline. The Despicables win by dividing families. We break the curse by standing as one."

For the first time in a long time, no one spoke.

The storm outside broke with a sudden thunderclap. But inside, the silence was sacred.

A covenant was just sealed. The rest of the night they sat around in the living room devising a plan to take down the Despicables.

Chapter Fifteen
Whistleblower

"Forgiveness without the opportunity for redemption or salvation is a vacuous promise to God."

— Author

Action commenced in a glass-walled executive suite atop PAINCO's New York headquarters in downtown Manhattan. The skyline glistened behind her. Jordan Mitchell sat behind a sleek modern glass desk, her tablet open. She scrolled through company correspondence with a steady focus.

She inherited some attributes from her father, including his determination and insight. She also possessed qualities she learned from her mother. A combination of social awareness; cunning street smarts with practical intelligence. She had that rare combination of class and "hood rat," when necessary, that captivated many; others enchanted with her. Monica refined and polished her like a 20-carat diamond, though not quite a rough diamond. After graduating from Princeton University, Jordan joined the Peace Corps and traveled to regions including Asia, the Middle East, Central America, South America, and Europe.

She became fluent in five languages, and her international experience contributed to her professional development. These qualifications supported her appointment as a director at PAINCO and were factors in Irolla selecting her to serve as his Executive Assistant after her role in Corporate Relations. Because she went by the last name Mitchell, Monica was able to omit or withhold that Jordan was Malik's daughter. It was Monica that placed her within PAINCO. She intended to groom her daughter to work for and with the Despicables. That was until Malik brought to her attention their current dilmena.

With honey-bronzed skin and sharply defined cheekbones, she moved with effortless grace and poise. Fluent in Spanish and Mandarin, as a former Peace Corps ambassador, Jordan was comfortable in any environment and held her own. She was a rising star in Corporate Relations and was assigned to John Irolla, CEO of PAINCO, as a special liaison. It was easy to see why Jordan fit in the Executive Suite and the reason why Irolla wanted her as his assistant. Malik did not like the idea of it, but he was certain Jordan could handle herself, any way needed.

Lately she got to see things she was not meant to see, but she never let on to those she came in contact. With the Genesis potential takeover, corporate activities in response to their move were on overdrive.

Emails coded in vague euphemisms. Off-site meetings that took place after hours. Vendors she could not verify. Payments routed through layers of shell corporations. Her role was to observe, report, and translate. But no one expected her to understand the total picture of all the information and transactions.

And she understood more than they knew.

Jordan closed her tablet, stood, and walked to the window. She stared out across the East River. In the reflection, her expression shifted from elegance to resolve.

"No one sees me coming," she thought. "Let them keep thinking I am the pretty face in the room."

What they did not know was that Jordan kept tabs on Gino Colucci's movements, already building a separate encrypted file with his meetings, connections, and expenditures, connecting the dots between Doug Venier's operations, Alessandra Bell,

Genesis, and the street-level commerce which Monica had disclosed.

She had Kendall secretly deliver the executive suite's internal mail to her. Jordan sorted through the executives' mail to intercept any mail that might tip PAINCO about what they planned.

The family watched from every corner of PAINCO.

It was not a corporate finance analyst. It was not a whistleblower. But a lawyer and his daughter.

It was Jordan, Malik's own daughter.

She worked closely with John Irolla, PAINCO's CEO, who was suspected of being a high-ranking operative within the Despicables. Jordan, ambitious, bright, beautiful, and eager to make her mark, gravitated to Irolla's orbit in search of mentorship. Irolla noticed her one day in the employee cafeteria. He chatted Jordan up and asked her to go see HR about a position he wanted to fill. Jordan passed the interview easily and served as Irolla's Corporate Relations Director. She had a high-profile position for someone who was just 28. She had access to rooms where Malik did not. She heard whispers of matters in corridors not meant for her ears.

At first, Malik worried she might be influenced by it. But Jordan was smarter than they knew. She did not just listen; she learned. Like a slave girl in the Master's Big House who listened to important conversations without the Master and his friends being aware she could write and read.

One night, after the Genesis fax detonated through the office, Malik met Jordan at a diner off 9th Avenue. She accompanied John Irolla on PAINCO's corporate jet from Chicago to NYC. She assisted him with whatever pressing matter was before him. She shared in detail the latest activities from the executive suit.

Chapter Sixteen
The Final Blow

"Learn to do good; seek justice, correct oppression; bring justice to the fatherless, plead the widow's cause."

— Isaiah 1:17

The burner phone felt heavier in Malik's palm. Its cheap plastic casing was no protection from the weight of what he was about to do.

He sat alone in a nondescript motel room off the Garden State Parkway, near his home in Asbury Park, a place chosen precisely because it would be forgotten. The walls were paper thin, the air stale, the TV buzzing faintly with static from a lost signal. On the nightstand beside him sat five letters: one addressed to Gino Colucci, another to John Irolla, one to Doug Venier, one to the board of PAINCO, one to Marion Raynor, and the last, folded and unsealed, to an unnamed recipient deep within a cartel structure. Monica provided the last name.

He picked up the burner cellphone and typed a message to Gino.

"I see that you call me every time you don't like what I type. Too late. What I write is true[9]. Stop gaslighting me. You know what comes next."

He paused, then typed another line: "Check your cell."

He hit send.

Moments later, across the country, a signal was received. Somewhere in the shadows of the underground, a man known only by a codename: Chaltwe, began his final descent.

Chaltwe wasn't a man in the traditional sense. He was a ghost. A phantom that governments whispered about but never admitted existed. No photo, no fingerprint, no record. But when Chaltwe moved, people and information disappeared… quietly, without a trace, without a sound.

In Manhattan, Doug Venier stepped out of his Upper East Side condo into the crisp morning air. Then the FBI agents descended upon him. Doug was not concerned. Someone else would take the fall for what just happened.

In Chicago, John Irolla glanced up from his desk just in time to see a blur pass outside his glass office wall; then darkness. The bullet entered in the center of the back his head as slumped back in his chair, blood oozing from the bullet wound. Change of plans. A necessary message was sent to those on the list.

From her Genesis office, Alessandra Bell sat at her desk staring at her computer screen just as the bullet shot out a computer monitor from the credenza behind her. She too slumped lifeless over her laptop.

A hour later, as Gino Colucci was about to enter his office, a silent shot pierced his throat. Those around him watch Gino grab his throat as the words gurgled through inaudible words. He dropped 15 seconds later.

By dusk, news broke of multiple unexplained deaths in PAINCO's leadership: heart attacks, freak accidents, sudden disappearances. But Malik knew better and he was not happy about it. This was not the agreement he had with Madam Erzebet. People on the list were not to die unless something happened to him and or his family.

The war had turned.

Later that night, Malik dropped the burner phone into a storm drain, watching it sink into the abyss.

"Let the dead bury the dead," he whispered to no one.

Then he walked away.

The backroom operation began at 3:33 a.m. in the Caribbean, the nation of Belize to be exact.

The Despicables' money transfer plans would commence at the start of the business day around 9 AM.

The family planned their strike over the last six months and left little to chance. Each went through their sketched-out roles and kept their communications to in-person meetings. Malik was certain the surveillance of his personal and work activities scaled upwards after the Oyster Bay meeting. He played along as if he was a "team player" to not draw any more unnecessary attention to himself. For the moment, at least, it seemed to placate Gino and Doug.

The wind-down of PAINCO Florida company operations was announced the prior year, so state government officials implemented the final stages of the withdrawal of the company from the Florida market. Once all the creditors, policyholders, employee benefits, including compensation, and "statutory" payments were made, any remaining funds held by the State of Florida went to "other disbursements." Other disbursements as in to grease the palms of all those in the cartel and the various organizations who provided cover from the local, county, and state officials, political party action committees, law enforcement, and those companies and/or individuals who participated in the Oyster Bay meeting.

This was how they money laundered revenue from their "street commerce" activities; masked by within the wind down of

PAINCO's withdrawal from the Florida insurance market. It was done in any numerous ways within the confines of a corporate financing. Ways that shielded street commerce from the watchful eyes of the FBI, IRS, DEA, DOJ, ATF and sine state governments.

The hour of spiritual warfare occurs when angels warred in the heavens and devils whispered to men in their sleep. But tonight, the war moved to earth.

Malik stood over the sink in his motel room off the Garden State Parkway in New Jersey. He splashed cold water on his face. His burner phone buzzed twice; no more, no less. The signal. Kendall was in.

Jordan was already in D.C., disguised as a Department of Labor contractor, using her real clearance to siphon data from PAINCO's shadow subsidy programs. Files labeled "Community Reinvestment" were code for shell-funded real estate grabs, gentrification plots, and weaponized entitlement fraud. She had downloaded enough to bring down wealthy billionaires, three senators; and possibly implicate a former Vice President.

Down in Atlanta, Monica sat in a glass tower downtown, posing as a financial auditor for Genesis's acquisition wing. She had embedded herself inside the very entity trying to dismantle PAINCO from within. Her voice was cold, clinical, as she whispered into her secure mic: "The flight manifests to the Bahamas include names of over 14 board members, three lobbyists, and a known Despicable international financier: Klaus Derringer."

Denai, meanwhile, walked silently through the hallways of a Fortune 50 insurance company's executive suite in midtown. She no longer played the passive VP. Dressed in slate-gray slacks, heels clicking like metronomes of justice, she entered the boardroom with a USB drive hidden in her designer clutch, containing footage of ritualistic abuse conducted at a Despicable retreat posing as a "Global Thought Leaders Conference." The video had been watermarked by a Shiloh contact in Croatia. Denai's job was to leak it to trusted investigative journalists before morning.

"We all good?" came Kendall's voice over the encrypted group line. "Upload is live. Blockchain mirrored on 12 nodes. If they try to erase it, we've got it scattered like gospel in the wind."

"Let the wind howl," Monica responded. "We need a storm." If only PAINCO were a property and casualty insurer, because they were about to experience the "risk of ruin" catastrophe.

Except this calamity was a man-made peril… Shiloh.

Chapter Seventeen
The Final Blow

*"But transgressors will be altogether destroyed; The posterity
of the wicked will be cut off."*

— Psalm 37:38

The end of PAINCO Florida came not with scandal or fire or natural disaster, but with the silent paperwork of a bureaucratic death.

A "strategic restructuring" was how it was framed for the public. In press releases, officials from the Governor's office in Tallahassee assured the public it was a normal sunset: part of a regional optimization strategy. Further, the exit of PAINCO would not disadvantage consumers in the marketplace. Behind the scenes, however, it was a controlled demolition.

Assets were liquidated in careful cadence and in compliance with regulations about the withdrawal of an insurer in the marketplace. Creditors came first to the trough: bondholders, reinsurance syndicates, claims-processing vendors. Then came employee compensation: back pay, pension and 401k obligations, severance packages, health benefits. Each disbursement wrapped in a bow of legality, quietly observed by handpicked liquidation agents vetted by Genesis Financial. With oversight by the insurance regulator as the last pig at the trough.

But the next tranche of disbursements drew darker shadows.

Political Action Committees, nearly two dozen of them, received donations masked as "philanthropic legacy gifts." State officials across Florida, Georgia, Texas, North Carolina, and other states received PAC-backed consulting fees for their "advisory services" on insurance reform. Several sheriffs' associations and law enforcement groups received bulk grants for crime prevention programs that had no receipts. Consumer advocacy groups who did not object to the withdrawal got their cut as well. And finally, the most protected and most damning set of transfers: the offshore accounts tied to the cartel figures present at the Oyster Bay meeting.

One transfer memo simply read:

"Global Advisory Committee – Emergency Stabilization Allocation – $115M."

The total sum was staggering. Had it been redirected, it could have fed every starving child in Gaza, rebuilt crumbling water systems in Flint, or erased entire blocks of student debt. But to the Despicables, it was just redistribution of power.

What they didn't know was that Malik, Monica, Jordan, and Kendall had already written the final chapter. A storm brewed unbeknownst to the Despicables.

Aldridge Financial Ltd. appeared on no American government list.

It had no U.S. registered agents, no IRS EIN, and no link to PAINCO on paper. Nor was Aldridge Financial Ltd. on any PAINCO organization chart. Not even with any company filings with the Florida Department of Insurance or any state Secretary of State Office.

But it was the linchpin of the Mitchell-Madison maneuver.

Monica had been meticulous. "The thing about deception," she once told Malik, "Is that it requires the truth[9] to be present, just hidden behind a velvet curtain."

While working inside Genesis, Monica had authored the asset transfer provisions for the Florida liquidation plan. Quietly, under the guise of "foreign risk reserve," she embedded Aldridge Financial Ltd. as a custodial agent for offshore compliance transfers. She knew the Despicables would overlook it: assuming it to be one of the dozens of dummy firms they themselves used.

Jordan made sure of that.

In the final days of Irolla's chairmanship, she presented him with a stack of documents for signature: routine, innocuous, bearing the name Alder Capital Corp., a well-known international auditor used in government liquidations.

Except... it wasn't Alder Capital Corp.

"Sir, these just need your signature to finalize the wind-down." She leaned over Irolla with papers for his signature with just enough cleavage shown for further distraction.

"Fine," Irolla said, barely glancing. His pen moved.

He never knew that the documents were for Aldridge Financial Ltd., the Belize-based vault Malik and Monica had prepared about a year earlier.

Kendall swept through the digital underbrush. His job was to retrieve any metadata or electronic footprint related to Aldridge. Search indexes, compliance logs, even AI-generated memos. All scrubbed, all rerouted into a secure node protected by military-grade encryption. Only one man could access the backup: Malik.

"We don't spend this money," Malik said. "We don't touch it. It's not for yachts but for safehouses, personnel and surveillance. This is our resurrection fund. For justice. For the Shilohs' rebuilding."

They had siphoned just under $100 million, a mere sliver of PAINCO's worth, yet enough to seed investigations, build a legal war chest, and protect those who would come after them.

And when the final dollar hit Aldridge's private vault, the last phase of the plan activated.

Wire routing numbers dissolved.

Legal documents shredded automatically via metadata triggers.

Encrypted phone records deleted in real-time.

In a nanosecond, Aldridge Financial became a ghost. Malik chuckled to himself.

He thought: "In business, you have to have a little larceny in your heart." Famous last words. He chuckled to himself as he thought of Gino who uttered those words once to Malik.

Malik stood on the porch of a rented villa in Placencia, Belize, watching the sun melt into the horizon. "It's done," Kendall said beside him.

"You'll have it," Jordan said. "Tomorrow's headlines will read: *'PANIC at PAINCO.'* Irolla, Colucci, and Venier are finished."

"Not until I send the letters," Malik said.

He opened his laptop. On his desktop were five files:

To Colucci.

To Irolla.

To Doug Venier.

To the Marilyn Raynor, Cartel

To the Board.

Each letter was a final blow: a confession, an indictment, a warning, and a declaration of war. The letters exposed deals brokered in blood and contracts sealed in children's tears from human, child, sex and drug trafficking. Each bore no signature, just a scripture and a poem:

"Be not deceived; God is not mocked: for whatsoever a man soweth, that shall he also reap."

— Galatians 6:7

And one final message contained in the note read:

WHISTLEBLOWER

"I am a whistleblower, hear me blow.

I am a whistleblower, I won't let your hatred, corruption

and sinister plans grow.

I am a whistleblower; you made me go low.

I am a whistleblower, see my falling star glow.

I am a whistleblower; you reap what you sow.

I am a whistleblower; it's my time to go."

He sent them. Gino received the Whistleblower text message over his cell phone just as he was to entered the PAINCO Manhattan office.

And just like that, it was over just as soon as it started.

Servers crashed in three countries. Financial regulators will issue subpoenas. Anonymous published internal CYA memos. The Vatican distanced itself from its own advisory board. Half a dozen Despicables vanished from public view.

By dawn, the headlines screamed scandal. But Malik didn't gloat. He walked alone through the early morning fog in Battery Park; Psalm 91 whispered on his lips like armor.

"He that dwelleth in the secret place of the Most High shall abide under the shadow of the Almighty..."

He was not safe. But he was seen. And heard.

Because tonight had been the crescendo: the swelling of justice from whisper to thunder. It was not a natural disaster that caused PAINCO the risk of ruin but a man-made disaster of their own making.

And the Despicables... they had finally heard the roaring rush of sound of God's wrath though it is doubtful they still understood it.

Chapter Eighteen
Belize

*"And the beast was taken, and with him the false prophet.
These both were cast alive into a lake of fire burning with
brimstone."*

— Revelation 19:20

The sun melted gently into the Caribbean. It cast a golden hue across the white sand of Placencia. Waves lapped the shore in perfect rhythm, and the scent of salt and lime wafted on the breeze.

Malik sat reclined in a lounge chair, barefoot, shirt unbuttoned, straw hat tipped slightly forward. A crisp copy of the New York Times lay folded on his lap, the headline bold and unapologetic:

"Insurance Giant PAINCO Crumbles Amidst Criminal Probe – Organized Crime Allegations Unfold"

Below it, a grainy photo captured three men in tailored suits, only one with his wrists in handcuffs: Doug Venier. The other were pictures of, and John Irolla, Gino Colucci and Alessandra Bell and descriptions about their assassinations Marilyn Raynor arrested in Oyster Bay.

Malik exhaled slowly. For once, not in exasperation or exhaustion, but in peace. A quiet, long-awaited peace. The storm passed. The web unraveled. The empire fell.

And his beautiful, broken, resilient family was together. They arrived in Belize one by one, like puzzle pieces returning to their place in the picture.

Monica was first. Her new passport bore the name Celeste Vaughn. She arrived in designer sunglasses and a wide-brimmed hat, looking every bit like a film noir heroine in exile. But her smile, when she saw Malik, was real. There was history between them. Fire and frost. But the ice thawed. The mission mended something deeper than pride: a different kind of love that bore of friendship and mutual respect.

Denai came next. Under the name Danielle Roberts, she wore a flowing ivory sundress and sandals. Her walk still led with her hips with long confident strides, and her presence was unmistakably elegant, formidable. She greeted Monica with a simple nod. What surprised Malik most was not the civility: but the laughter. The two women now sat under large beach umbrellas, drinking margaritas and occasionally bursting into conversation like old sorority sisters trading secrets.

"I never thought I'd see the day," Malik whispered to himself, grinning.

Jordan and Kendall traveled separately, with forged IDs issued through the Hungarian travel agent from Malik's contacts in Panama, presumably Shiloh. Jordan, now Jayla Mitchell, wore her braids up, sunglasses wide, lips glossed and strong. Kendall, now Kenneth Moore, kept quiet confidence, never far from his laptop, always scanning the perimeter.

Now, the two siblings stood waist-deep in the warm Belizean surf, laughing, tossing sea foam at each other, and talking quietly. Their bond, once strained by time, betrayal, and secrets, seemed restored by truth[9] and blood.

Malik looked out at them and felt something powerful, something unfamiliar: joy.

They did it. He had broken the curse.

The Mitchell bloodline no longer belonged to the Despicables.

They were once used. Monica as a pawn. Jordan as a tool. Kendall as a target. Even Denai, unknowingly, was surrounded by wolves. But now they were free.

And it was Monica and Jordan, the two he once doubted, who ultimately took the ride to turn the tide.

The breeze off the Caribbean whispered through the palms, carried with it the scent of salt and something older, something ancient. Malik sat in stillness, barefoot in the sand, watching the horizon blur where sea met sky. Around him, laughter echoed: Monica, Denai, Jordan, Kendall. His family. Whole. For now.

But he knew peace was not permanent. Not for him. Not in a world that still bowed to shadows.

The Despicables were wounded, yes. But not dead. They were not men: they were systems. Spirits. Strongholds wrapped in liturgy, law, currency, and code.

And the war?

The war was never about PAINCO alone. It stretched back to Babylon, through Rome, on the slave ships during the "Middle Passage," through the cathedrals and the boardrooms, the laboratories and the secret societies. They changed their names. Their faces. But hunger was always the same: control, deception, dominion, and corruption.

Malik closed his eyes and whispered a quiet prayer: not for rest, but for clarity. It included Psalms 91. For the strength to see what others refused to see. For the courage to always take the road less traveled when most preferred the path of least resistance. Somehow, he knew that if called upon, he would take that road less traveled, which led to its own lonely path.

He had crossed oceans, betrayed kings, faced death in silence. And still, he had breath in his lungs. That meant something.

Malik's survival and ultimate victory over the Despicables did not come from brute strength, inherited or stolen wealth, or the manipulation of power. Their empire was built on deception, coercion, and fear. His was built on something deeper: the quiet and often overlooked forces of intuition, spiritual growth. The ancestral history born of the indomitable strength endowed in the ancestors of former Black slaves who, through tragedy and injustice, gained a moral conviction through sheer self-preservation in the process.

Intuition gave him foresight, a way of sensing danger long before it manifested. It was the whisper of his ancestors, the guidance of the Shilohs, and the lessons born of silence. These were both his personal and spiritual truth and growth that gave him the capacity to endure suffering. Suffering without becoming consumed by it, to find meaning in his exile, and to see beyond the material illusions that blinded so many.

Morals and values were the compass that kept him from becoming what he fought against, even when influenced by political truth[9]. The Despicables thrived on compromise and betrayal. Malik chose fidelity to family, to justice, and to truth[9]. His intellect, the sharpening of the mind through discipline and study, enabled him to outthink his enemies, to decode their patterns, and to transform their traps into lessons. The Despicables believed they were intellect. Yes, the Despicables were intelligent, but on the lower end of that spectrum, more along the lines of cunning and instinctual habits, much like a predator infected by a parasite. But when the hunted became the hunter, the Despicables faltered.

Together, these forces fused into a singular truth[9]: that no system of oppression can fully bind the human spirit when it is aligned with its highest principles. Malik embodied the intersection of personal, political, and objective truths[9]. Personal truth[9] demanded honesty with himself; political truth[9] required courage against the machinery of power, and objective truth[9] demanded a steadfastness in the presence of GOD, even when in the face of man-like goodness. These principles always outlive empires.

In this convergence, Malik found the strength to resist, and to ultimately overcome. The Despicables, for all their perceived might, could never wield such a weapon against GOD. Because no weapon formed against him shall prosper.

Perhaps GOD wasn't done with him yet.

Perhaps the greatest battles still lay ahead.

And if so, he would be ready: not as a lawyer, not as a husband, not even as a father.

But as a Watcher.

A breaker of curses.

A witness to the fall of giants.

Epilogue
THE FALL OF A KING

"All this came upon King Nebuchadnezzar. At the end of the twelve months, he was walking about the royal palace of Babylon."

— Daniel 4:28-37

Once, there was a king whose power stretched over nations and tongues, whose palaces gleamed with gold and whose gardens climbed to the very sky. Nebuchadnezzar, ruler of Babylon, thought himself more than a man, he thought himself more than a god. He raised monuments and held parades as if to rival the heavens and demanded worship as though he were a god. His armies crushed rebellions, and protests, and nations, his edicts silenced dissent, and his pride reached beyond the clouds.

But what man has ever prevailed against the Most High?

One night, as Daniel the prophet foretold, the King's arrogance brought his ruin. His reason fled him, and the once-mighty Nebuchadnezzar was driven into the wilderness. He lived like a beast, his hair grew long like eagle's feathers, his nails like talons scraping against the earth. The throne he had clung to with iron became dust beneath his knees.

Only when he lifted his eyes to Heaven, confessing that dominion belongs to God alone, was his sanity and his kingdom restored. The fall of Nebuchadnezzar is more than history; it is **a** parable. Just as the Prologue spoke of Lucifer aka, Satan, the light bearer cast down from Heaven for exalting himself above the Most High, so too do earthly rulers who mimic that rebellion.

When pride and power corrupt, when leaders demand worship and silence conscience, they follow the path of both Lucifer and Nebuchadnezzar: a rise built on arrogance, false narratives, then a fall from divine justice is carved for them.

And so the story repeats itself in every age. From emperors who crown themselves gods, to dictators who silenced nations, to corporate tyrants, to political sycophants, and to felonious strongmen who believe their wealth or armies secure them eternally. Each stand upon Nebuchadnezzar's balcony, gazing over their empires, whispering to themselves: "Is this not the great Babylon that I have built?"

But the Despicables, like their master Lucifer, cannot escape their fate. Pride blinds. Authority corrupts. Accountability finds all. And power without humility devours itself.

The Epilogue closes as the Prologue began-with a warning: The separation of Lucifer from Heaven was not a singular moment in the cosmos, but a pattern written into the human story. Every age raises its Nebuchadnezzar. Every age must watch them fall.

They whisper of immunity, of systems too vast to fail, of wealth too great to audit, of laws crafted to shield the guilty. They forget that the silence after the collapse is not oblivion, but the space where the true record is kept. For the Most High does not require human courts to pass judgment, nor mortal armies to execute sentences. He merely waits until the proud man's vision clears, until the Beast looks up from the dust, and sees the majesty he sought to steal. Then, and only then, does the true kingdom, the one not built by hands begin its reign. And the name of the fallen, whether Lucifer, Nebuchadnezzar, or a Despicable, becomes merely a footnote in the scroll of Eternal Justice.

History repeats itself. But history only repeats itself if man fails to heed the warning; to learn the horrible lessons of the past. Man must yield to GOD by his own will or by GOD's divine providence and His infinite wisdom. Except, man rarely learns and so the wicked ways of the Despicables are destined to continue for generations to come.